2

LipstickDiaries

foreword by **Wahida Clark**

WHERE
**HIP HOP
LITERATURE**
BEGINS...

AUGUSTUS
PUBLISHING

© 2009 Augustus Publishing, Inc.
ISBN: 978-0-9792816-6-2

Foreword by Wahida Clark
Edited by Anthony Whyte
Creative Direction & Design by Jason Claiborne
Cover Photo by: Milo Stone / BigAppleModels
Cover Model: Olivia Jones

Augustus Publishing paperback December 2009
www.augustuspublishing.com

foreword

This young genre has spawned great storytelling, fantastic novels and raised a lot of important social issues. Hip Hop literature has given rise to numerous authors and presented the world with many new authors. A lot of them are females, mothers, sisters, daughters, and women who have not only seen it all, but lived the life. They are now writing the stories that will one day change how we view the world. This collection of great storytellers has grown and branched out to be some of the best in the game. Most of these authors are already on their way, watering their gardens of literature for the young ones coming up. Their works have served as inspiration to many. Educating and feeding the masses with words of wisdom, just like the great, Zora Neale Hurston, Alice Walker, Terry McMillan and others before them incited. African American female authors have risen. Their words like scars will live on in greatness, and be a testament, written on the flesh of society, showing the great people we are.

Lipstick Diaries Part 2 is an anthology that has produced rich storytelling with interesting characters and plots from the hottest female authors in Hip Hop Literature. Authors like Genieva Borne, Arlene Braithwaite, Sharron Doyle, Kiniesha Gayle, Brooke Green, Tracee Hanna, Katrina Jones, Caroline McGill, Jada Roberts, Aretha Temple, Zoe Woods, have continued to carry the torch.

In **Lipstick Diaries Part 2,** short stories range from coming of age, erotica, gangsta life, and the effects of the streets. Each story is different and offers an exciting voice in the book game. The only common element of **Lipstick Diaries Part 2** is that all short stories are by top female authors. All their voices are different. Their stories are the war cries to our sufferings, pain and glory. The authors are from different regions of the United States and offer readers provocative stories, all from a female perspective. These stories are guaranteed to raise consciousness of our readers.

I'm Wahida Clark, the Official Queen of Thug Love Fiction. I've been down with the game since 2002 and have witnessed the rise and fall of many authors, both male and female. A collection of rich strong and wonderful voices, **Lipstick Diaries Part 2** is the springboard for new authors and an enhancement for the established ones. Enjoy reading this wonderful collection from the woman's perspective and continue to support us. Because without you, the reader, we will not get to reach our highest plateaus.

Signing Out

Wahida Clark
The Official Queen of Thug Love Fiction

Daddy's Girl

SHARRON DOYLE

The perfectly cloudless summer sky was blue as a gas flame, when she stepped outside. Winds had driven off the smog and the day dawned crisp and clean. Sabrina staggered home glassy eyed and obviously stoned from the night before. She could not wait to get home so she could hug the toilet in private.

Home—if that's what it was. Her mother passed away when she was nine years old and it was just her and her father. Everything changed then. Things that she hated to go through or think about, but were as real and painful as anything that she had ever felt. There was nothing but pain since her mother passed, except her father—if that's what he wanted to be called.

She made it to the front door and fumbled for her keys. She knew her father was at work and that gave her some time to herself. Sabrina climbed the staircase and went straight to the bathroom. Up came the usual residue from a night of drinking with her friends.

She had to get ready to go to her part-time job at Popeye's and did not want to be late again. Plus Taisheem was coming back from vacation today and she did not want to look all worn-out even though that was the way she felt. He wouldn't understand and she was too embarrassed to confide in him.

Sabrina got under the shower and then lay back on her bed, waiting for the room to stop spinning. She felt like she was on a never ending merry-go-round. Turning on her side, she stared at her favorite picture, the one with her, and her mother at Great Adventure, when she was eight years old.

It was the last trip that she and her mother had taken before her mother passed away. Tears came to Sabrina's eyes like always when she looked at her mother's smiling face. Sabrina turned away from the picture, and set the alarm on her clock to ring so she could be to work on time.

Three hours later the alarm clock buzzed angrily and insistently. Sabrina reached over and hit the button. Rolling out of bed, she stretched until her back cracked. That felt good. She had less than an hour to get to work, so she went into her closet and took out the bottle of Alize in her shoebox. She checked her stash, noting that she was low on Grey & Goose and Henney.

Sabrina went into the kitchen and put ice in a tall glass. She carried the glass to her room and poured some Alize over it. She swallowed it quickly and then poured another one. Checking the time, she got dressed after having one last drink just to get out the door. That's the way it was with Sabrina, a sixteen year old alcoholic.

Taisheem was in the back counting out cashier drawers when Sabrina went on her break.

"How are you feeling today? You been awfully quiet," he said looking Sabrina over with concern.

"I'm okay," she said looking away from him.

She wanted to tell him everything but was ashamed. Unlike the thugs she hung out with, Taisheem was a good guy. He'd never understand what she was going through. He'd probably think that she was dirty because that's the way she felt all the time—dirty.

She turned away from him and went to her locker to get a cigarette.

"You really should stop smoking. Them things are going to kill you," Taisheem said taking the pack out of her hand.

"I know," Sabrina said turning to look at him.

"Am I going to see you tonight, or what?" Taisheem asked touching her face softly.

"Yeah, I guess," she said quietly.

If only he knew he wouldn't want to be bothered with her. He had so much going for him and if he knew he'd drop her like a bad habit. Sabrina often wondered what he saw in her. She was a high school drop out, a drunk and she was used up.

"All right then, wait for me when you get off and we'll take the train together to your house," he said.

"Um, no I'll come back and get you," Sabrina said reaching for her pack of cigarettes that he was still holding in his hand.

He kissed her quickly so that none of the employees saw them. Most of them knew that Taisheem liked Sabrina but still there were rules, employees should not fraternize. Sabrina went out front to smoke before her break was up. She had already taken lunch and she only had fifteen minutes. She smoked quickly, then went back inside and opened her register for the waiting customers.

Two thugs rushed to her line, "Oh you open? Good let me get a ten-piece and two large ice teas, and your number when you're finished," the first one said leaning on the counter. Sabrina ignored him and asked, "Is that for here or to go?"

"To go," the other one said pulling money out of his pocket. He put a twenty-dollar bill on the counter while talking on his cellphone.

The first one was still leaning on the counter, and asked Sabrina, "So what time are you getting off? Maybe I could come back and pick you up."

Sabrina gave the other one his change and then said, "I'm good but thanks anyway." She turned her back to get his 10-piece and the ice teas, hoping that when she gave him his food that he'd leave and not hold up her line talking shit. Those kinds of guys did nothing to impress her. She was a dime piece, gypsy-tan complexion, round heavy lashed eyes and perfect thick lips always attracted the guys. If that wasn't enough then her jade green eyes were mesmerizing. Sabrina was used to the attention men gave her.

She passed the food and drinks and said, "Have a nice day." Then she moved on to the next customer saying, "Next in line, can I take your order?" That was her nice way of dismissing cats that she had no interest in. The rest of the day buzzed by quickly, next thing, Sabrina was clocking out. She told Taisheem that she'd be back to pick him up.

"Alright, seven-thirty," he said, winking.

Her father was in the kitchen when she came home. Sabrina immediately went upstairs, hoping he didn't hear her. Sabrina was not in the mood not now— not ever, but that never stopped him. She closed her bedroom door, held her breath and listened. There were footsteps coming up the stairs.

"Dammit!" She said and sat on the bed, waiting for his knock.

"Bree honey, open the door," he said turning the door handle. Reluctantly she got up, opened the door and stood in the doorway.

"Are you okay, honey?" he asked stroking her face.

"I'm fine, daddy. I just want to be alone."

He stepped into her room and hugged her while stroking her long hair. She hated him touching her, and despised the way he looked at her. He cupped her face and forced his tongue in her mouth. Sabrina resisted, but he held her head and turned it back to face him. Picking her up, he carried her to the bed. Setting her down like she was a baby, he got on top of her, slowly grinding his body between her legs.

"It's been two days, Bree. I've missed you honey," he whispered in her ear while unbuckling his belt.

"Daddy, please...don't," she said, tears in her eyes.

Why did he do this to her? He didn't listen and he stood up and let his pants fall off. Sabrina curled up in a fetal position on her bed hoping that he'd go away but she knew better.

"Please Sabrina," he said giving her that sick look.

She knew eventually he'd take it if she didn't give it. Sabrina got up and took her uniformed pants off and then her panties. With tears clouding her eyes, Sabrina got under the covers. This thing with her father had been going on since she was ten years old, and every time it still hurt like it was the first time.

He took off his underwear and stood over Sabrina rubbing his manhood over her lips.

"Just a little bit," he said quietly, watching his pre-cum stick to her lips. She opened her mouth and let him in. She sucked him until he was fully erect and turned her head in disgust spitting out his juices that escaped.

Her father got on top of her and roughly inserted his penis into her.

She was still not responding because she had learned how to shut her body down. He fucked her while running his fingers through her hair. Sucking on her perky breasts, his breathing became labored until he was finally finished.

Sabrina rolled from underneath him, running straight to the bathroom, turning the shower on. She stepped under the water and cried as she scrubbed her body. Dirty, that's how she had felt since she was ten years old.

Taisheem was waiting for Sabrina when she got out of the cab. He spotted her and walked over.

"You're late. I thought you weren't coming," he said.

"Sorry, I had to do some laundry," she lied, avoiding his eyes.

"Are you sure you're okay?" he asked studying her.

"Yeah," Sabrina said and smiled.

"You always say that, but for some reason I don't believe you. Even when you smile, it never reaches your eyes," Taisheem said seriously.

Sabrina kissed Taisheem to distract him. She wanted so bad to tell him— to tell somebody but she was ashamed.

"Come on," he said, taking her hand. "My mom's waiting for us."

They walked to his house, and just like he said, his mother was waiting. Taisheem was a mommy's boy and that attracted Sabrina. He was eighteen but let his mother know everything he did. Unlike the thugs she had dealt with, all they cared about was getting money and fucking. No family values, respect for their parents, no merit.

"Taisheem talks about you so much. Please come in and have a seat, Sabrina. I'm Mrs. Beverly, Taisheem's mother."

She gave Sabrina a warm hug that felt familiar and was so needed. Mrs. Beverly took Sabrina's jacket and walked her to the living room.

"Thank you," Sabrina said following her into the living room.

Taisheem's father was sitting in front of the TV watching news. He stood immediately and took Sabrina's hand in a friendly embrace.

"Well it's about time we meet you," he said smiling at her. "I was starting to think that Taisheem had an imaginary friend," he laughed.

"Knock it off, dad," Taisheem said, walking into the living room.

Sabrina sat on the couch and crossed her legs. Taisheem's parents seemed both wonderful she thought. Wishing she lived in a household like this one, Sabrina remembered Taisheem saying that he had to be home for dinner on several occasions, but Sabrina really thought that only families on television ate dinner together.

Inside an alcove between the kitchen and the living room, a table was laid out for them. Taisheem said to Sabrina, "I'll show you where the bathroom is so you can wash your hands."

"Okay," Sabrina said following him upstairs.

He took her to one bathroom and then he went down the hall to the other bathroom. She went inside, locked the door, and sat on the toilet. The bathroom was lemon pine fresh. Sabrina opened her bag and took out a small bottle of E & J. She looked it up and down then took a long swig.

Standing in front of the sink, she turned on the water, and took another swig before closing the bottle. She put the fifth in her pocketbook. She washed her hands and then put two pieces of Spearmint in her mouth. Taisheem was waiting for her by the steps when she walked out.

"Let's go eat," he said taking her hand in his. He gave her a quick kiss before they got downstairs.

At dinner his parents asked Sabrina about her plans after she graduated. Sabrina talked enthusiastically about going college.

"How's your mom and dad?"

Sabrina heard but allowed the question to hang. She quickly filled her mouth with a fork full of rice and sweet potato combination. Fearing his parents would find out the truth about her, Sabrina did everything to avoid talking about her home life.

"Kudos to the cook," she said between bites, "This is really good."

She chomped on fried chicken and gravy petrified that Taisheem's parents would think she was no good for their only son. Sabrina ate heartily, smiling but feeling scared of being judged, and losing Taisheem. He was the only pure thing that Sabrina had in her life and didn't want to lose him.

After dinner they went into the sitting room and talked some more. She could tell that Taisheem's parents were very proud of him the way they talked about him as if he wasn't sitting there. Sabrina wished someone were proud of her.

"You have to invite your father over one evening, Sabrina. We'd love to meet him."

She heard Taisheem's mother speaking and quickly headed off any possibilities.

"He ah…works a lot and besides he's not very sociable," Sabrina replied.

"Oh well that's alright then, I guess. You're always welcome, Sabrina," Taisheem's mother said.

The rest of the evening went by sociablely correct. Later his father announced in a crisp voice, "Taisheem, it's getting late, why don't you use the car and take Sabrina home…?" his father offered, passing the car keys to Taisheem. "Straight there and back," he sternly continued.

"All right, dad," Taisheem said and looked at Sabrina. "Are you ready?"

"Not really, but I know we have school tomorrow."

As she got up off the couch, her pocketbook suddenly tipped over and the fifth fell out. Sabrina immediately reached for it but not before all eyes saw the bottle hit the carpet.

"I'm so clumsy, my father's. I have to hide it from him," she said embarrassed pushing the bottle in the bottom of her bag.

Taisheem had a stunned look on his face while his parents exchanged wide-eyed looks.

"Thank you for dinner. Goodnight," Sabrina said making her way to the door.

She knew that they would not want her in their house again or around their beloved son.

"I'll be right back," Taisheem said closing the door after them.

Outside Sabrina stopped and said, "Taisheem. I am soo sorry".

"Yeah, whatever," he replied getting into the car.

For the next three days Taisheem said nothing to Sabrina that wasn't work related. He totally shut her out since that night at his house. She understood how he felt and wanted to tell him why she drank and how she became an alcoholic, but would he understand?

She wanted to tell him that she wasn't a virgin like he thought, and that she was not even in school anymore and most important she wanted to tell him her father had been taking her since she was ten. She wanted to tell him that she had lied because she was terribly ashamed, and felt that lying would protect her.

That evening she had slept late and when she woke up her father was standing in front of her naked, masturbating. He wanted her again. She could tell he had been drinking and that he would be rough and it would take a long time for him to finish. Sabrina tried to get out of the bed and he pushed her down. She flopped on the bed. He was on her so fast, pushing roughly inside of her while holding her down. He bit on her neck, and with the other hand pulled her hair while thrusting in her.

When he was finished, he rolled off of her panting, and breathing heavy like he had just ran a race. Sabrina got out of the bed and ran out of the room.

"I'm not done yet," he called out to Sabrina.

The bathroom door slammed shut. She locked it and slid down to the floor with her back against the door. The dam had broken and she could not turn it off. Tears were running down her face.

"No more, no more," she repeated quietly to herself shaking her head back and forth.

Her father was turning the knob to the bathroom and banging on the door at the same time.

"Bree! Bree! Open this door or I'll take it down!" he yelled through the door.

Sabrina stood by the door with her hands on it holding it against the weight of him as he banged, heaving his shoulder at the door.

"Sabrina! Open this damn door now!" he yelled.

"Go away! Please leave me alone! Why do you do this to me!" she screamed still pushing her weight up against the door.

He kept banging the door so hard that the splinters in the frame were about to give way. Sabrina backed away from the door and bolted to the window. She frantically pushed the window up and then the screen. Her father was still banging on the door like a mad man.

It always happened like this when he was drunk. She grabbed a towel off of the rack and wrapped it around her. Sabrina stood on the toilet seat to go out of the window just as the door flew open. Sabrina scrambled pushing herself through the window. Her father grabbed her by the ankles and violently pulled her back through the window.

"Get in here you crazy girl!" he growled through clenched teeth.

Sabrina hit the floor hard, head first. Blood spurt from her mouth as her father dragged her out of the bathroom by her ankles, down the hall and into the bedroom. Sabrina screamed at the top of her lungs trying to get out of his grip. He slammed the bedroom door shut and threw her on the bed like she was a pair of pants. She tried to jump off the bed but he blocked her. He was much stronger than she was but she still fought, clawing and scratching at him.

Her violent, drunken father grabbed her by the wrists and with the other hand he punched her in the face. Her nose bled violently onto the bed. Sabrina screamed and yelled at the top of her lungs still trying to get out of his grip. She raked her nails down his face, drawing blood.

"Little bitch!" he scowled and slapped her face.

Sabrina continued to fight. He put a pillow over her face; held it down and then forced his self into her. Only muffled screams escaped while he rammed in and out of her young body.

"Stop fighting me," he ordered her while taking her roughly.

It seemed like forever but finally he was finished. Sabrina pushed him off of her and ran into the living room. She stood in the middle of the floor naked and crying. She was swollen; bloody and bruised from her father's attack.

She ran down to the basement and grabbed a baseball bat that her father kept from his playing days. Sabrina walked slowly back to her bedroom where her father had passed out on her bed like he always did when he was drunk. Sabrina stood over him with the bat in her hand. Her face was swollen and she could feel the skin over her eye stretching, her busted mouth protested in pain.

No more she thought and swung the bat hitting him in his shoulder. Her father jerked from the impact and tried to jump off the bed. Sabrina swung again using all her weight hitting him in his knees. He went down quickly, mumbling incomprehensible to her. She could see his mouth moving, but nothing registered to her. He tried to get to his feet again and Sabrina swung the bat perfectly hitting him in his face. She heard bone crack and blood spattered out of his nose. He fell, grabbing at his bloodied face.

"No more," she calmly said, standing over her father.

Sabrina swung the bat repeatedly until he stopped moving. She was covered with his blood, skull fragments and brain matter that had spattered with every head-crushing blow. She dropped the bat and walked out of the room in a trance. Sabrina picked up the phone and called Taisheem. The phone rang twice before he answered.

"Hello."

"Taisheem, please come...I don't know what to do," Sabrina whispered.

A short while later Taisheem stopped by. He saw Sabrina standing in the doorway covered in blood.

"My god what the hell happened?" he exclaimed. "What happened to you?"

Taisheem stepped slowly inside the house. Sabrina sat on the couch and put her head in her hands and cried. Taisheem closed the door behind him and walked over to where she was sitting. He stood over her, unsure of what to do. He wanted to touch her, to hold her but not with all that blood on her.

"Sabrina, talk to me... I need to know what happened. Where is your father?"

She pointed to the bedroom. Taisheem walked toward the staircase and slowly began climbing the steps.

"Oh my god!" he exclaimed when he reached the top of the stairs.

Then he came running down the steps almost falling over his feet.

"What the hell happened!" he yelled standing in front of Sabrina. "Talk to me dammit! Did someone break in?"

Sabrina cried harder. Taisheem bent down in front of her; his eyes pleading for an answer, "Sabrina...please you have to talk to me. What the hell happened here?"

When she stared blankly up at him, he noticed that her eyes were swollen and her lips were the size of a small fist.

"Who did this to you!" he yelled filled with emotion.

Time seemed to pass by slowly but then she raised her head and said, "He...he...rapes me. I could not stop him...he just kept doing it to me...I begged for him to stop but he wouldn't listen," she said between sobs.

Taisheem looked toward the staircase and asked, "Who? Your father…?"

Sabrina slowly nodded. She could see the confusion in Taisheem's face. He stood up and said, "We have to call the police. My dad's a retired lieutenant. He'll know what to do." He reached for his cell phone to call his father and Sabrina grabbed his hand.

"Noo…! I'll go to jail! They won't understand," she screamed jumping off the couch and snatching the phone from him.

"Please, Sabrina let me call him. He'll know what to do. He can help you so that you won't go to jail. Trust me on this," Taisheem said sincerely.

He knew that his father still had an influence in the department and he would help Sabrina the best way that he could. She stood there; hand shaking studying Taisheem wanting to believe him. With a shaky hand she slowly passed him the phone.

"Trust me," he said again dialing his home number.

His mother answered on the second ring. "Hello," she said cheerfully.

"Mom, I need to speak to dad," Taisheem said hurriedly.

"Um, he's down in the basement. Is there something wrong?" she asked hearing the anxiety in her son's voice.

"Mom I can't talk about it. I need you to get dad for me."

"Taisheem is everything alright? Where are you?"

"I'm at Sabrina's. Something has happened and… Well I think dad can help us," Taisheem said, trying to be patient with his mother.

"Us? What do you mean us? Has that girl got you in some kind of trouble?" she asked with a sudden fear in her voice.

"Mom, please," Taisheem said losing his patience. "It's pretty crazy over here and…well I just think that dad is the person that we need".

"Taisheem, I want you home this instant. I don't know what kind of trouble that girl has gotten herself in and I don't want you having any part of it. Now you get home this minute," she ordered Taisheem.

"Mom, I can't do that. It's her father…he's…well he's hurt pretty bad, mom," Taisheem said looking at Sabrina. He did not want to tell his mother that Sabrina had killed her father.

"Mom, if you won't get dad, will you come over?" Taisheem asked.

His mother hesitated and then asked, "What's the address?"

Taisheem opened the door for his mother when she rang the doorbell. She came in and demanded to know what the hell was going on.

Taisheem said, "Mom, I don't know how to say it."

"Say what, Taisheem? You better tell me what the hell is going on now. And where's that girl anyway?"

"She's upstairs cleaning herself up. Her father…he's…well he's upstairs. She called me and asked me to come over. When I got here, she told me that her father rapes her… and well…she hurt him pretty bad and he's not moving. There's blood everywhere and she's pretty beat up," Taisheem explained.

"Raped…?"

It seemed like that was the only word that registered with Mrs. Beverly. She took off her jacket, setting in on the chair.

"Where's her father, upstairs?"

"In her bedroom on the floor," Taisheem said pacing back and forth. "I think we should call dad and tell him before we call the police."

"No," his mother snapped. "Don't tell your father anything. I'll take care of this," Mrs. Beverly said walking to the staircase.

She could hear the shower running as she got to the top of the steps. She looked in the first bedroom and then went down the hall to the other room. On the floor was Sabrina's father just as she had left him. Mrs. Beverly bent down and checked for a pulse. There was none. Immediately she went to the bathroom and opened the door. Sabrina, still in the shower peeped out of the curtain when the door opened. She didn't have time to say anything.

"Get out and get dressed. We have work to do," Mrs. Beverly said, closing the door behind her.

She went downstairs and headed to the kitchen. Over her shoulder she asked Taisheem, "What did you touch in this house?"

"What do you mean? What are you doing?" he asked his mother watching her take dish rags out of the sink.

His mother stopped and sternly asked her son, "What did you touch in this house. I want to know everything that you touched".

Taisheem looked around remembering when he had first got there and replied, "Um, the door knob and the banister when I went upstairs. Why?"

Without answering, she ordered him, "Take these rags and wipe the banister and the door knobs."

She carried the rags in the living room. Taisheem stood looking at her filled with confusion. She stopped at the staircase and said, "Do it now."

Sabrina was coming down the steps and Miss Beverly said to her, "Come with me".

They went to the bathroom and Miss Beverly tore the shower curtain down and passed it to Sabrina. Then they went into Sabrina's bedroom and Miss Beverly said to her in confidence, "I know what you've been through and I understand the pain…do you hear me?"

Sabrina nodded in a knowing way. She understood clearly and it felt good that somebody understood what she had been through. Tears came to her eyes and Mrs. Beverly said, "It's no time for tears. Now help me get this bastard wrapped up."

Taisheem came up the steps and stopped in the doorway. His mother looked up at him and said, "Get over here and help us."

He stood there not believing what he was seeing. She stopped and said, "Now!" Taisheem did as his mother said and helped them lift Sabrina's father so they could wrap him up. He stared at his mother in disbelief. She was not only participating but orchestrating this act.

They wrapped the corpse in a comforter and carried it out the back door. Mrs. Beverly drove her car around, and the three hoisted the corpse into the trunk. Night had fallen and there was no one out, the job was easier.

"You two go to the house. Not a word of this to your father, Taisheem do you understand me?" his mother asked waiting for an answer.

"Yes," they said at the same time. She got in the car and before pulling off she reiterated, "Not a word."

"Okay, mom," Taisheem said.

Mrs. Beverly drove out to Chester County to a very familiar place. She hadn't been in thirty years and never thought she'd return to this resting spot. She knew exactly what to do when she had heard that Sabrina was being raped by her father. She carefully disposed of the body the same way she had done to her own father, for the same thing... Thirty years ago.

Satiated Desires

TRACEE HANNA

Two weeks in Osan, South Korea, three lovers, and one hell of a fucking good time. I never believed in kismet until recently. I'm all too happy to say that fate has a very unique, if not peculiar, way of shaking things out— being that wild card in my life just when I needed a jolt.

My name is Pearl Mosley. I am a newly divorced, thirty-four year old, lovely, brown skinned woman. I don't live an exciting life per se, however, I've had some splendid moments; none better than my first trip to Asia.

Although I didn't set out to have the kind of a vacation that I did, damn if it didn't turn out great. I visited South Korea to see my friend Trevon. He's very handsome, tall, and extremely charming, with sexy smoldering brown eyes, a decadent chocolate skin, and the most wickedly alluring smile. We were fuck buddies who developed an excellent friendship over the years. We shared each other's joy, pain, and pleasure. We always had each other's back.

So, when he invited me to visit him at Osan Air Force Base in South Korea, I was on the next flight out. Knowing Trevon and I were going to have the time of their lives, especially with all of the wonderfully wicked things that he was saying to me before I got there.

"Pearl, I am going to tie you to the bed and not let you go," he had said so wantonly.

"And I will let you," I had invitingly responded.

"You know, you might never leave."

"Good… I am boarding my flight right now."

On board Korean airline, I drank a few cocktails every hour, ate a few meals, and enjoyed some snacks all while watching movies. I was too excited to fall asleep, just as well because the time flew by.

I couldn't believe that I was on my way to the Orient. Hot damn! It was gonna be fun. When the pilot announced that we would land in under an hour, I hurried to the bathroom and freshened up. Ooh la-la! I'm going to be face to face with my wonderfully sexy friend Trevon, in no time at all. I smiled unbuckling the seatbelt and made my way to the bathroom.

There, I unloaded my toiletries, took off my ankle length black leather trench coat, stepped out of my jogging suit, and freshened. I always travel with little miniature toiletries and a wash cloth. I brushed my hair, washed my face, brushed my teeth and applied fresh makeup. I stepped into a sexy Santa suit, put my coat back on and stuffed the Santa hat into my coat pocket.

Once I was satisfied with my appearance I gathered my belongings and returned to my seat. I giggled as I got settled in. This was going to be so good, so hot, extremely passionate and electrifying. I'm going to make damn sure that you, Trevon Carpenter, was very happy and completely satisfied for as long as I am in your company. After all, that's what friends are for. I have never been so excited in my life. Come on plane land!

Customs was a piece of cake. I made my way to baggage claim and immediately started looking around for my friend. I turned in a complete circle looking for what would have been the only Black man in the airport. I didn't see him, so I decided to gather my luggage.

"Where are you sweetness?" I said out loud to no one in particular.

"Right behind you pretty lady," Trevon lovingly answered.

Instantaneously my smile stretched from ear to ear. I spun around to see his lovely face. He stood arms outstretched, inviting. I leaped into his warm embrace. Tears welled as we held each other tight.

"Oh my God…! My dear, I have missed you so much," I gushed.

"I've missed you too sweetie," Trevon responded.

It's been way too long. Dear God in heaven, I didn't want to let go of him. I took a deep breath before I pulled away just far enough to look into his eyes. Standing on tippy toes, I kissed Trevon on his cheek.

"How was your flight?" he asked flashing his brilliant smile.

"Long," I responded and closed my eyes in a slow blink.

"How're you doing?"

"I'm doing all right now," I smiled.

"You're not tired or sleepy are you?"

"Not at all, Tre… How was your day?"

"I'm overworked and tired as hell."

"Poor baby…" I cooed.

You, sexy man, are going to be doing much better in just a moment. The thought slipped into my head as I stepped back just enough for Trevon to have a full frontal view of my body. I unbuttoned my coat. I slowly opened it up and smiled.

"Now, see you're getting my dick hard already, you'd better stop."

"And if I don't whatchu go'n do?"

"Don't make me get atcha right here in this airport."

"I'm down if you are," I said, winking at Trevon, tempting him to go for broke. I licked my lips then dragged my teeth across my bottom one before speaking. "Come get me." I lifted up my left eyebrow for emphasis. I posed for a moment longer, smiling. The very second that I saw a glint of mischievousness in his eyes I quickly shut my coat and giggled. "I'm just kidding. I am not trying to end up in a South Korean jail."

"Good because if you wouldn't have shut that damn coat, I would've just had to push you up against the wall and have my way with you."

"Well damn! You wouldn't have taken me to the bathroom, or a broom closet or something—for privacy?"

"No!"

Jail would've been worth that shit, well, almost. Trevon read my thoughts. He immediately, took me by the hand and led me to a secluded spot in the airport, an area that was closed due to construction. He pushed me up against the wall. He pressed his body against mine as he kissed me deeply. He reached his hand into my coat, found his way into my panties, and slid his middle finger into my pussy.

I was so hot and wet that I was throbbing with desire. I sucked in a sharp breath while his fingers probed my pussy— rhythmically stroking my heated den, pushing me into climactic need. He inserted a second finger instinctively. I was instantly consumed with desire— ravenous.

"Ooh!" I held on tightly. "The crotch has snaps, Trevon. Hmm…!" He didn't move fast enough. "My panties unsnap, baby." With a flick of his wrists my Santa panties were undone—freeing up more room for maneuvering. "Oh yes!" I sighed as he continued to fingerfuck my pussy while massaging my G-spot expertly. "You have such wonderful hands, so talented."

Trevon heard footsteps approaching. He adjusted his body so that he was standing on his own, yet blocking any view of my half-naked body. He continued working his fingers in and out of my saucy pussy with his left hand all the while he smiled at the man approaching.

"Hello," the man spoke with a deep Korean accent.

"Hello," Trevon replied.

"No passengers allowed in this area," the Korean man said.

"I understand," he flicked my clit with his thumb making me sigh, "but she's not feeling well and I cannot go into the bathroom with her to make sure she is okay. I brought her over here away from the crowd, so that she could catch her breath."

The man looked at me. At that point I was so consumed with passion that I couldn't even react. I was still leaning up against the wall with my eyes closed. Hell it was all I could do.

"Are you alright ma'am? Do you need doctor?"

I rolled my head against the wall, and opened my eyes. Barely able to focus, I looked over to the man. Just as I was about to open my mouth and speak, Trevon drove his fingers, working deeper and faster inside of my pussy. I moaned my response.

"No, no doctor, I'll be alright."

My breath was labored. I was on the brink of completion.

"He… ah, he's helping me okay. He's helping me with everything," I stuttered.

I closed my eyes once more and turned my head away.

"She's suffering from a little inner ear problem which causes motion sickness. However, she took her medication… She'll be just fine in about ten minutes," Trevon offered.

Satisfied with his explanation the man turned and walked away, leaving us alone. Trevon's digits continued stroking my pussy until my entire body was shaking.

"I'm gonna cum sweetness! Oh I'm soo close!"

He stopped, withdrew his fingers, re-snapped my panties and then stepped away from me. I opened my eyes with a scowl.

"Wha…? What's wrong? Someone else's coming…?"

"No," Trevon said sounding amused. "It's time to go, that's all."

"You have got to be kidding. Right…?"

"That'll teach you to tease me. Now we're in the same boat."

"Aw…! All right! Okay!"

"What?" he smiled boldly. "Are you mad baby?"

"Nope, not at all," I retorted. "It's all good."

I am going to fuck the skin off of your dick! Damn it! I'll leave it raw! I was thinking as he smiled at me. I smiled back, and together we were feeling horny as hell. We gathered my luggage and left the airport. Once we were settled on the bus to the United States Air force Base in Osan, South Korea, Trevon whispered into my ear.

"I'm going to fuck you so hard your toes will curl. They're going to curl so tight that your toenails will feel like they just might pop off," he said, gently kissing my cheek, and looking into my eyes.

"You do that!"

Although I responded lightheartedly, my body quaked with expectancy. I rested my head on Trevon's shoulder and smiled. Let me tell you that was a long-ass bus ride. The very moment that the hotel door closed, Trevon tossed my luggage and grabbed a hold of me.

I was already trying to pull my coat off. However he took over, swiftly snatching my coat and pushing me face forward against the nearest wall. He pressed me there as he unzipped his pants and unceremoniously shoved his dick into my welcomingly, salacious pussy. I cried out instantly.

"Oh Trevon, I have missed you so…!"

I pushed back against his every stroke, thoroughly enjoying having him as my lover again. He gripped my hips and took complete control as he buried his dick into my hot hungry flesh, again and again fucking me against the wall hard and fast.

My passionate moans filled the room. I reached my orgasm and my ardent cries spilled into the hall. My pussy was so lubricious that my juices ran down my spread legs. The extra slickness was all that Trevon needed to reach his orgasm. He painted my vaginal walls white with his semen.

I must confess that was my dream just before landing. However it wasn't the way it went down.

Trevon did not meet me at the airport. The ride to Osan was long and lonely. I tried to be understanding. He was military and could not just take time off. I easily made my way to the hotel just down the street from the base and emailed him letting him know that I made it safely. I left him my hotel information. Thirty minutes later, he called, promising to be at my door by five the next morning when the gates o the Air Force Base opened.

He lied, although he did call. I wasn't tripping. The night before I showered, dressed and went out exploring. I met some fun people however I didn't hook-up with anyone. I came to visit Trevon, and as his honey-lover-friend he was first. We met at the base entrance. I waited behind the enormous black, irongate filled with anticipation.

The moment I saw him all my ill feelings vanished. He gathered me in his arms and held on tight. We walked back to my hotel and fucked once... He was tired, at twenty seven, after fucking once— yeah right. He fell asleep. Okay so, I ain't stupid and I wasn't tripping either.

I know he wouldn't have invited me if he had a girlfriend. He probably had a shorty on the Base. No problem, more fun for me, if I had to share. I left him sleeping, and that set the tone for my trip. We didn't see one another everyday, however he promised to come get me on Valentine's Day.

There I was on Valentine's Day in Osan City, South Korea, in my hotel room feeling hurt, frustrated, and confused, trying my level best to turn pain into anger. If only I could get mad instead of feeling hurt, then I could spring into action and do something about it. So I spoke aloud, reiterating everything that had gone wrong since arriving in Osan City. All the while, I was taking swigs of Jack Daniels straight from the bottle.

"God help me I want to cry so badly right now. Oh shit this hurts! Your girl is in your room? Your muthafuckin' girl! Ain't that a bitch! Well damn, that explains the past few days. Now I understand. I can't do this man. There's no way in hell I'm going to sit here, in my hotel room while you're spending Valentine's Day with your damn girl. I can't believe this shit! See, if you would've told me that you had a girl from the get-go, then I would've had a different mindset, and I definitely wouldn't have crossed our friendship line… Well maybe once or twice, but that's about it. That's our understanding. But nooooooo! You left that little tidbit out and I know damn well that you did it on purpose. What, you didn't know how to tell me? We tell each other so much. I just couldn't believe that you'd choose to leave out that important bit of information. Fuck it then. I came here to play and have as much fun as I possibly could, and that's exactly what I'm gonna do. I will not let you make me cry. I won't let any man make me cry, not from hurt feelings. It's not that kind of party and never will be. I can't believe this bullshit though. I remember telling him, "If you have a girl… I will find other ways to occupy my time."

But what was his response?

"No, there is no one here. I am just laying in the cut. The girls on base have fucked up attitudes."

So I'm like, "Okay, but if your situation changes just let me know."

What did you say? "No pretty lady, that's not likely."

"It's not as if I wouldn't have come to Osan City. I missed him way too much not to come see him. Not only that, there was this uncanny need to make sure that he was all right. I even told him that I'd be Cousin Pearl— it would be alright. I wasn't trying to mess up anything he had going on over here because he had months of living in Osan City, but I would only be there for two weeks. Damn it man! You are such a piece of shit. I need to keep drinking. I need some company. I have been so mistreated by you Trevon Carpenter. I swear that if I didn't love you so much I would not talk to you at all. However, I do care a great deal for you so I just need to cheer myself up. I can't believe Trevon hurt my poor delicate feelings, especially when it was so unnecessary."

I was pacing back and forth again and again. Willing my alter ego to kick in, wanting her to take over, I like her. She doesn't allow anyone or anything keep me down. She's a real saucy bitch and men love her too. I took a really big drink then staggered back falling onto the bed. I was able to keep a hold of my bottle of Jack without spilling a drop.

"Damn it all to hell. Fuck this shit! I mean it… Fuck it all! Okay I love him, and…? What's the good of loving someone if he doesn't love you back or even care enough about your feeling to show a little bit of common courtesy? Oh but he cares enough to come and try to fuck my brains out a couple of times then run off."

"Oh yeah, that was the highlight of my trip thus far. After he left my room that first day, he said that he would be back that night but he didn't come back. I didn't hear from him until I was online late the next day and even then he promised to come see me but did he? Nooooo he sure didn't! He stood me up again!With the plane ticket, hotel and passport I spent a grand just to come see him, but we are friends more that anything else, so it was worth it to me. See, that right there is precisely why I don't allow anyone to get too close to me. What good is love when it is not returned? Why Trevon…? Why the hell are you treating me so badly? I don't deserve it! I didn't deserve to not hear from him for days. I told him that I needed to use the ATM. I can't go around broke in a foreign country. He sends me nicey-nicey instant messages, but still no Trevon. Another man took me on base. So here it is Valentine's Day and he has the gall to tell me that he's with his girl, in his room, and he has to go now. What the fuck was that shit all about? How the hell am I supposed to process this shit?"

I took another long drink. At that point was breathing hard from the effort to remind myself of how I was wronged. I think that I must have been screaming at the top of my lungs or something or just not breathing properly because I was spent. I was at my wit's end and in that moment, just when I needed her to, my alter ego took over.

Poor me, poor-poor me, come on now dear, let's get you pretty, and then we're going to go find a way to cheer you up, okay? Okay! I got up, went to the bathroom and turned on the shower. I picked out something sexy to wear and laid it out on my bed while the water warmed up. I was a woman on a mission. I had to get out of my hotel room! I had to get cheered up! I had to play with somebody, hell, anybody. I just wanted to have some fun.

After I got showered, perfumed, and dressed, I left my room in a salacious state of mind. I exited my hotel and noticed that the streets were practically barren. Damn, just my luck, there is no one out tonight. Oh well, I am finally out of my room; I am going to just walk around to see if there's anything at all going on. Hell, maybe I can find the cigars that I have been asking Trevon for since I got here five days ago.

I walked passed a fast food restaurant and noticed a young man staring at me. I smiled and kept on walking. I don't know exactly what I was looking for but I figured that the party was not in there. I walked a little bit further, thinking to myself. Maybe I can get something started without a crowd. I turned around and went back. I walked up to him.

"Were you just staring at me?" I asked boldly.

"Yes I was." He responded smiling down at me.

"Why?"

"You are beautiful and I was just wondering who you were."

"I'm Pearl, a civilian visiting a friend."

"Charles, this is my last night here. I was stationed in Osan for a year."

"So, how are you going to celebrate?"

"I have no plans."

"Well I'm on my way to get something to drink. I'm headed to the base. I will be in the first bar that good music is coming out of. Come find me."

"I'll definitely go looking for you."

I was at the bar on my second drink when he walked in. I smiled as I spoke, "You found me."

"Are you staying on base?" he asked looking around. "I don't want any trouble."

"No, I have a hotel room just down the street."

"It's Valentine, isn't your friend going to be looking for you?"

"I doubt it. So what do you have in mind?" I asked, raising my left eyebrow.

"I just wanna lick your pussy. I am like a starving man. I haven't had any good African-American pussy in a good year."

"Really...? That's a damn shame," I smiled.

"I will do to your body whatever you want me to do," he assured.

Oh really now? How the hell do I say no to that? I mused. "Let's go," I said inviting him boldly.

Charles was fabulous. He had a beautiful, well chiseled, coco brown body that made me hot the minute I saw him naked. He licked my pussy until I creamed all over his face and then he licked it dry. He ate my pussy in every position imaginable, but the position that I loved the most was doggy style.

His tongue darted in and out of my pussy and asshole over and over again until I was begging for him to fuck me. Although he was not very well endowed, I had pussy-control. I clamped my kegel muscles down on his dick and let him fuck me with all of his might.

After our third round of him doing everything for my personal pleasure; licking, fucking, sucking and salad tossing, I asked him how many times he had ever came in a one night stand. To that he responded four.

My reply was simple, "Tonight you will reach an all new personal best."

At the end of round five I told him that I wanted him to fuck my mouth. He was a bit hesitant because of his size but I reassured him that he was thoroughly exciting me and that was exactly what I wanted.

I sucked his dick until he was ready to cum but he wanted to cum inside my pussy again. I opened my legs welcoming him as I clamped down my pussy muscles tight, yet again. I watched him with an idle curiosity as he held me still and fucked me soundly. He ground his hips with every plummet making sure that he the whole length of his dick was inside of my greedy little pussy. We fucked until we both quivered. He came so hard that he cried out. Charles collapsed back on the bed struggling to catch his breath.

"I'll bet you don't forget this night," I said cockily.

"No I…" He took a deep breath. "I won't, not ever, but I have a question for you."

"Shoot."

"You came for me a whole lot tonight. Your bed is soaked. When was the last time you had sex?"

"When I got here five days ago," I answered honestly.

"Your friend is stupid. There is no way in hell I'd have given up a good pussy. This was the best night of sex that I've ever had in my entire life."

"Thank you, but it is not over yet."

"I can't I…"

"You can and you will. Now get on your hands and knees and lick my pussy good." He promptly did as he was instructed. "Stroke your dick while you eat me. I need you to cum inside of me one more time before we call it a night."

"I like being told what to do, it really turns me on."

"Good… now shut the fuck up and eat this pussy!"

He licked my pussy, fucked my pussy with his tongue until his face was glistening. He plunged right on in with his dick the moment that it got hard again. We fucked like jack rabbits for real. We moved together until we were both spent. It was definitely a happy Valentine's night—sinful—naughty.

The next day I heard from my friend, Trevon. And let me tell you, he was not very happy, not at all. It was brought to my attention that he called me the night before but I didn't answer my phone. So when he asked about the goings one of my Valentine's night, I told him the truth. He showed up to my door in a flash.

Men are so incredible... so amazingly stupid and predictable. The minute he got to my hotel room he made is intentions very clear. He started to undress but I didn't.

"Why do you still have your clothes on?" he asked perturbed.

"I have no idea."

"Get naked and get into the bed. I've missed you so much," he said in a voice that was oddly convivial.

"All right," I practically sang.

I knew what he was up to. He told me long ago that he'd never hit a woman. He had other ways of chastising them. I was about to find out exactly what he meant. I was curiously aroused.

The very minute that I was in position my punishment began. He fucked me so hard that my ears rang. He was relentlessly brutal, but thrilling. Trevon had no idea how much I love being angrily fucked. I could barely breathe as he pounded my pussy, sending his dick deep. He was grinding inside my body and stretching the walls for more.

With every shockingly arduous thrust he whispered in my ear, "I miss you." Trevon's words were fallacious—devious. He fucked like a mad man—mincing me. Time moved slowly. The mixture of pleasure and pain sent me into an orgasmic high. Damn the pain! He was giving me what I needed.

All I could think after he was done with me, as I lay there with my body quaking uncontrollably was, hell yeah... If he had fucked me like this the first time I wouldn't have fucked anyone else. His time to make a power play was long gone. Therefore when he broke his word again, that very night, I played.

I didn't find anyone that was fuck-able right away. However I had a wonderful time dating, dancing, and drinking my nights away. It took a few days to find some good trouble again.

KB ruined me for life and I enjoyed every fucking minute of it. I met KB in a bar in Shungdan, South Korea at eight o'clock in the morning three days after I last saw Trevon. It all started with me going to the convenience store to get some orange juice after a night of heavy drinking. I approached the counter and a man walked into the store smiling at me, so I smiled back.

"Hello, my name is Phil. How're you doing this morning?" He smiled as he spoke.

"Hello Phil, my name is Pearl. I'm doing fine. How about you?"

It was so easy to be cordial.

"I'm good. Can I buy you that?" he asked pointing to my juice.

"Sure, thank you."

"No problem," he said paying for my drink before handing it to me. "I'm going over to the Monaco with some friends. Would you like to join us?"

"What's the Monaco?"

"It's the only club that's open at this hour. We just got done with a field exercise so we're all going to hang out and get our drinks on."

"Okay but I need to go back to my room and fix myself up a little better. If you don't mind waiting, you can come with me to my hotel."

"Bet."

Although he tried, Phil was not what I wanted. I agreed to spend the morning with him at the Monaco, nothing more. However, the moment that I walked into the bar I found what I was looking for. I saw this handsome mixed breed that I will call KB. I couldn't help but stare. I'm one of those cocky women that will never ever take a second glance, but with KB I was stuck. I did everything that I could do, without doing anything overt, to catch his attention. It worked, lucky me. KB slipped a note into my pocket as he walked by. The stage for deception was set.

"Why are you staring at ol' boy?" Phil asked. "Do you know him?"

"What man?" I asked with a puzzled look on my face.

"That one...!" Phil pointed at KB.

Damn, I thought I was being discreet. I'm going to have to do better. After all Phil was nice enough to invite me.

"Him...?" I asked undaunted. "What makes you think that I was staring at him?"

"I saw you."

"Don't be ridiculous, I was reading the writing on the wall," I responded with a chuckle. "Unlike you, I've never been here."

He calmed down, took me by the hand and led me to the bar. He ordered a large glass of Soju, a lot like vodka only sweeter. In an effort to get me drunk but it didn't work. After a very short period I began playing darts with one of KB's friends. I purposely grazed my ass across KB's dick every time I switched turns at the board all the while smiling at Phil. I was a bad-bad girl—Machiavellian.

As the morning continued on I began to feel the effects of the Soju. I told Phil that I wanted to get something to eat. He insisted on going with me across the street in hopes of talking me into going back to my hotel room. I peeped game quickly and throw game even faster. I asked the fellas that I was playing darts with if they were hungry, however, everyone said no. I asked KB again if he wanted a burger. I love smart men. He said yes and gave me a reason for returning. By noon I had run poor Phil off. The moment Phil left the bar I audaciously kissed KB and invited him back to my room. I handed him my ID as we walked.

"This is the fastest way of getting to know one another," I said boldly.

"Indeed," he agreed.

He handed me his ID. It turned out we were both from the same state and lived about five miles from each other.

"We are practically neighbors?"

"Yes, I see that." I was just as fascinated as he was. "This is Kismet."

Our bodies were intertwined in a lascivious escapade that took my desires to an echelon of pure enchantment. Every stroke, every thrust calling forth my essence into full blossoming concupiscence, pushing me even further with his unrelenting rhythm into the sea of ecstasy where we basked in prolific pleasure—ecstasy. Thirteen inches long with a seven and a half inch circumference; gentle yet fulfilling. He was truly gifted. So much so, that I spent the next two days adjusting to his monolithic dick.

We fucked for hours, three days in a row: including a couple times in the Monaco's bathroom. I took every inch of his dick deep inside my pussy that last day. I agree with the song; a man can stroke it, he can lick it, but he ain't done a damn thang to it if he can't stand up in it!

KB stood like a true soldier and fucked like a champion. My pussy will never be the same. My sexual fantasies were fulfilled my desires were completely satiated. Thank you KB!

It was my last night in Osan, and God help me but I had been acting as naughty as possible, there were no rules, no lines that I wouldn't have crossed if presented as an alluring copulatory temptation.

I love men and men love me. They are my only weakness in life. I am delighted by everything about a man, the way that he sounds and smells, the way he looks at me, touches me, kisses me, and especially the way that he feels inside of my flesh.

I absolutely adore the strength of a man. I am completely turned on by his boldness, his confidence, and his sense of self-worth. I never knew what it would take for a man to win me over. However I do look forward to being enticed. It excites me to no end to watch the seduction unfold. I am at my very best when my mind is clouded with passion. I am happiest relishing in lasciviousness, and basking in carnal desires. Sterling pleasure for me is the complete acquiescence of my body to a powerful knowing man. And um, let me just say this, I had my fun.

Oh, I don't want this to end! However, it's time for me to go home tomorrow morning, so let me start packing. The last thing that I needed to do was put it off for the last minute, especially since I have no idea what was going to happen next.

Alright, it was six pm and if I hurry up and pack now I will have the next eighteen hours to do whatever I wished. I turned up the music and got down to business. Just as I was packing my last suitcase the phone rang. I had no idea who was on the other line; however I was excited to have my night start off so early.

"And the fun begins!" I said out loud before I picked up the receiver. "Hello?"

"Hey," Trevon sounded less than thrilled. "What are you doing?"

"Packing..." I would not allow one iota of happiness to leave my voice. "What about you?"

"Oh okay. I just got off of work. Have you eaten?"

"No."

"Well, I was going to go get something to eat."

"Okay."

"Would you like something?"

"What? Do you want me to meet you somewhere?"

"No I can come to get you."

"I think that it would be easier if I just met you out."

"No, I will come to your room."

"Alright," I agreed reluctantly, "About what time?"

"I've got to get changed first then I will be there."

"Okay, I'll see you later."

Damn! That is not the call that I wanted to get. Oh, he sounded so solemn. It seems to me that our friendship should end here in Osan. After all he has been less than amiable and I've been more than friendly and accommodating with everyone much more than I've been with him.

Stop that, I chided myself. What happened, happened and I couldn't change it now, so just take a shower and get ready for whatever the night holds.

An hour later, Trevon arrived at my room. He knocked once before the door opened. We walked together to the restaurant making idle conversation about nothing important. Talking and laughing as if nothing was wrong between us, it was wonderful yet deceptive. Dinner was lovely. We joked, laughed and took pictures. Even the walk back to my hotel after dinner was pleasant and friendly. However, just as I anticipated, everything changed shortly after we got back to my room.

"I am going to put these leftovers in my refrigerator and then we can go get some drinks, my treat since you bought dinner."

Trevon did not respond instead he took off his coat and took a seat at the table. He looked at me. His face was expressionless; his eyes unreadable.

"Or…" I couldn't get a handle on his mood so I kept talking.

"If you are not ready to go yet, we can just sit here for a while and let our food settle."

"You didn't eat." He responded in a matter-of-fact tone and demeanor.

"I ate all my shrimp," I nervously laughed.

What the hell are you thinking Trevon? I thought folding my hands in my lap and sitting on the bed.

"I am sorry that I didn't spend more time with you." His apology took me by surprise. "I will make it up to you."

"Well maybe we can meet in Hawaii in May, for like a four day weekend or something. Are you still coming home in May?"

"As far as I know..."

"Okay, we'll talk about it some more later on," I said as he stood up and so did I. "Are you ready to go now?"

He walked toward me; within three steps he was standing in front of me—toe to toe. I was not paying any attention to him because I was straightening out my clothes. I looked up to smile at him, trying my best not to show how much he startled me, however, before I could focus on his face, he pushed me down onto the bed. He pushed me hard enough to make my legs fly up as I fell backwards. Just as they did he grabbed my legs by the ankles with one arm and flipped my shoes off of my feet with his free hand.

"Well damn…"

I was unusually calm considering the circumstances. Not everything can be done with everybody however it was my Trevon.

"Is it that kind of party?"

"Hell yeah..."

And he sounded hellbent. I didn't even think about putting up a fight.

"All right," I was ready for anything. He snatched off my pants. "Oh my…!"

I couldn't help but smile, thinking sarcastically, ooh he's mad. He got on the bed, gripped my panties in his fist, and ripped them off. Damn… this is going to be good. I thought with a smile. He dove on me plunging full force with every ounce of his strength, the full weight of his body. His drive was absolutely mind-boggling; however my shirt kept getting in the way.

"You know, I can take my shirt off if you need me to," I offered obligingly.

"Could you?" He asked earnestly.

He backed up off me a little bit giving my just enough room to maneuver but not enough space to try to attempt a get away.

"Sure, you want me to take my bra off while I am at it?"

"Yeah, take that off too."

"All right," I said, sitting up as much as I could, removing my clothing, and laying back. "There ya go... Now where was I?"

I spread my legs for him making sure that I got back in the exact position that he originally had me. I allowed him to have his way with me. Because I was lying across the middle of the bed I kept slipping over the other side.

"Sweetness, I'm half way off the bed. Can you pull me back up please?"

"Quit running!"

"If you weren't trying to puncture one of my lungs with your dick, I wouldn't be running."

"We're going to fix that right now."

He lifted me up and positioned me so that my head was on my pillows at the head of the bed.

"Now, you won't be scooting away from me."

"All right..."

Trevon gave me all that I could truly stand. He had me pinned down to the bed on my side driving his dick inside of my body as if his sanity depended on each stroke. He spanked my ass as he spoke and drove his dick deeper and deeper inside me.

"This is my pussy." Slap! "Don't you ever give my pussy away ever again!"

Each syllable was punctuated by another whack or smack!

"Whose pussy is it?"

Smack! Slap!

"It's your pussy Trevon!" I screamed with wanton delight. "Oh my God it's yours! It's yours!"

I have never in my life been so consumed by someone, so dominated, but the pain was exquisite. I was lost in an abyss of sadistic ecstasy—sadomasochistic taboos—pleasure clouded by agony drowned in orgasmic bliss. My mind couldn't separate the pleasure from the pain. My ears rang and I clenched my teeth, only realeasing to shout his name over and over again.

"Trevon! Trevon," my voice squeaked.

I could barely breathe. I arched my back and buried my head under my pillows.

"Oh please! Trevon…!"

He threw the pillows to the floor. I dug my nails into his shoulder gripping as tight as I could, holding on for dear life. Hell it has been almost a year since he has touched me. I'm having flashbacks writing this shit. God help me, but no one has ever, ever been able to take me to the level of sexual bliss and total abandonment.

My desires sated with pain and climactic delight. I was exploding too many times to count—complete acquiescence. I have never given myself so completely before or since. Our final goodbye left a lasting impression on my mind, in my heart, and all over my pussy.

Cold Blooded

ARLENE BRATHWAITE

A candy apple red 848R Ducati exited the thruway. The rider made a right turn at the stoplight and then turned onto First Street, pulling up behind a black BMW parked in front of a brick house.

The potbellied, white man in the BMW stepped out. The rider climbed off the bike and removed her helmet.

"I hope I didn't keep you waiting long, Hugh," Paris said as she took off her gloves and sashayed toward him.

Her hour glass shape could easily be seen in the vacuum-sealed leather outfit she was wearing. Paris was creamy-brown complexion and very attractive.

"Oh no," Hugh said, tugging his suit jacket over his stomach. He shook her hand and stared at her for a moment. "I knew there was something different. You had braids the last time we met."

"Yes," Paris said, touching her Rhianna-style short 'do. "It's the new me."

"I like it," he said staring at her.

"Okay…so, can we get down to business?"

"Yes, of course. If you'll just follow me," he said, retrieving the house keys from his pocket. "Everything is just the way Emma left it."

She followed him into the house. Paris looked at the pictures of young children hanging along the living room wall.

"She had a lot of foster children," Hugh said.

"Yes, she did. I was one of them."

"Serious?"

"Yep, that's me right there," she said pointing to a little girl in a group photo.

"That is you," Hugh said, checking out the little knocked-kneed, braces wearing girl. "I don't remember seeing you around."

"I ran away when I was 14. I went back to the Bronx to find my mother."

"Did you?"

"No, but I did hook up with people who later became my family. Now, here I am twenty-eight, wondering why Emma would leave me her house."

"I wish I could answer that question for you."

They entered the dining room. Hugh opened a folder he had laid there earlier. "The house has been paid in full and there are no back taxes owed. All I need for you to do is sign these papers and the house and everything in it is yours."

"I still can't believe she's gone," Paris said, shaking her head and signing on the dotted line.

"We are going to miss her, especially the kids."

Paris walked him to the door.

"Here's my card," he said, handing it to her. "If you have a question or need anything, don't hesitate to call."

"I won't, thank you."

She closed the door and took a tour of the house. When she walked down into the basement, she was shocked. It looked like one big game room. There were pool tables, ping pong tables, card tables set up down the center. She walked into another part of the basement and saw nothing but video games. There were X-Boxes, Play Stations and hand-held video games. She picked up a Game Boy and looked at it. She tucked it in her pocket and went back upstairs to the bedroom. She took off her back pack and pulled out the denim outfit she was going to wear to her first day of work tomorrow. Work, she thought to herself. I've never worked a day in my life.

The next day, heads turned as Paris rode into town. She parked in front of the bookstore and took off her helmet. Dismounting, she caught the bookstore owner staring at her through the window. He met her at the door.

"Paris?"

She took off her riding gloves and shook his hand. "It's good to finally meet you in person, Neal."

"My aunt didn't tell me you–"

"Rode a bike?"

"No, that you were so damn beautiful."

"Hey, you're the boss; I'm supposed to be flattering you." She looked around the bookstore. "This place is nice."

"Let me show you around."

Paris followed him down one of the aisles as he gave her the rundown. Neal was easy on the eyes. Light skinned, chiseled features, fresh fade, she quickly tore her eyes from his butt as he turned around.

"Any questions…?"

"Huh? No, no questions."

"So, basically, you'll be working behind the counter."

"I think I can manage that. So, are you from around here or…?"

"I'm from Brooklyn, originally. What about you?"

"The Bronx. What did your aunt tell you about me?"

Neal hopped onto the counter. "She called me and told me a friend was moving into Emma's house. She said you would need a job. I said no problem."

"That's it?"

"Is there something I should know?"

"No." Paris quickly answered and placed her helmet on top of the counter.

"Yo, Neal!"

They both looked toward the front door. A 13 year old kid came rushing in. "Whose bike is that? That shit is crack, yo." His eyes focused on Paris and saw her helmet on the counter. "That's your bike, shorty?"

"Shorty?" Paris said.

"I didn't meant it like that, shorty."

"Her name's Paris," Neal said, cutting in. "And Paris, this pain in the ass is Scratch."

"You got a man?" Scratch said.

Paris had to laugh. "Boy, if you don't get away from me…"

"Don't come in here harassing my new employee, Scratch."

"She's working here? Everybody's going to be coming up in here, now."

"If you ain't buying nothing beat your feet," Neal said.

Scratch swiped the new Don Diva and Street Literature Review Magazines off the rack. "I'll take these." He pulled out a wad of bills and peeled off a twenty. He put it in Paris's hand. "Keep the change."

"Scratch–" Before Neal could finish his sentence, Scratch was out the door.

Scratch must have ran his mouth off to everyone he knew. Two hours later, mad dudes came into the bookstore to see the new eye candy. Three hours later, Neal had to kick dudes out in order to close.

"If I would've known that a pretty face would boost my sales two hundred percent, I would've hired one a long time ago."

"Sales went up two hundred percent?"

"Listen, there were dudes in here who brought books who don't even know how to read."

"Stop playing."

"I'm dead serious." Neal looked out the window. Paris followed his gaze. Two tricked out vehicles coasted by the store. The first vehicle was a white Tahoe with tinted windows, sitting on twenty-fours. The second was a burgundy Lexus with a gold stripe running down the middle. When they got to the corner, they made a U-turn and parked in front of Paris's bike.

Paris watched a slim guy hop out of the Tahoe. She chuckled as the baggy jean, Timb wearing diamond in the ears having hustler dramatically looked around before bopping toward the bookstore.

The kid in the Lexus got out and leaned against the hood of his car. His woman stepped out and slid under his arm.

The slim dude knocked on the door. "Yo Neal, what up?"

"We're closed."

"C'mon I know you ain't going to do me like that."

Neal dug in his pocket and pulled out his keys. Slim smiled when Neal opened the door. "What up?" He slapped Neal five.

"Same ol', same ol'…"

"That's not what I'm hearing." He looked at Paris. "I'm Cyrus."

"I'm –"

"Paris, I know."

"Word travels fast," she said.

"This is a small town," he smiled.

"It's getting late, Cyrus, so…" Neal started to say.

"I won't keep y'all any longer. I just stopped by to say hi to our new neighbor."

Paris grabbed her helmet. "I got to go."

"See you tomorrow," Neal said.

"I'll be looking for you at the lounge tonight," Cyrus said.

"Don't bother; I won't be there."

"You don't hang out?" Cyrus asked, getting a good look at her as she walked from behind the counter.

"Goodnight, Neal."

"Ouch, it's like that?" Cyrus said.

Paris walked outside.

"What up?" The girl snuggled up under her man's arm said to Paris as she walked by.

Paris acknowledged her with a nod before putting on her helmet. She started her bike and revved it. She locked the front brake and popped the clutch. She made a donut in the street before peeling off.

"That was hot," Ramel said.

The girl under his arm, Tee, elbowed him in the ribs. "I saw you looking at that dyke bitch's ass."

"She got a fat ass," Ramel laughed.

"And you about to have a fat lip."

Over the next couple weeks, Paris realized Hudson, the little town right outside of Albany, wasn't the rural place she remembered. There were a lot more Blacks here, drugs and cliques were slowly taking over.

Cyrus's gang was by far the biggest. They were from Albany, but were here to sell drugs and recruit young kids. Cyrus's thugs came into the bookstore on a regular, kicking their weak game. Paris would smile and politely shoot them down. The chicks in Cyrus's clique definitely weren't feeling all the attention their men were giving her. Paris just shrugged off their glares and jealous remarks. She didn't want their wannabe, hood-rich boyfriends.

Besides, she was having too much fun working a real job. It wasn't as hard as she thought it would be, and Neal was good company. He wasn't trying to get with her. Paris pulled up to the bookstore bright and early one morning. She stopped in her tracks. Neal was in the center aisle, stacking books on the shelf. His G-Unit tank top was fitting him right.

"Hey," he said, looking up. "What are you doing here so early?"

"I woke up early this morning, couldn't go back to sleep, so I figured I come on down."

"I don't have a particular dress code. If you want to wear short sleeves or a tank or whatever, I don't mind."

"You don't like my blouse?"

"Yeah, I like it. I just noticed that you wear long sleeves a lot. I didn't know if you did because you thought I wanted you to or…"

"I prefer to wear long sleeves when working."

"Okay, no problem."

Neal finished stacking the books and walked over to the counter.

"Hand me that log book right above you."

When Paris reached overhead to grab the book, her sleeve slid back to the middle of her forearm.

"Is that a tattoo?" Paris quickly pulled her sleeve back down. "It looks like it goes up your whole arm."

Paris handed him the book and pulled out her Game boy.

"What does it say?"

Paris continued to ignore him.

"Is that why you wear long sleeved shirts?"

"You don't quit, do you?"

"My bad... Sometimes, I don't know when to shut up."

Paris continued playing the game.

"I see you have a different Game boy."

"There's like twenty of these things in the basement, and that's not counting the Play Stations and X-Boxes."

"Emma's house used to be the neighborhood hangout spot. All the kids would go there after school."

"I was wondering why kids kept hanging around the house."

"I guess they miss hanging out in the basement, but they must be too scared to ask you if they can."

"Too scared…?"

"You're the 'biker broad'; that's what the kids call you."

"Biker broad…? That sounds so…rough."

"It's just a name. I'm sure they'll stop calling you that once they get to know you."

"Umm, hmm, I hear you."

When Paris pulled up to her house, she noticed two boys, no more than 9 years old, sitting on her porch. They immediately jumped off and started playing by the curb. Paris walked by them and stuck her key in the front door. She looked back at the boys and sucked her teeth.

"Hey, did y'all know Emma?"

Both boys nodded.

"When is she coming back?" One of the boys asked.

"She's gone, she's not coming back."

"Why?"

"Why? Because…" Paris felt a lump forming in her throat. She didn't cry when she first heard that Emma passed away, but having to tell the kids that she was dead made it more real for her. "Y'all want to come inside and play in the basement?"

"Yeah," both boys said at the same time.

A couple weeks later, the neighborhood kids had their hangout back.

"Peace to my peoples," Scratch said, as he walked into the bookstore.

"What's happening?" Neal asked.

"Ain't nothing. I just came in to get some CDs for the throwdown. You stopping by later on, Paris?"

"The barbecue…?"

"Where else…?"

"I was thinking about it."

"If you need a date…" Scratch started to say. Paris tried to snatch him up and punch him, but he was too quick.

"You're going to make me go upside that coconut head of yours, boy."

Scratch purchased five CD's and left.

"You should head over to the barbecue after work. Every one's going to be there, including me," Neal said.

"What's that supposed to mean?"

"I'm just saying, if you think you won't know anyone…"

"I knew everyone in this small-ass-town the second day I got here."

"You got jokes."

"Besides, I don't want the townspeople to think the 'biker broad' is crashing their party."

"Check this out, as your boss, I'm ordering you to go to the barbecue and have a good time."

"I'll think about it."

Paris rode into the park and pulled up along Neal's car.

"Glad you could make it," Neal said, eyeing her brown leather pants and cream shirt.

"You gave me an order, remember?"

Neal got out of his car as Paris was getting off her bike. "People might think we came together," he said.

"You got a problem with that?"

"Heck nah." He held his arm out. She intertwined hers with his.

"A lot of people are here," she said.

The kids ran up on them. "Paris, can you ride me on your bike?" A young girl asked her.

"Maybe later, baby."

"I see you got a little following," Neal said, looking at the kids trailing them.

"What can I say, biker chicks are cool."

"Yo, yo," Scratch called out to them. He left the crew of youngin's he was with. "I knew y'all were coming." He slapped Neal five and bumped fists with Paris. "Y'all want something to eat? I'll get my little soldiers to get y'all something."

"Your little soldiers…?" Paris echoed.

"Yeah," Scratch said, pointing to the boys he just left.

Paris recognized a lot of them from hanging out in her basement.

"I'll get my own food," Paris said.

"Whatever. I'm a holler at y'all later, deuces."

"Kids today," Paris said shaking her head.

She peeped Cyrus and his crew in a corner of the park they had locked down. That was the area Scratch and his little soldiers were heading. Cyrus and his crew were corrupting the youth of the town, but she didn't seem to care. Now she was becoming emotionally attached to some of the kids.

"Leon," she called out to one of the boys in Scratch's group. The little boy turned around. "Come here." He looked at Scratch and then at Paris. "Boy, you hear me calling you, get over here."

He ran up to her.

"Where's your mother?"

Leon shrugged.

"What you doing with them boys?"

"Nothing…"

"Well, being that you're not doing anything with them, you can hang with me."

"Yo, Leon," Scratch called out to him.

"He's hanging with me," Paris shouted.

Scratch shrugged and herded his crew, ages twelve and under, toward Cyrus's side of the park.

"Can you hold on to this for me?" she asked Leon, handing him her helmet.

He nodded and took it.

"This town wasn't always like this," Neal said.

"No town ever is," Paris said. "What's up with the sheriff?"

"Why'd you have to talk him up?"

Paris looked to her left and saw the sheriff heading right for them. "Good afternoon."

"Sheriff," Neal said. Paris nodded.

"You must be the pretty little thing who moved into Emma's house," he said to Paris.

"Yes, I am."

"Sorry I haven't had a chance to introduce myself before now. My name's Ernest Krupp, pleased to meet you."

"Likewise," Paris said, shaking his hand.

"You ah…work with Neal at the bookstore?"

"Yes."

"He's a good man."

"Yes, he is." She stared into Neal's eyes.

"Y'all enjoy the festivities."

"We will, sheriff," Neal said.

"Like I was saying, what's up with the sheriff?"

"You see what's up with him. He's an old white man who's probably making more money on Cyrus's payroll in one week than he sees on three of his paychecks."

"And I bet it's safe to assume that his deputies are just as corrupt."

"It's safe to say that."

"And I can't believe people are just sitting back and not doing anything."

"What are they going to do, go against a drug dealer, his gang and the police?"

"Fuck it. If they don't care, I don't care."

They hung and tried to enjoy the atmosphere of the barbecue.

Paris pulled into her driveway and started to head inside.

"I remember you."

Paris stopped and looked over on her neighbor's porch and saw an old lady rocking back and forth in a chair.

"Excuse me?"

"Emma used to have to beat your behind every other day. Ooh you were a little bad ass."

"Do I know you?"

"You broke her heart when you ran away. No matter how many kids came and went, she always talked about you."

Paris walked over to the old woman's porch. "Who are you?"

"I used to say to Emma, 'Don't you worry none, Emma, that child is going to find her way back home, you'll see and she's gonna take care of the children."

"Ma, you okay?" A young woman came to the front door. "I thought I heard another voice out here."

"I didn't mean to disturb you," Paris said to the young woman. "Your mother was just telling me –"

"Don't pay her any mind. She has Alzheimer's; she just rambles on and on about any and everything."

"Alzheimer's? But she remembers me from when I used to live next door."

"My mother can't even remember her own name. It's time to go inside Ma."

"Okay mommy."

"See? I'm the daughter and she calls me mommy."

Paris watched the young woman help the frail woman up and walk her into the house.

She remembered me, Paris whispered to herself. She went home, undressed and got into bed. She racked her brain trying to remember the old woman next door. She said she remembered her, remembered when Emma had to beat her butt. She was right about that. Paris couldn't remember a day Emma didn't have to slap, hit, or punch her.

"Miss Belle," she said out loud. "Oh shit, I remember you, Miss Belle." She was the dentist assistant who held her hand when the dentist was putting on her braces. "Damn, Miss Belle, you got real ah... old."

Paris was staring at the ceiling, thinking of her family. The one she left down in the city. She was missing them something terrible. She reached for her cellphone on the table and stopped. She wasn't ready to talk to them yet. She kicked off the sheets and put her clothes back on. Paris decided to go out.

She walked into the lounge and immediately regretted coming. Tee and four girls from her clique were sitting at a table tucked in a corner. She rolled her eyes at them and headed to the bar.

"What can I get you?" The bartender asked.

"Five shots of vodka," she replied.

The bartender arched his brow. "Five?"

Paris held her hand up. "Five."

"Coming right up…"

"I thought you didn't hang out," Tee said, walking up on Paris.

"I don't."

"It looks like you're hanging out to me."

"I'm just having a drink."

"Here you go," the bartender said, placing five shots in front of her. Paris threw back the first two right off the bat.

"Damn, you an alcoholic or something?"

"Why are you talking to me?"

Tee put her hand on her hip. "I just wanted to let you know to stay away from Ramel."

"What?"

"You heard me. I see the way you be looking at him when he comes into the bookstore."

"Bitch you bugging."

"Bitch…? You sure you want to go there with me?"

Paris downed her third shot. She pulled out a twenty and placed it under one of the empty shot glasses. When she got up to leave, Tee blocked her way.

"Where you think you going, bitch?"

Paris shoved her out the way and left. She didn't get half way down the block before Tee rushed out of the lounge with her four girl crew.

"Where's your bike, Dyke?" The girls laughed at Tee's remark. "Hey, Dyke, I know you heard me."

Paris stopped walking.

"Yeah, bitch, that's what I'm talking about," Tee said, walking up on her. Her girls surrounded Paris.

"You need to grow the fuck up," Paris said.

"You need to shut the fuck up."

Tee swung on her. Paris deflected the blow and backed up into one of Tee's crew. The girl pushed her back into Tee. Tee got a punch off to Paris's cheek. Paris got off three. One to Tee's jaw, another to her forehead, and the last one to her temple. Tee backed up and looked at Paris in shock.

"Gena," Tee yelled out to one of her girls. "Shoot this bitch."

Paris looked at the girl Tee was talking to and watched her pull a .25 out of her jacket pocket. Gena looked no more than seventeen years old.

"Yo, put that away!" Gena saw Cyrus and immediately stuck it back in her jacket.

"What the fuck are you doing?" he asked Tee.

"This bitch disrespected me."

"Go back inside, now."

Tee sucked her teeth and headed back to the lounge.

"What the fuck are y'all still standing here for?" Cyrus said to Tee's girls. They headed back to the lounge.

Paris started to walk off.

"Where's your bike."

"I walked."

"You walked all the way here by yourself?"

"My house isn't far from here."

"It's dark as hell."

"I'm not afraid of the dark."

"The dark is the least of your problems out here at night."

"I can handle myself."

"Yeah, I peeped that. I never saw a chick hit another chick that hard and so many times."

Paris picked up her pace.

"Hold up, let me give you a ride home."

"Nah, I'm good."

Cyrus ran to his truck; he pulled up along side her. "Hop in."

"I said I'm good."

"C'mon now, I'm not going to let you walk home in the dark."

Paris stopped walking.

"I'll drop you off and breakout, no funny stuff."

She opened the door and climbed in.

"I heard you used to live here."

"I used to."

"Is that why people flock around you?"

"People don't flock around me."

"Sure they do. The kids hang out at your house, people who never stepped foot in Neal's bookstore, are now in there half the day kicking it with you. You're like a hometown girl who left, became a famous movie star and then came back."

Paris laughed. "You're funny."

"I'm dead serious. I've been watching you. I recognize real when I see it."

"You're so full of shit."

"See, that's what I'm talking about, realness. You don't bite your tongue and from what I saw back there, you definitely don't hold back any punches. You would fit in just fine with my Albany team."

"Albany team...?"

"That's where I'm from. I run all of downtown."

"So why are you here in this small town?"

Cyrus took one hand off the steering wheel and rubbed his thumb and first two fingers together. "Opportunity… And now I'm offering you one."

"Not interested."

"I can take care of you."

"I take care of myself, been doing it for years."

"Well, maybe it's time for you to let someone else take over that responsibility," he said pulling up to the curb in front of her house.

Paris opened the door and got out. "The next time someone from your crew pulls a gun on me, you're going to see just how real I can get."

Cyrus smiled. "I like your style, mommy."

Paris slammed his truck door. Cyrus pulled off as she headed up her steps.

"You okay?"

Paris turned around. "What are you doing here?"

Neal walked up the steps. "Jerry called me from the lounge, he said Tee and some girls were trying to roll on you. When I got there, I saw you hopping in Cyrus's truck." He saw the light bruise that Tee's punch left on Paris's cheek. He tried to touch it.

"It's nothing," Paris said, turning her head.

"You don't have to act tough all the time."

"Who said I was acting?" She didn't move when he touched the bruise. She could see the anger and hurt in his eyes. The last thing she wanted him to do was go get himself into trouble.

"You want to come in for a while?" she offered.

"It's kinda late," Neal said.

"Do you have a curfew?" she asked.

"You're something else, you know that?"

They headed inside.

"Just so you know," Paris said, as she took off her jacket, "you ain't getting no pussy."

"What about some head?"

She threw her jacket at him. She disappeared into the bathroom and came back with an ice pack for her cheek. "Can I get you something to drink?"

Neal was in the living room looking at the pictures on the wall. "I'll take a beer."

Paris grabbed two bottles of beer out of the fridge and entered the living room. She handed him one. "Thank you," she said.

"For what…?"

"For coming to check on me," she smiled.

"I'm going to have a long talk with Cyrus. His clique is getting out of control."

"That won't be necessary. Cyrus and I had a little chat on our way here."

"He has to hear it from me, as well."

"And why is that?"

"He has to know that I'm not just going to sit back and watch you being fucked with."

"That's so sweet," she said grabbing his hand. "But don't get yourself killed on account of me."

"Cyrus's not going to put a hand on me." His face softened. "So which of these is you?" he said, pointing to the pictures.

"That one right there," she said.

"Oh shit."

"What?"

"You were an ugh-mug."

"Fuck you," she said, pushing him. He grabbed her arms as he stumbled back. He fell on the couch; she fell on top of him. Paris didn't move, Neal didn't say a word. Neal's body was hard and warm. Paris felt her temperature rising. She stood up.

"I'm not ugly, anymore."

"No…you're not," he said sitting up. He studied a picture on the wall.

"What?"

"He stood up and walked to the picture. "That's Scratch."

Paris looked at the picture of the 8 year old. "That is him."

Neal studied the rest of the pictures more closely. "I know a lot of these kids. Most of them are still here in town." He was studying the pictures so hard that he didn't notice Paris standing on the side of him, staring at him with lust in her eyes. She reached out and touched his lips. He turned to her. He grabbed her hand and kissed her fingers. She closed her eyes.

"Neal?"

"Yes."

"Remember what I told you earlier about not getting any pussy?"

"Yeah..."

She pulled her hand away. "I wasn't playing." Neal stared at her, smiling. He kissed her on the forehead.

"I'll see you at work tomorrow."

"I'm off tomorrow and Sunday," she smiled.

"Well, then I'll see you Monday," he said walking out the door without looking back. When he shut the door, Paris exhaled.

Monday morning, Paris stepped out of her house she saw the newspaper on her welcome mat.

"What the hell is wrong with this boy," she said, referring to the paperboy.

She told him on three different occasions that he kept dropping the paper at the wrong house. She picked it up and headed next door. "Good morning, Miss Belle."

"Good morning, Emma," Miss Belle said, as she rocked in her rocking chair.

"No, Miss Belle, I'm not Emma, I'm Paris."

"Paris is a good girl. Give her some time, she'll come back, you'll see."

"Miss Belle, Emma's gone."

Miss Belle looked at her. "Paris will be back, you'll see."

Paris laid the newspaper on Miss Belle's lap. "I have to go to work; I'll talk to you later."

"Okay, Emma."

Paris walked away and hopped on her bike. "That was creepy."

When Paris walked into the bookstore, Neal was holding his head.

"Neal, what's up?"

"You didn't hear?"

"Hear what?"

He shoved the Albany Times Union to her.

Jermaine Thomas A.K.A. Scratch, age 13, was gunned down in the Arbor Hill section of Albany last night, in gang retaliation. Jermaine escaped from a DFY facility 2 years ago and hadn't been seen since. The names of the other teens involved are being withheld until their guardians are contacted...

Paris dropped the paper on the counter.

"That's fucked up," Neal said.

"That's fucked up," she said, pointing to Cyrus's Tahoe parked in front of the diner. "He drove them kids to Albany to do his dirty work. Now, they're dead and he's having breakfast like nothing happened." She walked off.

"Paris, where are you going?"

She walked across the street and barged into the diner. The look in her eyes silenced everyone in the eatery.

As she walked toward Cyrus's table, Ramel stood up. "What's up?" She pushed past him. "Yo."

He grabbed her by the shoulder. Paris spun around and banged him in the face with a left, then a right, another left, and a right, then an uppercut. He hit the floor face first and didn't move.

Cyrus stood up, eyes wide. Tee, Ramel's girl shook off the shock of seeing her man getting knocked out by a chick and charged Paris. She ran into a left jab and a right hook. She screamed and grabbed her coochie after Paris kicked her in the crotch with a steel-toed boot.

Cyrus yoked her from behind. Paris struggled to break free. She stomped on his feet, kicked him in his shins, clawed at his arms, but Cyrus refused to break the hold.

The sheriff ran through the door with Neal on his heels. The sheriff grabbed Paris while Neal held Cyrus back.

"This fucking bitch is crazy!" Cyrus shouted.

"You're a murderer!"

Paris broke free and charged him. Neal got caught in the middle of the blows coming from both sides.

A deputy ran in, grabbed Paris and wrestled her to the floor. He handcuffed her and dragged her off to his cruiser.

Paris sat on the cot in the holding pen staring out the window when the sheriff approached the cell.

"I've talked to the young man and woman you assaulted. They don't want to press charges." He opened the cell. "I advise you to slow your roll. Next time, you may not be so lucky." He walked her to the curb. "Hey. Why don't you do everybody a favor, sell Emma's house, take the money and go back to where you came from."

Paris walked off on him and headed to the bookstore to retrieve her bike. Neal walked out the bookstore when he saw her.

"You okay?"

Paris hopped on her bike. Neal put his hand on her shoulder. She shrugged it off and started her bike.

"What are you going to do?"

She peeled off, leaving him in a cloud of burned rubber.

Paris sat in her living room staring at the pictures on the wall. The old woman's words from next door replayed in her head. Why me Emma? Why leave me this house? She looked out the window when she caught light reflecting off of something shiny. She dived to the floor as the guns went off. Glass shattered all around her as she crawled out of the living room and into the bedroom. Moments later, she heard tires peeling off into the night.

The deputy looked up from his note pad.

"And you didn't get a look at who shot at your house?"

"No."

He flipped his note pad shut when he saw the sheriff approaching. Paris stared at him as he stared at her back pack.

"Going somewhere?"

"I'm taking your advice."

The sheriff looked around before spitting out a glob of chewing tobacco.

"I'll follow you to the town limits and make sure you get out safely."

The sheriff followed her a little past the town limits before slowing down and swinging a U-turn. Paris rode into Clifton Park and got a motel room.

She threw her back pack on the bed and pulled out her cellphone. She scrolled down to the number she wanted and stared at it. She knew once she made this call, there was no turning back. Paris closed her eyes and thought about Scratch, then she hit dial.

"Talk to me," the voice on the other end said.

"Sid…I need you."

"Where are you?"

Paris gave her the name of the motel and the room number.

"And Sid, bring the family."

Four thirty in the morning, a black Dodge Charger drove up into the motel's parking lot and stopped in front of room 103. The Charger's passenger side door swung open and out stepped Sid, all six-foot, two hundred and twenty pounds of her. She wore her black trench closed, fitted cap just above her eyes and Timbs laced to the top. She walked up to room 103. Before she had a chance to knock, Paris opened the door. Paris looked up at her and couldn't stop smiling. Sid could tell that she had been crying. She hugged her and stepped in.

"Who we got to kill?" she asked, shrugging off her trench and tossing it on the bed. She stood in the middle of the floor, clenching and unclenching her hands.

Paris stared at the Kevlar vest and .45 tucked in Sid's shoulder holster. "Where's the rest of the family?"

The hotel door banged open. "Be careful what you wish for," Mimi said. She ran in and hugged Paris. "I miss you."

"I miss you, too."

Twelve more women walked in behind Mimi and hugged Paris.

"Jamie?" Paris said, looking at the last girl to walk in.

Jamie pulled up her sleeve and proudly flashed her *COLD BLOODED* tattoo snaking all the way up her arm. "I'm family, now." Paris ran to her and hugged her tight.

"So, who we gotta kill…?" Precious asked. She was all business, no play.

Paris gave them the rundown. "There's this kid out of Albany who calls himself Cyrus. He's got half of Albany on lock and he's expanding his enterprise into my town; and he's killing the children."

"Killing the children?" Mimi mused.

"He's using them as soldiers to knock off his competition. Two nights ago, four teens from my town were shot and killed up in Albany in what the papers are calling gang retaliation." Paris started to tear. "He's got to go."

Precious folded her arms. "And how did this become our problem again?"

"This motherfucker is killing kids," Paris said.

Precious pulled up Paris's sleeve. "This is what we are," she said, pointing to the tat. "Kids die everyday, get over it."

"Precious is right," Sid said. "This has nothing to do with us."

"Yes it does. This is what we're about," Paris said.

"Getting paid by any means necessary is what we're about," Precious said.

Paris looked to Sid. "I ran away from this town when I was fourteen to find my mother. I had nothing but the clothes on my back. I hooked up with some bikers and…I did what I had to do to survive. And one night when I was being passed around like a blunt, in a shit house bar, in busts this six foot, big bitch and kills the head of the bikers with her bare hands."

Sid looked at Mimi who was crying. "Those motherfuckers left Mimi for dead in that dumpster. It was only a matter of time before they did the same to you."

"You and the family lit that bar up. Only three of them got away that night."

"And we hunted their asses down," Mimi said. "And they paid for what they did to me, and for what they did to you."

"What was the family's motivation, back then?" Paris looked around the room. "All of us have a horror story to tell. Me and Mimi gang raped by bikers, Jamie raped for years by different foster parents, and you…"

She walked up to Precious." You were only 6 years old when your crack head mother started prostituting you out to support her habit."

"Fuck you," Precious whispered.

"And you, Sid. You were kidnapped by your boyfriend's connect when he couldn't come up with the fifty thousand he owed him. Instead of him hustling up the loot that he owed, he left you for dead. How long did they keep you down in that basement, chained to the radiator? Ballers from all over the neighborhood paid a king's ransom to come down in that basement to fuck and sodomize the ex Queen of Philly."

Sid slapped her. Paris continued staring her in the eye. Sid slapped her again. Paris didn't flinch.

"My little biker chick, tough as shit," Sid said looking around at her crew. "Ladies, I don't know about y'all but just thinking of putting my .45 in this motherfucker's mouth and pulling the trigger has gotten my pussy dripping." Everyone started laughing. Sid grabbed her trench off the bed and put it on. "Let's do this."

Neal looked out the window when he heard Paris's bike. He did a double take when she walked in. She was wearing a tank top, jeans, and Timbs. As she approached the counter, he could see the *COLD BLOODED* tat swirling up her arm.

"Paris?"

"Where can I find Cyrus?"

"How would I know?"

"Neal, we're cool and everything, but don't fuck with me. Where is he?"

Neal turned to the window when he saw three black Yukon's pull up.

"Neal," Paris whispered, "just tell me what I need to know. They won't ask nicely."

"I'm not a snitch, Paris."

Paris looked toward the window and shook her head. The doors on all three trucks flew open. Sid and the rest of Cold Blooded swarmed into the bookstore like a nest of angry hornets. Neal backed up against the wall when Precious leaped over the counter and pressed her gun against his forehead.

"Okay, okay, I'll tell you."

Cyrus and Ramel were in the living room smoking a blunt and watching TV when the front door almost flew off its hinges.

"What the fuck?" Ramel reached for his gun on the table. Precious had her .38 in his mouth before he got to it.

Cyrus ran out the living room, toward the backdoor. He opened it and caught the butt-end of Jamie's shotgun with his mouth. He fell on his ass.

Paris walked in and kicked him in the face. "Get your punk ass up," she said, kicking him in the stomach. He got up and limped back to the living room. Paris shoved him to the couch.

"Scratch would be alive today if it weren't for you."

"Scratch knew what he was getting into."w

"He was only 13. Don't you feel anything over his death and the other kids who died with him?"

"It's all part of the game."

"You just made doing what I have to do that much easier."

"And what are you going to do?"

Sid walked into the house and closed the front door. "He's pulling up."

"Who's pulling up?" Cyrus said.

"Shhh..." Jamie said pointing her shotgun at his chest.

"Cyrus?" the sheriff called out as he stepped onto the porch.

Sid opened the door and snatched the old man off his feet. The sheriff landed on his back in the center of the living room. He reached for his pistol. Mimi stomped on his hand before he could get to it.

"What the hell is this?" he asked looking up at the women.

"Justice," Paris said, snatching his pistol out of its holster. "You're a hero, sheriff."

"A hero?"

"Yes, you came here and took out these two drug dealing thugs all by yourself. You busted in and shot Ramel twice." Paris shot Ramel twice in the chest with the sheriff's gun.

"But then, Cyrus got to Ramel's gun and shot you in the stomach," Precious said, shooting the sheriff in the gut with Ramel's gun.

Cyrus jumped off the couch. Paris shot him three times in the chest with the sheriff's gun. "You were able to shoot Cyrus three times before dying from the two bullet wounds you took in the stomach."

"Wait –"

Precious shot him again in the stomach. Everyone looked toward the top of the stairs.

"I found her hiding in the closet," Jamie said.

"That's Ramel's girl," Paris said.

"Get out of here," Sid said to Paris. "You can't be seen here. Remember, stick to the plan."

Two months later, Paris rode her bike onto the sidewalk and stopped in front of the bookstore. She climbed off and walked in.

Neal looked up from the book he was reading. "Hey."

"Hey." Paris looked around. "How's business?"

"Business has dropped two hundred percent since you left."

"Don't try and make me feel guilty."

"Would it make you come back?"

"No. The kids need me."

"I need you."

Paris walked behind the counter and kissed him. "And you have me."

"Since you opened that youth center in memory of Scratch, I'm seeing less and less of you."

"Tonight, you're going to see a lot of me," she said kissing him again.

He wrapped his arms around her waist and pulled her close." You are so beautiful."

"You're getting some pussy tonight, so you don't have to gas me up."

"Are we going to have the house to ourselves? You know I can't…do my thing with Sid and them around."

"They intimidate you?"

"Hell yeah…!"

Paris started laughing.

"And I'm not ashamed to admit it. When I'm around them, I feel like a goldfish in a tank with piranhas."

"They love you."

"Like cat loves mice."

"Well, you will be pleased to know that Sid told me that they are going back to the city this weekend."

"Thank you God."

Paris punched him in the arm. "Don't say that. It was because of them that this town is back to normal."

Neal nodded. "You're right. I can't take that away from them. We owe them big time."

"And don't you forget that."

On the outskirts of town, a black Yukon pulled into a barn. Precious and three females from the clique got out.

Sid walked into the barn. "Talk to me."

Precious opened the cargo area of the Yukon. "According to Ramel's bitch, we just hit the last of Cyrus's stash houses in Albany."

Sid looked at the kilos of dope and nodded.

"So what's the plan?" Precious asked. "We got a whole lot of coke and dope."

"We're setting up shop."

"Where…?"

"Right here."

"In Paris's town…?"

"What better place? We have no competition."

"I don't think Paris will approve."

"Paris is going to do what the fuck I tell her to do."

"And if she doesn't?"

"Then, she goes into the ground like the sheriff, Ramel and Cyrus."

"That's cold, Sid."

"No, bitch, that's *COLD BLOODED*."

Find Me An Angel

KATRINA JONES

I was scared to turn around. I could feel the anger all in his voice.

"Angela you better turn around and answer me," Tony said.

Though I knew that this would exasperate him even further, I couldn't fix myself to turn around. I stared at the wall, "My sister…" I answered in a low voice.

"Bitch!" he said and my face hit the wall.

Pain surged through my entire body. Holding me firmly with one hand wrapped around my head, and the rest of me almost part of the wall, he breathed heavily into my ear. She was predicting things were about to get worse as they normally did.

He locked his arm around my neck and pulled me back with such force, that when my head hit the floor it split. I laid there dazed with blood running from my dome. My throat burned with such intensity, it was hard for me to catch my breath. I couldn't utter a word if I wanted to.

What he didn't know was I was ready to die. The only thing that kept me here were my two kids, but maybe this is how it was suppose to be from the beginning. Take me out of my misery I thought, and with that I smiled.

Taking the smile as a form of disrespect, Tony kicked me twice in my ribs.

"You wanna be a disrespectful, bitch, huh?" he said.

I was already in so much pain I didn't think it could get any worse. Tony climbed over me, bent down and punched me in the nose. Every thing went black after that.

When I finally came to, I was in bed with a bandage over my head and a headache the size of Queens. My body did not seem functional at all. All I could do was lay there. I heard footsteps coming from down the hall. I knew that it could only be one person, the man responsible for my current condition. I didn't know what to expect but I prayed that this meant the beating was over.

Tony was the love of my life and father of my two children. We were married a year ago and things were wonderful. After about nine months into the marriage and our second child he started changing. Staying out some nights, he sarted talking to me very disrespectful, and would occasionally slap me. I always rationalize it to be caused from stress, and never really said much about it.

When his six foot frame entered the room he had a glass of water in his hand and what I hoped were pain killers in the other. He walked up to the side of the bed that I was occupying and smiled. I didn't want to upset him again so I just smiled back.

"Here take this," Tony said, bending down to give me the pills.

I was very skeptical and allowed him to drop the pills into my opened mouth. He gave me some water to swallow.

"Being that you're in no condition to pick the kids up from school, I will get them, and don't worry about dinner, I will pick something up on the way home," he said then turned and walked out the door.

I couldn't believe he had the audacity to even say that to me, when he was the reason I couldn't pick up my kids, or make dinner. I looked up toward the ceiling and closed my eyes.

"Lord, why didn't you take my life?" I silently prayed. "It would've been so much easier if I was gone. Now look at what I've gotten myself into. If I would've turned around then this wouldn't have happened. I don't know why I can't do anything right. How good am I if I can't even please my husband and all I do is make matters worse. Lord, please forgive my husband, he's just going through a lot and I'm just putting more pressure on him. Please help my marriage. I don't want to lose my husband, I love him too much."

Before I knew it, I was fast asleep. I woke up from the aroma I knew all to well, Soul food from Amy Ruth's. I looked up at the clock it was already five in the evening. I heard little voices coming from the kids' room. How I wish I could just get up, walk in their room, and hug my kids. I was still too tired to get out of bed.

Lying there in my dense state, I started to think of my life. How I felt when I graduated from high school, the things that I accomplished when everything was stacked against me. My dream wasn't to be a lawyer but that was where I was heading. It gave me a sense of power. In reality, my life consists of insecurities and loneliness. The first time I met my husband was when I thought I had a chance for happiness.

He understood me, accepted my flaws, and loved me for me. Now I feel the distance widening between us. I know he loves me and as usual I find a way to mess things up.

"Mommy, you're up."

I heard the voice and looked toward the door. A little startled Michael and Michelle were there.

"Yes babies, mommy's up."

"Mommy, daddy said you hurt yourself," Michael said.

"Are you okay?" Michelle asked.

"Yes, mommy did hurt herself, and yes, mommy will be fine. I just need to rest, okay? So that means not too much noise."

"Okay mommy," they chimed with innocence.

I looked at my children and had to hold back the tears. I loved them both dearly and felt like I disappointed them too. Michelle, the younger of the two asked me if she could get on my bed and brush my hair. All I could do was smile.

It was something in her that rang when people are sad. She always tried within all her power to make the person feel better. Tony appeared in the doorway. Our eyes met and I could tell by his expression that he wanted to say something. I gave him a look of disadin letting him know I expected an apology.

"Alright y'all, it's time to eat. Go take your places at the table," Tony said to the children.

"Can I eat here with mommy?" Michelle asked.

"No, you know you gotta eat at the table," Tony replied.

I didn't mind if she ate in here with me, but didn't want to say anything to piss him off. I remained quiet and watched the kids leave the room on their way downstairs to the kitchen.

"Are you hungry?" he asked me.

I was very hungry but I was too sore to help myself. So I said, "I'm fine."

He walked out leaving me with my thoughts. The struggles I had to bear, sacrifices that had to be made, tears came. I was feeling too sorry for myself. .

"You need to get yourself together," he said.

I couldn't believe what I was hearing. I tried to sit up in the bed and felt a pain shooting through my spine, so severe my eyes started to tear. The nerve of this man damn near beat me dead.

Again not wanting to piss him off I agreed and he walked out the room. I knew I was in bad shape but I knew I had to find a way to get out of bed, before this man finds another reason to use me as a punching bag. I laid there another minute trying to gather up my strength.

Once I felt I could get up I held my breath and heaved myself up. It hurt like hell but I did it. My feet felt wobbly. As I stood it felt like I was going to faint. I held on to the bed post until the feeling passed. I heard the front door slam. Tony had just walked out the door. I slowly made my way to the bathroom, scared of what I would see in the mirror.

When I reached the bathroom I went directly to the toilet, sat on it for five minutes releasing my full bladder. I was too afraid to look in the mirror, so I kept just sitting on the toilet until I got up enough courage. Tears ran down my bruised face when I looked. It was not unbearable but it was not me. My body on the other hand had all kinds of bruises and swelling.

I felt better enough to make my way downstairs. I wanted to check on Michael and Michelle. They were in the living room watching *Dora*. Before disturbing them, I stood there watching them, so innocent and unaware of life. How could I do right by them if things aren't right with me, or the home that they live in? I had to ask myself. I felt like I don't deserve them, but looking at their little faces always light up my day.

"Okay guys, let's go. It's time to take a bath. Michelle it's your turn to go first Michael went yesterday," I said to them.

"Alright mommy," Michelle said.

It took all I had to get the kids bathed and into bed. It was now time to clean up. I cleared the table, and washed the dishes, thinking of how unfair life had been to me. The things I didn't have when I was younger, turning out to be the same things I can't get now. I couldn't blame Tony for hitting on me. Something about me probably needed to be fixed.

After all the cleaning was done I decided to take a bath. I wanted to soak my aching body. I turned on the water and watched the tub filling up. I reluctantly removed all of my clothing and stared at my body in the mirror. Despite the swelling and bruises, it was still in good shape. I stepped into the tub and let my body disappear under the water.

A relaxing feeling came over me. I closed my eyes and let my mind take me to another place.

I don't know what's going on with me. I have a wife and two beautiful children. My wife once meant the world to me. I could never forget how beautiful I thought she was when I first seen her. When she spoke to me, her voice was soft, and to the point. We spoke about a legal matter that a mutual friend was having. She blew me away, once she told me she was only nineteen and already a paralegal wanting to further her career and become a lawyer. Still, I knew her experience was still inexperienced and I wanted to add to her knowledge, I had to have her.

I was a manager in a McDonald's restaurant. I let her know that from the beginning of our conversation. I was twenty-two at the time and was kinda proud of my own success. Everything was beautiful in the beginning. I wasn't mad that Angela made more than me, or that her circle of friends was so much different than mine. After awhile it bothered me when we had to go to one of her little functions and I had to make small talk with a bunch of lawyers, and the up and comings.

Even though no one has ever said anything about what I do for a living I could feel them looking down on me. Angela never said or showed that she was embarrassed by me, and if anyone said anything about it she never let on to me. I pretended until I couldn't any more.

I promised myself that I would do better so she wouldn't have to work. The vibration of Tony's cellphone broke him out of his trance. He retrieved his phone from his pocket and looked at the screen.

Shalone calling... Tony answered the phone.

"Hello," he said.

"Baby, where you at?" the person on the other end of the phone whined.

"I'm downstairs. I'll be up in a minute," Tony said.

After hanging up the phone, he cut off the car and got out. He knew what he was doing was wrong but circumstances taught him how to control his wife, and in return he could do whatever he liked.

When he walked in the building he spoke to the security guard and went to the back where the elevators were located. Once the doors opened he walked inside and pressed eleven. The ride up was fast as usual. He exited the elevator made a right and went to room 1101. Before he could knock on the door it flung wide open. Shalone came out wearing a red see through gown and nothing under. She jumped into Tony's arms and wrapped her legs around him. Kissing him passionately she made sure he knew just how much she's missed him. Carrying her inside, Tony kicked the door shut and brought her over to the bed.

Placing her down on the bed, he never let her go. The two continued kissing passionately. He moved his hand up her leg, caressing her soft thick thighs. Shalone moaned. She removed her hands from around his neck ready for him to explore her body. Tony moved down to her neck, his kisses sending chills racing down her spine. She always loved how attentive he was when it came to pleasing her.

Shalone was ready for him. He stuck his ten inch thickness inside her inviting love box, she moaned from pure pleasure. She continued meeting his thrust perfectly, she felt herself about to climax. Shalone wrapped her legs around Tony and made him dig deeper inside so he could feel all that she had.

He could not hold on any longer, and started to pump faster and faster until he released inside her. He lay on the bed next to her, both breathing heavily with nothing left to say for the moment. Then they both fell asleep.

I woke up from the chill of the water. What time is it how long have

I been in here? Sitting up, I let the cold water out and turned on the faucet, runing some warm water. I must've been very relaxed.

While hot water poured into the tub, I grabbed the washcloth and body scrub, lathering. I was trying to do it as softly as possible, being careful not to scrub the parts with bruises too hard. Later, I wraped a large towel around my body, walked into the bedroom, to see if it was still the way I'd left it.

I could feel an unusual queasy feeling in my gut. My husband was doing something wrong. I don't know what to do with that man. As I was putting lotion on my body, I turned my head up to the ceiling and started to pray.

"Dear Lord," I began. "I come to you as a willing servant, and ask you to help my husband. When I took my vows it was for better or worse. Right now things don't feel as if they can get any worse but I know they can be. I ask you to forgive his life of adultery. I have no proof but I do know what is right. Please Lord, I also pray for strength. If he cannot overcome that devil, then please give me the strength to do what's right for my kids. I know that I'm not the best, Lord, and I blame myself for the things that he does. Please help me to better myself. Maybe it's something wrong with me—"

"Mommy," it was Michelle's voice interrupting.

I opened my eyes and looked at my daughter, standing in the door way with sleep filled eyes.

"Yes baby," I answered.

"I had a bad dream. Can I lay here with you?" Michelle asked her mother.

I could tell that she was frightened.

"Of course, honey."

Michelle climbed into the bed with me.

"Amen…" I said finishing the prayer.

"Mommy, what were you doing when I came into the room?" Michelle asked.

"Mommy was praying," I replied making my way to the dresser drawers to retrieve some underclothes and pajamas.

"What were you praying about, mommy?"

"I prayed for strength, forgiveness and thanked God for my two beautiful children."

I had to smile when I said that. Michelle was my twin. With smooth, dark complexion, she had slanted eyes that almost made her look Asian. We both had long jet-black hair and a smile that can light up a room. Michael looks more like his father with broad shoulders and chestnut complexion. He was blessed with eyes like mine, but he still was the splitting image of his father.

After putting on my pajamas, I got in bed with Michelle. Michelle said good night to me and was fast asleep. I held my daughter like someone threatened to take her away. Life was about two beautiful children and I knew things needed to be right for them.

Tony never hit me in front of the children but I don't want it to come to that and they see how daddy beats on mommy. I was back to thinking about how much I'd given up for that man. He was insecure and because I loved him I did everything in my power to make him feel like a man. It's not like I had a problem with his profession, it was just that he couldn't get comfortable knowing that I made more money than he did.

When my son was born, everything changed. He said that I didn't need to return to work because I needed to take care of his son. I remember times he made me feel so low I had to believe that what he was saying was true.

It was now three o'clock in the morning and my husband still wasn't home. I pray that he was okay, but I knew that he was more than okay. Everything ran through my mind and I thought about it all until my eyes could no longer stay open.

"Why did you call her?" Tony asked.

Still lying in bed on her back with both hands behind her head, Shalone just gazed up at the ceiling.

"Shalone…" he called.

"I just wanted to check on her. She's still my sister right?"

"Wrong," Tony answered with more bass in his voice now. "You think she'll want anything to do with you if she found out that you were sleeping with me?"

Shalone lunged up in the bed looked down at Tony with disdain.

"Do you think she'll want to be bothered with you if she found out that you were sleeping with me?" Shalone asked.

"I'm her husband. I pay the bills and take care of her and the kids," Tony said in a sly tone.

Shalone wanted to respond but she also knew that Tony had a bad temper. He was one of them, Jeckyl and Hyde type.

"I wanted to speak to my niece and nephew," Shalone said instead of saying what was really on her mind.

"What part of that-is-no-longer-your-family, don't you understand?" he asked. "Because of you my wife couldn't pick up her children or make my dinner."

"Because of me…?" Shalone yelled.

"What do I have to do with her not picking up her children?" Shalone asked.

"She disobeyed my rules, so she paid the price."

Shalone looked at him with fury and worry in her eyes.

"What did you do to my sister?" she asked.

Tony was now the one with his hands behind his head gazing up at the ceiling. Shalone jumped off the bed and ran to the closet to get her phone so she could call her sister. Tony jumped up when he realized what she was trying to do. Tony grabbed the phone, Shalone wouldn't let it go. They swayed back and forth fighting for the phone Shalone tripped, stepping off balance she fell forward hitting her head on the table, before falling to the floor. She let the phone go as her arms went limp.

Tony panicked when he saw that she wasn't getting up. He bent down and shook her. She would not get up. Tony then checked for a pulse. He felt it so he knew that she was still alive. He started smacking her face, trying to see if there was any response.

After about a minute Shalone started to stir. She opened her eyes slowly. Shalone looked up at Tony with a quizzical expression on her face. Tony lifted her up and carried her to the bed. He gently laid her down then retreated to the kitchen and got some ice. With the ice trays in hand, he suddenly stopped.

"Another fall on the head, what the hell am I trying to do, catch a murder charge?" he said to himself.

How did life become so complicated? I remember when being a manager in Mc Donald's meant a lot to me. I took pride in my job. Then I fell in love and was intimidated by the woman I loved. Instead of making things right for us, I wanted her to need me. When I felt like she hadn't done a good job in making me feel good, I beat her. I loved the feeling that I got when she begged me. I made sure that I was all that she needed. Snapping back to reality Tony cracked the ice trays and placed the ice in a towel, before walking back.

Shalone was on the bed, quietly trying to control the headache she now had. Tony sat on the bed and waited for Shalone so he could put ice on her head.

"I'm sorry, baby. I didn't mean to hurt you," he said caring for another bruised throbbing head. "Things got out of control and you lost your balance," Tony explained.

Shalone was now lying in his arms while he held the ice on her bruised head. Not knowing what to say, Shalone just looked in his eyes. How did she fall in love with her sister's husband? She could no longer do this. Her heart was the only thing that mattered to her at one time. But she missed her sister and she knew that this man would keep her away from her.

She knew that she was taking a risk telling her sister what was going on and may lose her anyway. That was a risk she was willing to take. All she could think about was what condition her sister was in. She knew Tony had a problem with his hands, but didn't know that he had forbidden my sister to talk to me.

I made sure I stayed away because I didn't want to hear anymore good news about Angela and her success some how it always ends up being my down fall. Shalone knew this would be the last time she would be with Tony so she just laid there wishing the time would pass so she could get to her sister.

About an hour later, Tony got up to leave. He made sure she was okay and walked out of the door. Shalone waited awhile to make sure that he was gone. Then she jumped up and ran to her phone. It was late but she had to get to her sister before this man got home. Her hands were shaking as she dialed the number. The phone rung and she waited on the other end with anticipation.

After about four rings Angela answered.

"Angela," Shalone rushed to speak. "I need to meet up with you tomorrow. Please give me a call and let me know when we can meet up this is urgent so please call me." That said, Shalone hung up the phone.

It was all about to go down, and whether she left with her sisters love or not she knew she could no longer do this to her. Yes, she was jealous of Angela, because Angela always got whatever she wanted. This had been her way of getting back at her sister, but she fell in love with Tony. Feeling dizzy she decided to rest and wait for the storm to come. She wished Angela would understand but that was not likely.

Tony walked into the door, looked around, and saw that everything was clean. He hoped Angela was asleep upstairs. He didn't want to have to look at her. Tony walked up the steps to his room. When he opened the door the lights were off. He glanced at the bed and saw his daughter in the bed with his wife. He was glad, but felt so guilty he couldn't face her after all that had taken place tonight. He walked back out the door and closed it behind him. He went down the steps and slept on the couch.

I pretended to be asleep and hoped he didn't hear me on the phone with Shalone. When I first heard him come in, I'd jumped back in the bed and curled up next to my daughter. When Tony walked into the room, I could feel his presence. I couldn't hear him moving around so I didn't know exactly where he was standing.

Finally the door closed and I opened my eyes. I had sleep in my eyes from being awoken by the phone. I did not see him anywhere in the room. A sigh escaped and I laid back. I really didn't know why Shalone wanted to meet, but it sounded really urgent. I don't know how I'm going to meet up with her but I'll think of something.

When morning came, I got up still sore from the beating. I went to the kids' room and woke Michael up for school. Michelle was already up. Tony came into the room and kissed his kids good morning. I was shocked when he kissed me on my cheek and said, "Good morning."

"Good morning," I said with a half-smile, thanking the Lord that this morning was not a trouble filled one.

Once I got the kids together, I put on a robe and led them outside to wait for the schoolbus. When it pulled up, I kissed Michael and Michelle and told them to be good. I walked back inside the house, leery of my husband's presence. I went to the kitchen and made breakfast for him.

He showered, dressed and came downstairs for breakfast. We sat down at the table and ate in silence. I decided to break the silence.

"Could I have some money to buy the kids some new clothes and sneakers?" I asked.

Tony was already feeling guilty and he couldn't look at my face.

"Yes," he said with his head down and continued eating.

When he was finished, I cleared the table and started to wash the dishes. Tony got up from the table and went back upstairs. I was surprised at how cool he was about the situation and was happy he didn't argue about me leaving the house.

Sometimes when he was wrong he'd blame it all on me and want to fight again because he couldn't bear looking at the bruises that he left on me. Tony came down the steps ready to walk out of the door. He put the money down on the counter and kissed me good-bye. Maybe the Lord had answered my prayers I thought. I knew it could have been only guilt.

After cleaning up, I jumped in the shower so I could start my day. I wanted to call Shalone but decided to wait just in case this man decides to double back. Showered and now dressed, I threw my sunshades on and headed out the door. Tony had taken the car so I walked to the avenue and caught a cab.

When I arrived at the mall I made sure my first stop was to a pay phone. I dialed Shalone's number and waited for the phone to ring. After the third ring Shalone answered. I told her where we could meet and hung up. I walked into the mall and went into the store to do some shopping for my children while I waited for Shalone.

Twenty-five minutes later, Shalone showed up. We greeted each other with a hug and continued in the stores doing some shopping. I was anxious for her to begin but I knew my older sister and didn't want her to retreat into her shell.

"What's up? Why did you sound so worried on the phone?" I asked walking up and down the aisle of a kiddie's store.

Shalone was scared to reveal the truth, but knew she couldn't turn back. She stalled and tried to make small talk asking about the children. I quickly dismissed that, telling her the children were well and asked her if she was okay. Shalone looked up at the glasses on my face.

Going from store to store Shalone could not find the right words to say. She started by telling me that she was jealous of me as a child and couldn't stand that I always got what I wanted. I was confused, trying to figure out where all of this was coming from.

"Before you say anything please let me finish," Shalone said.

She continued telling me how she resented me for being able to establish the things that I did. I was listening but still didn't understand where the conversation was going. Shalone stopped and took a slow breath.

"I'm telling you all of this to let you know my state of mind."

"Okay," I said paying attention.

Shalone knew it was now or never and blurted, "I've been sleeping with Tony for seven months now."

I could not believe what I was hearing. There was weakness in my knees. This had to be a dream. This couldn't be happening I must be getting punk'd. I looked around for cameras but there weren't any. Shalone stepped back. It took me a little while to be able to compute what my sister had just told me.

I smacked Shalone with such force she fell to the floor.

"How could you do something like that to me?" I screamed. "My husband…? I don't give a damn about your jealousy, or anything other than what you were secretly dealing with. You stoop that low to sleep with my husband to get back at me."

I was fuming but had no more to say. I stepped over my sister and walked out of the mall. There was pain in my heart and tears flooded my eyes. I couldn't understand how my sister could be so cruel. I caught a cab and never looked back to see if Shalone was coming behind me.

Siting in the cab, I thought about everything. Is that why he beat me yesterday, because he was scared she would say something? Or why the beatings started in the first place?

My pain turned to fury, and I thought about all the things I wanted to do to the both of them. The cab pulled up in front of the house, I got out and walked quickly to the door. I dropped everything on the floor and went straight to the cupboard that held the liquor. I opened a bottle of Grey Goose, and drunk it straight out the bottle.

Hurt and confused, I didn't know what to do. The house phone started to ring and I knew who was on the other end. I took another shot of

Goose. I had prayed for revelation, but this wasn't what I had in mind. I felt I could've forgiven anything that man did, but to sleep with my sister. He had overstepped all his boundaries.

"Fuck him!" I said.

After all that I had done for him and the things I gave up just to make him feel like a man. The more I thought about it the more it made me mad. I had a trick for the bastard when he did roll up in this house.

I ran up the stairs, I had to pack some clothes and take them to mother's house. After gathering all that I needed, I walked back out the house enroute to mother's house. When I got there, I explained what was going on to mother, and like most mothers, she was happy to help. It was almost time to get the kids off of the bus when I got back home. Today was one of the days they were scheduled to be dropped off.

When the children arrived home I got them off the bus. Walking back to the house, Shalone pulled up in front. I didn't want them to see anything so I sent my children inside the house. I ran over to Shalone and punched her in the face.

"Don't you ever show up at my house again," I screamed.

Shalone staggered back and covered her face.

"I just wanted to say I'm sorry," Shalone said in a low voice.

I stormed away saying, "I no longer have a sister and just forget about ever knowing me."

I slammed the door once I got inside and found the kids in the living room watching *Sponge Bob Square Pants*. I tried to calm down before the children detected something was wrong. The front door swung opened.

"Why the hell was Shalone in front of the house?" Tony screamed.

Fury was already flowing through my body. I stared at my husband, remembering the kids were there so I said, "Not now," before walking away.

"Bitch you lost your mind?" Tony asked.

He followed behind me.

"Not in front of my children," I said with a fierce attitude.

Tony grabbed me from behind, swung me around and smacked me in the face. I sent a stiff left hook to his jaw. The fight was on. Tony grabbed me by my hair and threw me against the wall. I lost my breath when my back crashed against the wall, but I couldn't give up. I attacked Tony's face trying to rip his eyes out of the socket. Tony punched me in my face, and that stopped my assault.

Michael and Michelle ran in the kitchen to see what was going on. They saw their father hit their mother for the first time. It scared the both of them and they started to cry. Tony did not heed the cries of his children. He threw me to the floor. I balled myself into a fetal position.

He walked over to the draw with all the kitchen utensils. Tony picked up a knife out the draw and walked back to where I was. I peeked from my position and saw the knife in his hand. I didn't want the kids to see anymore so I begged them to go upstairs to their room and told them that everything would be fine.

Michael and Michelle kept crying. Tony got on top of me and turned me around. Raising the knife high about to stick it through my chest, I just knew it was over and wished my kids didn't have to see their mommy leave them forever.

"Tony, look I won't fight you if you want me dead, but please spare your children. If you kill me you're all that they have," I cried.

I was speaking from the heart. I didn't want the kids to be witnesses to anything like this. He wouldn't listen to what I was saying and held the knife in position. He knew I knew the truth about him and my sister but felt I still belonged to him.

Michelle ran to my side, all the while yelling at her father trying to get him to stop. She would never leave.

"I won't allow it!" Tony screamed. "I won't allow it!" Then he brought the knife down hard and fast.

I woke up in the hospital and asked for my baby. No one wanted to tell me that my daughter died by her father's hands. I cried every night asking the Lord why. I wish it had been me. I entered the church thinking. I just couldn't come to grips with what I was about to do. It was taking every prayer, and every bone in my body not to jump in that coffin with my baby, my twin.

"I have to stay strong for Michael. He has been crying every night with me. I know he's going to need to speak to someone when he gets older. It scares me, what do you say to a child who has witnessed his father sticking a knife through his sister and his mother. At the age of seven, he has to say goodbye to the only other sibling he had. Michelle will always be a part of me and I will miss her," I said, trying to finish the service before I broke down.

I ran from the room and collapsed in the hall.

"My baby…!" I screamed. "He took her from me," I cried.

After the burial I didn't want to be bothered. I went home and into my kids' room. I picked up her pillow and sniffed it. I picked up her doll and thought how I was still here without her. I thought the heart only worked as a whole. I moved on to her dresser and saw her face. I lay in her bed, I fell asleep.

She spoke telling me, I had too many marks already. She didn't want to see no more on me. I smile. She continued, telling me to go on and live everything was fine. I tell her I can't. I have to that is the only way I can help people. I cry. My dream, she knew it. I love you she says before she drifts away.

Tony got twenty-five years to life for murder and attempted murder. Shalone still tries to apologize but I'll never accept it. Let her apologize to my daughter and hope like hell she's that angel and forgive her. My mother stayed by my side through all of this and I know it will be a long road but I have people to help. Michael is doing better every day and he sometimes comes to talk about our situation and explain what domestic violence can lead to. Even though they only witnessed it that one time. No one will ever hear Michelle's side of the story and Michael wishes he didn't have a story to tell.

Rooms of Allurement: Part 1

CAPRI LOVE

I want him, was my thinking as this fine man glided past me. My sister and I were at Passion, a new nightclub in New York City. I was looking to have a good time, but back to this man. He had a glass of Grey Goose in his right hand and I didn't see a ring on the left, so I was happy and horny. He was well-dressed in a Sean Jean button down and a pair of jeans fitting him well. His hair was freshly braided back with two diamond earrings in both ears. His wrist was laced with a Cartier. I could smell money.

He turned around to get his boy's attention and best believe his boy was looking right too. He looked up and our eyes met. He licked his lips and nodded his head to say hello. I sexily waved back and squared my eyes, letting him know that I wanted him to the fullest. He smiled as his friend and him, walked off smoothly.

I was a little upset but from the look in his eyes he wanted me too. I knew this game that he was playing was far from over and I intended to be the winner by the end of the night.

"Hey Raine, girl I was looking for you. I met this sexy-ass man, and he told me to bring you over. They're in the VIP section. So I told him that we were going to chill with him and his friends," my younger sister, Skye explained.

"And when did you meet this sexy man?" I asked.

"Oh we were dancing and he said that he was here with two of his friends," Skye said.

"Hmm, what's his name and what's his age?" I asked being overprotective.

See, my sister was just nineteen and I was twenty-three. I knew what was on the minds of girls her age. This was a twenty-one and up club, the sexiness in me got her in. But now she was enjoying herself a little too much.

"Raine," Skye said whining. "Don't be trying to rein me in, I need an answer to what I just asked you," I demanded. "Ok, his name is Monte and he's the same age as you," she quickly added.

"The same age as me. You know what I don't even care, just as long as his friends are cute. Oh, I seen this fine man, he was looking good!" I exclaimed as we both started to laugh.

We made our way to VIP and there he was. I knew him, even with his back turned to me. Walking in, we immediately caught each other's eyes. He was sitting with his other friend who I saw earlier and another fine man. The other fine man stood up and made his way toward Skye, so I assumed that he was Monte. She was right. He was beyond sexy, all three of them. I had to stop my thoughts right now because I could see myself boning all three of them. It really didn't matter but I quickly shook the fantasies.

"Monte, I want you to meet my older sister, Raine. Raine, this is Monte," Skye said, introducing us.

"Hey Raine, how're you? I see good looks run in the family," Monte said while kissing my hand.

"I'm fine, thank you. You have good taste in women I see," I replied.

"By the way, these are my two best friends, Damonte and that's Pierre," he said, pointing.

They both stood and Damonte walked over since he was closer and I could tell that he was instantly attracted to me. Shit! I can't lie, I was too. He hugged me and kissed me on the cheek.

"Nice to meet you Raine," Damonte said sexily. Damn, his voice was invigorating.

"Nice to meet you too, Damonte," I replied.

Next was the one who I really wanted, Pierre. Just saying his name got me drenched. Pierre slowly walked over, passing Damonte and stood in front of me.

"So we meet again, beautiful," Pierre said while stroking the cheek Damonte kissed me on.

"So we have, I think it was meant to be," I smiled, leaning my face towards his hands.

"I think so. I was meant to be in your presence," he smiled, leaned closer to my ear and whispered, "Or maybe I was meant to be in your essence."

I was thrown back for a minute with his comment. It took me awhile to process it but trust me I eventually did. He moved from my ear and kissed me on my forehead. Then, just like that he walked away and sat down again, staring right at me, if you know what I mean. Damonte patted the spot between him and Pierre so that I could sit down between them.

"What brings you and your sister here, Raine?" Damonte asked me while Monte and Skye was in their own little world.

"She told me about Passion and that it just opened up. She wanted me to go with her since she was too young to get in," I said.

He smiled at me. "Oh, she knew her sexy ass sister could get her in huh?" Damonte asked.

"You're exactly right and what brings you and your boys here?" I asked.

Pierre started to smile also then he answered my question, "We are the owners of Passion."

I was in shock. No wonder we were in VIP. That made me more excited to be with him now.

"Oh ok, well owners, I'm enjoying your club," I said while looking at Pierre then at Damonte.

"I'm glad you are. We invested a lot of dough in this club to make sure women like you enjoy the spot," Damonte said.

I loved his way with words. He was the type who could talk you out of your panties without you even realizing it.

"Well I'm definitely enjoying myself. I know for sure that Skye is enjoying herself too," I said.

"Yeah, we can see that. I think Monte really likes her. He rarely approaches women in a club," Damonte explained.

"I hope he is. I don't want to whoop his ass because he used her," I smiled.

"Oh don't worry. We don't roll like that. We have respect for women in every way," Pierre said.

Damn, they both had a way with words. Pierre scooted closer to me and placed his hand on my thigh. I had decided to wear a skirt tonight with a halter to show off my best assets. It seemed like it was working, so I was happy. Damonte looked at his hand and started chuckling to himself.

"What's wrong Damonte?" I asked him.

"Nothing, it's just that Pierre likes taking what I want. He can never find someone for himself. Then, we always like the same type of women," he replied, looking at Pierre.

"Well Damonte, if you would stop looking at the ones I want then I won't have to take them, now would I?" Pierre said to Damonte.

Damonte gave him a look that was unexplainable. It was a pissed off kind of look in his eyes but then his slick smile showed that he was playing with Pierre. Personally, I think Pierre made him mad, but he didn't want to show it with me being here.

"You're right, but if you wouldn't take them, I wouldn't have to get them back. Like I always do...now would I?" Damonte said putting the emphasis on take and I's.

Pierre smiled at Damonte and put his arm around me. I was confused with all these little games that they were playing, so I decided to join in. "Well Pierre and Damonte, if the woman doesn't want to be taken or taken back, then where would that leave you all?" I asked catching them off guard.

Before they could even reply, a brown-skinned man with a suit on came walking in.

"What's up Dewar" greeted Damonte as they gave dap.

"What's up with y'all. I seen you and Pierre across the room. Y'all tripping again?" Dewar asked.

With that comment, I assumed this has happened too many times.

"Naw, we cool. We were just talking to this sexy woman right here," Pierre replied.

Dewar looked over and smiled at me. What's up with all the smiling, but I wasn't complaining.

"Hello Miss, how are you?" Dewar said, reaching for my hand.

I stood up and he caressed both of my hands. "I'm fine, my name is Raine," I said.

Damn! What is the Lord trying to do, set me up? These were the four sexiest men I had ever met in my life.

"Beautiful name for a beautiful woman... You already know my name but its nice meeting you," Dewar said.

He did the same thing as Pierre and leaned forward, "Can you rain for me baby?" he asked smiling.

I was really in shock and then he winked at me and sat down on the chair across from the sofa we were sitting on.

"What's up, Monte? Who is the lovely lady?" Dewar asked.

It's amazing how all of them had a way with words.

"Hey Dewar, I didn't know you were coming too. Anyway, this is Skye, Skye this is Dewar. Skye is Raine's younger sister," Monte replied.

"Nice to meet you Skye. I decided to come because I didn't have anything to do. Plus, I called Ishmael and he said he was going to swing through with Storm," Dewar said.

I looked up at him because my other younger sister was getting cozy with this new man, but that's all she had told me. I wondered if this was the same Storm that I knew.

"Hold up, did you just say Storm?" I asked him.

"I sure did, sweetheart. Why do you ask?" Dewar said.

"My sister's name is Storm. She's light skinned—" I began.

"With long hair and she's always laughing at everything," Dewar said, finishing my sentence.

Now I was getting a little mad because this tramp did not tell me about him.

"So she's met all of you?" I asked.

"Naw, only Dewar because Ishmael mentioned her name but hasn't brought her to meet us," Damonte answered.

"Oh ok," I replied.

I couldn't even explain it but I know I was turned on to the fullest.

"Yeah, well you'll get a chance to whoop your sister's ass when she gets here," Dewar said laughing.

"You're right, I'm definitely going to beat her ass," I replied.

I was talking to Pierre and during the whole conversation I kept seeing Dewar eyeing me from the corner of my eyes. I knew he wanted me too, but trust me the feelings were mutual. I felt a little bad. I actually felt like a ho, but my momma always said men do it, so why can't we. I definitely wanted all of them, well at least these three.

Damonte got up and asked, "Would you like to dance Raine?"

I looked at him and then at Pierre. They were both smirking at each other and I liked the competition.

"I'd love to. I'll be back Pierre and Dewar," I said while taking Damonte's hand.

He guided me onto the dance floor and at that same moment T-Pain's *I'm in Love with a Stripper* blasted through the speakers. I was excited beyond excitement. Damonte stood behind me and wrapped his hands around my hips. I moved to the beat of the song while Damonte whispered the lyrics into my ear, occasionally rubbing his lips across my earlobe.

I started rolling my ass on Damonte, very slowly. I was trying to get the feel of him. He was already hard from what I felt. I instantly became wet by his hardness on my ass. Moving so sexual, he rolled his groin against my butt. He wanted me to feel all of him and I was surely feeling it. I was into my own world while pleasing myself and Damonte. It was like we were both showing each other how we wanted to fuck the other, slow and sensual.

Damonte stopped and whispered something else, "Look baby, I think we got some admirers up there."

I looked up and saw Pierre and Dewar staring down at us. The look on their faces suggested jealousy but arousal at the same time. I kind of liked the thought of them looking at us and I knew for a fact that Damonte loved it.

While we were dancing, Ishmael and Storm walked in and headed straight to the VIP area.

"Hey, what's up? What y'all doing? Who or what are y'all watching? Cause whatever it is, it's really doing some serious shit," Ishmael said to Pierre and Dewar.

They looked back and smiled. "Anyway, what took your ass so long? I spoke to you on the phone, over two hours ago," Dewar said while giving Ishmael dap and hugging Storm.

"The Mrs. and I had to take care of some business," Ishmael said.

"We're just watching Damonte dance with the girl that I want," Pierre said.

"You mean that we want," Dewar said smirking.

"Damn y'all all want the same girl. She must be fine as hell. Let me see," Ishmael said, looking at the dance floor.

"I'm Storm by the way, since Ishmael forgot his manners and didn't introduce me," Storm said, looking at Ishmael.

"Nice to meet you, he's like that sometimes. Ol' forgetful ass," Pierre said, laughing.

"She's fine. No offense baby, but she is," Ishmael said.

Storm walked over to see also. She gasped as she looked surprised. "That's my older sister, Raine, who I was telling you about, baby. It looks like her and your friend having a hell of a time," Storm said.

"She said that she had a sister named Storm. I guess you were the one," Dewar said.

"Ishmael, what you doing here…? I thought you was staying at home tonight," Monte said while giving dap to Ishmael.

"I was but I decided to come anyway. To make sure y'all niggas are under control," Ishmael laughed.

"Sweetheart, I want you to meet someone," Monte said to Skye.

Skye walked over and immediately became shocked.

"Skye, what're you doing here?" Storm asked looking funny.

"Raine and I came together. The question is when were you going to introduce us to your man?" Skye said making emphasis on man.

"Whatever, we'll talk later. Ishmael this is my younger sister, Skye. Skye, this is Ishmael," Storm said as Ishmael and Skye exchanged greetings.

"Well it sure is a lot of introducing tonight. I guess we were all meant to meet somehow," Pierre laughed.

"Shut up, Pierre" Monte said laughing also.

Back on the dance floor, Damonte and I were still dancing three songs later.

Ginuwine's *When We Make Love* came on.

"May I have this last dance?" Damonte asked.

I smiled and replied, "But of course."

We had become quite acquainted with each other while dancing and were now dancing face to face. His arms found my ass and stayed there. I wasn't complaining. It was something about his touch that was so pleasurable. He moved his hand around to the front of my skirt, then down my thigh. It stayed there for awhile until he moved his hands up further and further. His hands now were playing with my panties. He started to sing again in my ear, *"That's what it sounds like when we make love."*

All of a sudden I felt his finger enter me and he asked, *"Do you feel it?"* Following the song, I moaned, "Yes!"

I couldn't believe what I was doing. Here I was supposed to be dancing and his fingers were dancing inside of me. No one noticed because of the darkness of the dance floor. He entered another finger, then another. I was fully coated as he drew his fingers in and out of me.

I was moaning just like Ginuwine and the woman in the song. He looked in my eyes and I knew he was getting off by seeing my face and the look I was giving him.

"You like that Raine? Rain on me baby, rain on my fingers for daddy," he whispered in my ear while kissing it.

I looked up again and seen Pierre and Dewar looking at me once again. This time they looked really aroused. I'm guessing they knew what Damonte was doing to me. I liked it more. I came on his fingers. He took his fingers out of me and started licking his fingers.

"You taste just like rain, baby," Damonte said as we walked off the dance floor and re-entered the VIP room.

I looked over and Pierre and Dewar were following my every step.

"Had fun?" a female voice asked. I looked over and there was my sister with her man.

"It depends, should I tell you? Since you didn't let me meet your new man," I said jokingly.

We both started laughing. She introduced me and Ishmael. I introduced her to Damonte afterwards. I was a little thirsty so Dewar had the bartender bring some drinks up for us. We were having a good time laughing and flirting with each other, me, Pierre, Dewar, and Damonte.

I had to go to the restroom, so I excused myself, "I'll be right back. I have to use the ladies room."

"Go ahead sweetie, I'll be right here when you return," Dewar said sexily.

I winked and walked out, knowing for a fact that they were all watching my ass.

I went downstairs to the restroom to do what I had to do. I was exiting the restroom, when suddenly I bumped into a tall figure.

"Going somewhere?" the voice said.

He was playing with me and I decided to play along.

"It depends on where you're taking me," I replied kissing his neck.

"I can take you where ever you like," he said.

"Take me to ecstasy," I said rubbing my hands down his chest.

He picked me up and I wrapped my legs around his waist. Luckily for me, no one was coming at that time. He took me down a hall and into a room that had the word 'Kinky' written on it. I was curious about the word on the door. It was like the room was hidden for some odd reason. He unlocked it with a key and I looked around.

The room was lit with a red light. It had a sexy vibe to it. Definitely one I could make love in. He walked us over to a large sofa and laid me down. He was looking at me like he could rape the hell out of me. At this time, I wanted him to. He leaned down and started placing soft kisses on my neck and collar bone. He had found one of my many spots. He lifted my shirt up and placed butterfly kisses down my stomach. He took his kisses all the way down until he reached my navel. Swirling his tongue in my navel, he pushed up my skirt and took down my panties. He was smooth with it and I was waiting for his next move. It was something about his touches that was different from Damonte's. They were more passionate. When ever he touched me, it was like someone was lighting a match at my feet.

"You want what I got for you, Raine?" he asked.

"I want whatever you're going to give me. I want everything you got!" I said as I felt his lips caressing my clit.

From that one touch, I knew I was going to have one hell of an orgasm. I could tell that he took pride in his oral work. He was a teaser and I liked that. He was taking his time pleasing me and I was taken back by that. You wouldn't necessary think that he would be this way. Even though I'm making an assumption about him, I was totally wrong and that's why I tell people all the time not to make assumptions about a person. I was loving the way he licked my precious jewel while kissing me.

I grabbed a hold of his head and started pulling him head toward me.

"Go deeper, Pierre. Give me more, baby. I want you to taste all of what I got," I whispered in a low sultry tone.

Maybe I shouldn't have said that but at that moment I felt his tongue finally enter me. It was like I was in another place, another era in time. I couldn't take it any longer while I tried to hold my climax, it was becoming so unbearable and he knew it.

"Let it go, Raine. Show me how much I please you," Pierre said grabbing a hold of my legs.

I was trying to get away from him. With that tongue, I could fall in love with this man. Ooh, with Damonte's finger and Pierre's tongue, I would be set off for a good little minute. That is until, I wanted the real thing!

"Don't run, go ahead and let it flow. Cum like running water that's overflowing in a bathtub," he said, going deeper then I thought a man could ever go.

Before I knew it, I was cumming like a raging river and he licked up every drop that ran out of me. I just laid there. Paralyzed from the pleasure of his tongue, I couldn't move.

"You all right, baby?" Pierre asked.

I just looked at him and moaned. He started laughing. I pulled him up and kissed the hell out of him, enjoying tasting myself. I felt something when our lips meld. I couldn't explain the feeling, but he could kiss—really, really well. We kissed for about thirty minutes straight.

At the same time, I wanted to know how blessed Mr. Pierre really was. I moved my hand down his stomach until it rested on his dick. My hand started roaming and he started to rise. I heard a moan escape his lips and I was satisfied with the size of him. I was going to enjoy fucking him. He pulled me up as he sat up.

"You like what you felt, baby. Maybe if you're good, you'll get it. You taste good though, Raine. You really have that flavor mami,"

Pierre said in his Puerto Rican accent.

Laughter escaped and I kissed him again. We both stood up and he pulled my skirt back down, putting my panties into his pocket.

"I might need these later," Pierre said spanking my butt as we walked out.

He let me walk into the VIP room first. He said he would come up fifteen minutes later. When I walked in, Dewar and Damonte was burning a hole through me. I looked around and noticed that Skye and Monte were not there. I knew then that they probably were in one of the other rooms I just came out of. I was laughing to myself. Go head Skye, get yours girl.

"Hmm…" I heard Storm mumble and I looked in her direction.

She immediately winked at me and I smiled. We always gave each other signals to what we just did. So she knew, I had already a little taste of Damonte and now Pierre. My next victim, maybe Dewar, who was I kidding? Hell yeah, he was my next victim.

"Where have you been?" Dewar asked me looking suspiciously.

I loved the jealousy they all bore.

"I told you that I was going to the restroom. A man approached me and asked me to dance," I lied perfectly.

He looked at me and gave me a look like he knew I was lying but he smiled instead. It was something about all this smiling that they were doing. Maybe it was some type of signal they were using. Indeed, Pierre came prancing through the room fifteen minutes later, licking his lips.

It was a sign to Dewar and Damonte that he had tasted me. Damonte looked at him and put his finger in his mouth. Pierre grinned and sat down beside me. Damonte was letting him know that he had the pleasure of tasting me also.

"You think you're slick, Pierre?" Damonte asked.

"I don't think, I know Damonte," Pierre answered.

"Well who cares who's slick or not?" Dewar asked in a frustrated tone.

He was mad that he hadn't had the chance of feeling nor savoring the taste of me. I was mad also but trust me he was going to receive his chance.

"Don't worry Dewar, you can be slick also," I said while opening my legs for him to see all of me.

He turned his head to the side and stared at me.

"If you say so, Raine" Dewar said.

I knew exactly what he meant when he said that and they did also. I looked over to where Storm was sitting with Ishmael and I caught Ishmael's eyes on me. I looked straight into his eyes and right then I knew that he had just seen what I did. He smiled and rubbed his hand across his goatee. I guess he had the smile too. I rolled my eyes flirtatiously because he too wanted a taste of Raine.

By the time they had looked at me, I had already re-crossed my legs. We had an understanding now. He was happy with knowing that his time would soon come.

"Pierre, take my cue and learn later, okay," Damonte said.

"Okay, then you can take my lesson and study it, Damonte," Pierre replied.

I admired their relationship. You could tell that they were the closest out of the five. I was now thinking how to get Dewar all to myself. After awhile, Monte and Skye returned to the VIP section all happy go-lucky. She looked at us and tilted her head. Storm and I looked at each other and smiled.

Right then and there, we knew that Skye had put it down and by the way she was smiling, we also knew that Monte put it down. I'm not going to lie to you. I wanted a piece of Monte and Ishmael. Monte had these luscious lips that I knew he could do damage with. I was curious and wondered what all he could do with them. Ishmael had this look about him. Something in his eyes told me that he didn't play when it came to doing the do. He had a twinkle that no one else had but I had made up my mind to just leave Monte and Ishmael to them, since I had three men anyway.

Storm and Skye called me over to where they were. As I walked over, I could feel five set of eyes all over my ass. Knowing that, I threw it harder. I wanted them to want me so bad that they couldn't take it.

"Yeah?" I asked them.

They looked at me and smirked.

"You think you the shit don't you?" asked Storm.

"I know I'm the shit, Storm. It's just a matter of time before you know too," I replied.

"Yeah, yeah, if you say so... So what are you planning?" Storm asked.

I looked over at Dewar and seen him looking right at my ass. Even though he was talking to the rest of them, he couldn't keep his eyes off of me. He couldn't wait to get me alone.

"I'm planning on getting what I want," I told her.

"What do you want?" Skye asked me.

"I want the dick, all three of them. I can't have five because y'all ho's keeping me from getting it," I said.

Skye smiled and said, "Good, you don't need my shit. He's all mine, the dick and all."

"And you know you ain't getting my dick so you better settle with three…you ol' greedy ass. You always want it all but maybe I can arrange something for you," Storm said as Skye and I looked on surprised.

She was the sister who did the weird sexual stuff so I was a little bewildered by that comment.

"What are you talking about, Storm?" Skye asked.

"You want to know how Ishmael performs in bed? Let me add Monte also cause I see the way you were looking at him," Storm began to explain.

"Storm are you thinking what I think you're thinking?" Skye asked.

"You bet. How about I take Ishmael into one of the rooms cause I know you and Skye been to one also? I'll take him and fuck him. Skye, you take Monte into the same room and do the same—" Storm began to say until I interrupted.

"Where do I come in at?" I asked.

"Raine, are you slow or something? Maybe you need to just get the dick so you can get some of your intellectual cells back," Skye said.

"I mean really, if you would let me finish explaining. Now where I left off, while we're fucking the hell out of them, you come and watch. I'm not letting you in on the fun but then you'll see how they perform in action. Meet us in room 'Rapture' in like ten minutes," Storm said.

I thought for a beat when we were walking out. I had remembered seeing five doors and on each of these five doors there were different words on the door. So the room Pierre had taken me in earlier had to be his room. I started wondering which room belonged to Monte or Ishmael. I agreed to her arrangement. Only she didn't tell me the other arrangement she had made.

They left me and walked over to Ishmael and Monte. My sisters whispered something in the guys' ears. All four of them got up and left, leaving me in the room with my men. Pierre looked over and licked his lips at me. I had to stop myself from lying down and having him insert his tongue back into my cavern.

I waited about ten minutes then left walking down the stairs. On my way out, Damonte let his hand rub across my ass. I guess they all like ass since that's one of my assets they have been paying close attention to all night. I turned back around and winked at Dewar. I was telling him soon baby, very soon with my eyes.

I proceeded to walk down the hallway and into room Rapture. This room was lit with a blue light which added a little mystery. The mystery was no longer there because that's when I seen my two sisters having sex in the same room. There was a chair sitting in the middle of the room. Assuming that it was for me, I sat down and got comfortable. Storm and Ishmael were on the right side of the room. Skye and Monte were on the left.

There was a bed and a sofa in the room. It was similar to Pierre's but Pierre only had a sofa. I was wondering now what the other three rooms held. I remember the names on the other three. They were Erotica, Sensation, and Kama Sutra. All of them had me curious but most of all, I wanted to know what room belonged to who. I knew that the words told how the sex was and how they performed. I turned to Ishmael and Storm first. He was on top so I concluded that he liked the control. I watched the way his movements were. He would move slowly then speed up a little bit. I noticed his roll action. He rolled from the ass to make sure I received it all. He was fairly quiet except the increased breathing. My eyes went to Storm. I watch her meet his pumps. I watched her face every time he went in. She was really benefiting from the sex with Ishmael. She looked over at me and moaned his name. I smiled at her and she winked.

It was now time to watch Skye and Monte. They were totally different. She was on top. She liked dominating her man just like me. I figured he liked the domination too. I decided to watch Skye first. I observed the way she rode him as his hands gripped her waist. He was helping her ride him. So by noticing that, I came to the conclusion that Monte was really packing. You're probably wondering how I know. I'll tell you this but I'm a pro at riding. I'm going to have to teach Skye a little bit more on how to handle any size dick. I never need help riding, just roll and dip the hip. She was fucking him but his eyes were on me. I was concentrating on his stare, trying to read his eyes. He loved it! But somehow I got the feeling that he wished that I was the one on top.

After watching them both, I felt a pair of hands touch me. I tried to turn around but he stopped me. He stood me up and started to rub all over my body. He took his hands down my back and traced my spine. That sent chills up and down my body. If he keeps on I am going to be dripping all over this nice carpet.

I was still wondering whose room is this. Whose sex was rapture? He moved the chair from in between us and unzipped my skirt. It fell to my ankles and I stepped out of it. Wanting to turn around to see who this was, he stopped me again. Stooping down, he placed soft, gentle kisses on my butt. Cheek by cheek, he massaged and loved my ass. Now this was different, I had never had this done before. By this time, Skye, Monte, Storm, and Ishmael were watching me. They were watching my facial expressions and the person who was behind me.

"Bend her over," demanded Monte. I looked at him and just that quick, the person bent me over. Before I could say anything else, I felt his tongue on my ass. I think I came right then and there. I had never felt anything like that before. He traced his tongue up and down my butt, occasionally touching my beauty with his tongue also.

"Play with your clit as he lick you" ordered Ishmael.

So all five of them were in on this, huh? I can't lie, I loved what he was doing to me and I loved the way they were watching me getting it done.

"Make sure you cum hard for my boy," Monte smiled.

"Cum like you never did in your life," Ishmael said.

They were so right because I came like hell from him tossing my salad. Then, he went and caught every drop.

"You loved the rapture Raine?" he asked me turning me around.

I came face to face with Dewar. So this is his room. I had to give it to Storm this time. She really showed her ass on this one.

"I loved it Dewar," I said turning back around to the others.

"Nice ass Raine," Ishmael said smiling.

"I agree with you Ishmael," Monte said.

Dewar walked around to the front of me and smiled. At that same moment, I heard a knock on the door.

"Come in," Monte, Dewar, and Ishmael said all at once.

All of a sudden, Pierre and Damonte walked in, smiling their asses off.

"Nice work Dewar," Damonte said.

I looked at Damonte and immediately knew that they were watching us. Pierre pointed to the corner of the room and there was a camera.

"So you wanted to video tape me, Pierre?" I asked.

"Not me, Dewar did. We just watched. We watched all of you," Pierre replied.

Damonte walked over to me and Dewar.

"It's not over yet, Raine. We got one more little surprise for you baby," Damonte said leaning over and kissing me.

While he was kissing me, Pierre came over to me and took off my halter. Then, Dewar unbuttoned my half bra that I had on and all my clothes were on the floor. Here I was naked in front of my sisters and these five, fine men. Damonte pulled away and I moaned, telling him that I liked the kiss. He smiled and licked his lips. Damonte picked me up with both hands to carry me out the room.

"Where are we going?" I asked him.

"You're going to a place where you have never been before," Damonte said.

We started walking in the direction of the door. Skye and Monte in front of me went in the room Kama Sutra. Storm and Ishmael were in front of them going into room Erotica. Next, I came in front of Room Sensation. Dewar and Pierre weren't behind us. I wondered where they could be. He unlocked the door, this room was lit with a green light. It had a big-ass bed. He carried me to the bed, and we started kissing again.

I glanced to the side of me, and there stood Pierre. He was walking in Damonte's room so smoothly.

"Are you taking my cue yet, Pierre?" Damonte asked him.

"Yeah, as long as you're learning my lesson, Damonte" Pierre replied and they grinned.

That's what they were talking about earlier. They had this whole thing planned from the start.

"You had this whole thing planned out from the jump huh?" I

asked Damonte as Pierre made his way toward my breasts.

"Not him Raine, us. All three of us had this planned out. We all wanted you but no one wanted to let the other have you, so we decided that we all would have you," Dewar said, walking in.

You should have seen my face. It was definitely a Kodak moment. I had experienced a threesome before but a foursome with three men and one woman, never. Oh boy! I was ready for this. Anxious is not even the word to describe what I was feeling. I was going to have three dicks in one night and I was fully lubricated for them. Pierre lowered his head towards my left breast as Dewar made his way towards my right.

"Let me see what Pierre was talking about when he said that you had the tastiest platter you could ever eat," Damonte said as I felt his mouth engulf my purring kitty.

Damonte started to taste my pussy and lick my clit causing me to become wetter.

"Hmm…" I moaned as his tongue went in deeper.

Pierre stopped fondling with my breasts to kiss me. It was something about my lips that he loved and I sure wasn't complaining either.

"Ahh, yes…" I moaned as I came over all over again for the tenth time tonight. By that time, Pierre was standing watching me release while Dewar was still on my breasts. I figured he was a breast man.

"I can't wait to get inside you" Damonte said.

Then, he kissed me as Pierre traded places with him. Pierre stood over me as I demanded him to take off his shirt. I watched him with intensity as I noticed his nice, broad, milky tan chest. He bent down for me to lick his chest. Starting at the nipples, I licked them one by one as Pierre gave off a pleasurable sigh. I pulled his head back by his braids while my tongue lashed out at his neck.

"I like this Raine!" he said calling out my name so sexy, "but I'm running this."

He unbuttoned his pants and I pulled down the zipper, showing off his black boxers. I reached into them and pulled out his nine and a half inch dick that was pulsating with so much desire. I'm absolutely like a ruler when it comes to measuring. Even through his clothes, I was still a good guesser.

"Ooh…" I moaned.

Just from him sticking the tip in, I was already moaning. He was most certainly thick in all the right places. The thickness of his dick had me wetter than a waterbed. He pushed it all the way in. I was a little uncomfortable at first but good at the same time.

"Ahh…" Pierre moaned from the feeling of sliding in me.

He was pulling in and out trying to get me wetter and wetter.

"I like how your pussy feels tight to my dick. It doesn't want to let me go. The way it's wrapping around my dick feels so good," Pierre said.

He started working his dick even more.

"Hmm, Raine your pussy feels so damn good," he said moaning even louder.

He started pulling and pushing in and out of me at a steady pace.

"I want you to watch me make love to you," Pierre said staring into my eyes. It was like he was hypnotizing me.

"The way you're looking at me is making me so excited Pierre. I'm cumming baby," I whispered in a low tone.

"Cum for me… Shit, you have me sweating," he said as I moaned.

His movement became faster from the sounds I make. He was humping me while repeating my name over and over.

"Hmm, I have never felt pussy like this before. I'm cumming too, Raine. Ahh!" he said leaning his head back.

He kissed me passionately while pulling his dick out of me. But there was something different about his kiss this time. He looked at me strange, and at the same time he got up, putting on his clothes, "You're mysterious to look at. I don't know about you."

Pierre finished putting on his clothes as Damonte steppped closer to me. He stood there and licked his lips so nasty.

"I want your shirt off" I ordered him while ripping off his shirt.

To my delight, there was a wide, tasty, chest underneath. I rubbed every inch of it as he relaxed to my touch. He began to zip down his pants to reveal his nine inch.

"Nice…very nice," I said.

He bit his lips as he stared at me.

"I'm going to love you good. Then, I'm going to fuck the hell out of you. Pierre you hold her right leg and Dewar hold on to her left leg,"

Damonte ordered.

I liked the bossy nature that Damonte had. He loved control! He put his dick in and I moaned right away from the feeling. He started thrusting in and out me. Using his right hand to finger my clitoris, he gave me the ultimate pleasure. His left finger was inside my mouth and I immediately start sucking. Oh damn! His dick and finger felt so good working all at the same time. I'm sucking on his finger while moaning like a pussy cat.

"Uh, Damonte baby, I'm cumming all over you…"

He pulled his fingers out of my pussy and mouth and reached down to tongue kiss me.

"I love the way you cum for me, Raine, and the way you call my name," he said, pumping inside of me.

He looked down and said, "I love watching my dick slide in and out of you. Hmm Raine, you make me crazy. Your pussy shouldn't feel this good."

He pumped harder inside me while continuing to moan and groan.

"Shit girl, my dick wanna do something crazy," Damonte said, tilting his chin up.

I began sucking on his neck like a vampire. He licked his lips. He was pumping even faster, "Ahh…" he said over and over again.

I knew he was about to explode. Louder and louder, he was pumping faster and faster. "Shit! Shit! Raine oh yeah... I'm cumming, ahh, I'm cumming…" he screamed kissing me deeper. "You make a nigga work for it. You had me loving the desires of you and the fucking touch of you. Hmm, you're dangerous to touch," Damonte said putting on his clothes.

I guess I was saving the best for last, Dewar. It was something that kept me wondering about him the whole night. It was like he was keeping something back and I intended to find out. Dewar contoured my body as he caressed my breasts, gently squeezing them, taking his tongue and licking around each one. He watched me while sucking and biting my nipples, putting his teeth into it.

I moaned low as he teased and pleased my nipples. He sustained from kissing me to control the situation. He kissed down my stomach until he reached my navel. I rubbed his head to relax him for a few minutes then he stopped me, staring at me. I thought two can play that game. He took off his shirt before I could tell him to and my eyes looked up and down his chest until our eyes met. The width of his chest turned me on. I bit my lips so that I wouldn't loose my mind. I sat up to kiss him. Not realizing, he kissed me back.

He pushed me back down on the bed. He licks his lips, looking down at his blue jeans. I could see that his dick was demanding attention from me and he knew it too. He took two fingers down to my clitoris.

"Ooh…" I moaned moving my body to his fingers.

Climbing up on my stomach, he guided his ten inch dick between my breasts. Squeezing them lightly, he slid his dick between my breasts. Stopping to kiss my neck, I started to nibble on his ears.

"Hmm…" he moaned as I stuck my tongue deeper into his ear. I had found a hot spot!

Putting his big dick into my pussy, he went to work. He was bigger than Pierre and Damonte and my pussy was reacting to it. The size of his dick had my walls gripping a hold of his dick more.

"Yes, ah shit," I moaned.

He started to fuck me like a dog in heat, going deeper and deeper.

"Are you trying to hurt me?" I ask him.

"No, I'm trying not to love you. Ohh Shit! You can't possibly feel this fucking good," he said.

Sitting on his lap, I wrapped my arms around his neck. I moaned, riding the shit out of his dick as he stroked my clit.

"Ooh, ooh Dewar baby, I'm cumming. Oh ah I'm cumming…" I yelled while he kissed me as I came.

He laid me back on the bed, picking me up from my hips. He started to put his back into it, pumping me like hell. He was humping me and kissing me like a wild man.

"Raine, you can't feel this good. Shit! Baby, I'm about to cum all in you. Ahh, I'm cumming, I'm cumming a lot. Aww, Raine!" Dewar said while his lips were trembling.

"You're hard to figure out baby," he said putting his clothes on.

"Got-damn…!" I said.

I was floating five levels pass cloud nine. It was so amazing that five friends could all be excellent in the bedroom. I mean, it's hard to find a man with a good size dick, let alone one who can work it. I was thrown back from endless enjoyment. The room was quiet and all you could hear was us breathing. I guess neither one of us had anything to say. I knew I didn't.

I couldn't find the words to say. What do you say to three best friends that you just got through fucking in front of each other? Your answer is as good as mine. So I'll leave that comment until next time.

Scorned

Kiniesha Gayle

Silence captivated the courtroom. Jasmine's eyes were fixated on the empty chair, the one the judge usually sits. Her patience was slowly running thin as she awaited the verdict. She cringed on the inside, the mere thought of what the verdict might be bothered her. Especially after Jay played tapes he secretly recorded. To the left at the far end of the table sat Jay, her ex-husband. His six foot, dark-skinned frame was looking really good in the blue suit, the suit she bought him. Every now and then he would either blow kisses, or winked at the whore he called his girlfriend.

"She satisfied me," she remembered him saying. "She doesn't fuss or quarrel when I asked her to suck my dick."

Jasmine chuckled at such notion. Shoot, even she would suck his dick every hour if he was shelling out the same amount of money he was shelling to Jhonelle. He wouldn't have to ask twice.

"Are you okay," Laura her lawyer whispered.

Jasmine gave her a don't–ask-stupid–questions look and drifted off in her thoughts.

"Only if I didn't say I do," she thought. "I wouldn't be in this mess."

"All rise," the baldheaded court officer ordered.

The doors to the judge chambers open, a wrinkled faced man,

looking like he was overdue for retirement with patches of gray hair, sat on the bench. He adjusted his glasses and opened the folder. Judge Lakinberg looked at her then her ex-husband. Jasmine felt his decision was not going to be good.

"Before I make my decision, I want it to be clear that I listened to both sides of the argument, reviewed the documents thoroughly, and I came to a fair decision," Judge Lakinberg said, clearing his throat.

"Think positive," Laura said, squeezing Jasmine's hand.

"Easy for you to say," Jasmine whispered.

"Mrs. Blackwell," the judge referred to her, looking over the rim of his glasses.

"It's Ms. Lee," she countered.

"Jasmine," Laura turned to her, red faced. "Do you realize he's about to make a verdict and if you piss him off, he could make it worst."

"Who cares? I am Ms. Lee."

"Counselor," the judge interrupted. "Could you remind your client I did not grant her the divorce as yet. She is Mrs. Blackwell."

"Yes, your honor," Laura answered.

"Jasmine, please calm down."

"After tabulating your assets, I will reveal what your husband is entitled to, and who will gain custody of the children. Sole custody will be granted to Mr. Blackwell. Mrs. Blackwell will have supervised visits once a week for two hours with her children…"

"What!" Jasmine said jumping up. "You cannot do that," she announced, banging her fist on the table.

"Mrs. Blackwell, I want order in my courtroom. Sit down and stop interrupting," the judge said pointing his index finger.

"Ma'am," the court officer touched her. "Sit down!" He ordered.

"Get your fucking hands off, before I knock you down!"

"Your honor, may I take my client outside to have a word with her?" Laura asked.

"Under the circumstances that'll be a good idea," the judge replied sarcastically. "While you're at it let her know that one more outburst and I'll hold her in contempt."

Laura and Jasmine headed out the door.

"Are you nuts? He can hold you in contempt. Listen, if things don't work out, we can always appeal."

"Appeal...?" Jasmine repeated. "I don't want that whore raising my kids."

"Listen to me," Linda grabbed her shoulders, "I understand, but the reality is that whore will be helping to raise your kids for the time being until things are sorted out. For now we have to do things the legal way."

"Screw that, Laura. All my life I have been doing things the right way and I got fucked, Laura. Bottom-line is, he's not taking my kids even if it means going out in handcuffs."

"Jasmine, don't screw this up," Laura warned.

"Everything has already been screwed up the day that heifer took my man. She crossed the line," Jasmine said holding onto the handle of the courtroom door.

"Jas," Laura called out.

It was too late. Jasmine had already walked into the courtroom. Everyone reconvened, and the judge continued.

"Sole custody will be given to Mr. Blackwell with Mrs. Blackwell having supervised visits. Mrs. Blackwell will pay three thousand a month in child support and alimony. The house will go to Mr. Blackwell, since the children are in his care."

The judge banged his gavel. Jasmine sobbed, the thought of having supervised visits with her daughters was too much. She slowly raised her head to see Jay handing her a piece of tissue.

"Dry your eyes, and start writing," he spoke "I don't want my check a day late either."

Jasmine didn't even respond. She grabbed her things off the desk and headed out the courtroom.

Five Years Earlier

The rain pelted against the balcony of Oheka Castle. Most brides would've seen this as a curse on their wedding day, but Jasmine saw it as nothing more than raindrops of blessing. As the hairdresser bumped the last curl on her weave, her phone vibrated, she glanced at it.

Hey baby, are you nervous? The text from James read.

No, are you? She responded and immediately placed the phone on the bed.

Taking a look in the mirror, she smiled at her beautiful reflection.

Her phone went off again.

No. I just can't wait to see you walk down the aisle. Are you going to show up?

Maybe, she typed, she couldn't resist laughing. *That is if I don't get cold feet.*

Cindy, her hairdresser just happened to glance at what she wrote. Lightly punching Jasmine on the shoulder she spoke, "You are mean."

"Naw," she smiled. "Let him sweat abit," Jasmine chuckled.

The phone went off again.

Don't play with me. He wrote. *Don't embarrass me. Let me know if you're going to show up.*

The president of a big financial company on Wall Street, Jasmine always looked her best. Her wedding was no exception. There was an immense amount of jewelry sitting in the Tacori box sitting on the nightstand. She walked over and opened it placing the diamond and sapphire necklace on her neck the matching earring hung from her ear. The set wouldn't be complete without the matching bracelet. Jasmine also made it her priority to ensure that James had matching cufflinks. She demanded the finest things, so should her man. Looking at her crystal-laced, Anne Barge gown, she closed her eyes allowing herself to reflect on how she and James met.

Stern's financial group organized a retreat on the island of Turks and Caicos. Although she was there for business, she didn't hesitate to dabble in a little fun as well. There wasn't a night when Jasmine wouldn't go to the bar situated on that beach of Sandals Resort. Chatting with the bartender, he always made her a specialty drink. The Jasmine's punch, he called the concoction and he always entertained her with conversation.

"So, do you always make special drinks for every girl on the island?" she sipped on her punch.

"I never came across a special girl, so I had no need for a special punch."

"Is that so," Jasmine stared at him. "She must be one special girl."

"Gorgeous too," James replied cleaning a glass. "Her hazel eyes is memorizing under the Caribbean moonlight. And her short haircut helps to bring out the beauty in her light flawless skin."

Jasmine blushed. Using the straw, she stirred the punch. Jasmine withdrew the straw and sucked on the bottom of it. Juices from his concoction accidentally fell on her exposed cleavage.

"I got it," James said, coming from behind the counter.

Ensuring that none of his superiors were around, his tongue glided across her breast. The sensation of his tongue shook her entire frame. That night they made sweet love under the shinning light of the Caribbean moon, watching the water beating against the shore. After visiting the island twice that year, Jasmine requested he joined her in New York.

"Hey you only have an hour left," Tameka her coordinator said. "Get ready. You'll not be late under my watch," she reinforced.

Jasmine got out the bed, picked up her dress and shimmied into the gown. Mrs. Lee, Jasmine's mother, entered the room with ear-filled eyes and gave her a hug.

"You are beautiful," she smiled.

Jasmine's father boycotted the affair. He didn't approve of James. He felt his daughter was too good for James, and besides, Mr. Lee felt James was nothing but a gold-digger. Her father's lack of support hurt, but Jasmine was set on marrying James. With five hundred people in attendance, her million and half dollar wedding was on. This was her day and she was going to be happy. Jasmine ignored the butterflies forming, grabbing her bouquet, she didn't heed the warnings. The wedding went really swell. Life was too…

Three Years after Wedding

"I have a reservation for two." She told the host at Le Bernardin.

Jasmine's philosophy was always, be your husband's girlfriend and not his wife. Once you became addicted to the phrase 'you are his wife', then you became too comfortable and sexiness will walk out the door. Le Bernardin was one of the best French Restaurants in NYC located on 51st Street. It was their third year anniversary. Each year had brought growth and the relationship got better. She wanted to show off her curvy figure and wore a black, strapless Ralph Lauren dress with matching Miu Miu shoes.

Seated at her table, Jasmine ordered a bottle of their favorite wine. She couldn't stop thinking how lucky she was to have a husband like James. Not only were they celebrating their wedding anniversary, they were celebrating James obtaining his green card as well. Time slowly passed. Jasmine's call to James' cellphone went straight to his voicemail.

"Hey dear, I am here at the restaurant, hope everything is well…"

She ordered appetizers. All around her people were laughing and enjoying their food. Time slipped by and Jasmine became worried, James still had not shown up or called. She dialed his cellphone again– straight to voicemail.

"James where are you? It's been twenty minutes and you haven't called."

"Would you like to order dinner?"

"Can't you see? I'm on the phone," she snapped at the waiter.

"Sorry…" he apologized.

"Call me back James…" Jasmine's tone was disgruntled.

"I'm fine. Just write me the check," she replied, sounding agitated.

She quickly rifled through her bag. When she finally found her American Express card, her hand shook, nervousness was kicking in. She was not sure what was going on. Embarrassment stung her face as she left the table and headed for the door. Hailing a cab, she hopped in the first one. After providing the cabbie with her address, she placed her hands across her chest and rode in silence. Jasmine tried James' cellphone. Once again the call went straight to voicemail.

"Is James using me for green card purposes?" she questioned. She couldn't help to wonder if her father was right about him all along. "No," she convinced herself.

James was a good man. There had to be an explanation. The cab pulled up to a home in Hartsdale, New York. The lights were off. She saw the Range Rover and the Benz in the drive way.

"That's weird," she spoke aloud.

Jasmine paid the driver, and walked cautiously to the entrance. She wanted to ensure there was no sign of a break in. She entered the apartment and called his name.

"James…"

Walking over to a well stocked bar, she grabbed a bottle of red wine, and poured a glass. Couple glasses later, an intoxicated Jasmine reclined on the sofa. Rays from the sun peaked through the blinds. Rubbing her eyes, she awoke with a pounding headache. Jasmine slowly got off the sofa. She poured a glass of water, and popped a pill in her mouth. She was beginning to feel nauseated. Walking from the kitchen holding her stomach she called for James throughout the house. There was no answer.

Stripping off her clothing, she headed for the shower. Half an hour later, she sat in the backyard on the lawn chair reading, while drinking orange juice. It wasn't long before a cab pulled up to the driveway. She didn't bother looking. She knew it was James. Jasmine watched him from behind her shades. He strolled up the driveway, realized she was in the back, and headed toward her. She said nothing and continued reading. He kissed her on the cheek.

"Instead of giving me a kiss, what you need to do is explain where the hell you been for the last twenty four hours motherfucker."

She smacked him right across the cheek. A look of shock creased his face. He rubbed his cheek.

"I am sorry about last night," he paused, looking at her. "The guys took me out for a drink, and I guess I had a little bit too much. And I don't know how I wound up on Bill's sofa but I did. I should've called, but the alcohol clouded my judgment."

He tried kissing the center of her chest, and was getting ready to fondle her nipples with his tongue. Without a warning, Jasmine smacked him again.

"Don't you dare put that dirty tongue on me!"

"Bitch!" he held his face as he stared at her.

"Please reserve that word for the whore you were screwing last night," she said removing her shades.

"You fucking crazy!" he shouted.

"I will show you crazy," she yelled, getting up off the lawn chair and throwing the wine glass at him. It smashed against the pavement.

"You lucky you is a woman. Or else I would have beat the shit out of you!" He warned in a Caribbean accent.

"Try it asshole, I will send you to jail faster than you came here."

She followed behind him. They both headed in the house. Jasmine watched him packing his clothing. Without warning she jumped on his back and began pounding at him.

"You ungrateful bastard!" she yelled.

James threw her onto the bed.

"Stop it!" he grabbed her by the shoulders and shook her.

Jasmine's strength began to weaken as nausea took over. She began throwing up all over the bed.

"Are you okay?" James asked.

"I'm fine," she answered and headed to the master bathroom, slamming the door behind her. James pressed the stop button on the tape recorder and headed out the door.

A Week Later

Jasmine sat nervously in the doctor's office, awaiting the test result. Dr. Albert entered the room carrying a chart. She looked at him for answers.

"I have good news the doctor told her." He looked at the paper and replied, "You're pregnant."

Jasmine was in disbelief and did not know how to react. She wasn't sure if she should call James and tell him the news.

"And you're pregnant with twins."

Her eyes opened wide. Now she was extremely shocked. A million and one thoughts crept across Jasmine's mind as she contemplated what to do. Her marriage was on the rocks, James walked out. Now it seemed like she was going to be a single mother. This was not the life she envisioned, especially with kids involved. Picking up the phone, she slowly dialed James' number.

"Hello," his husky voice answered.

"I am pregnant and I am pregnant with twins," she replied.

"Is it mines?"

"Man…you know what!" she abruptly hung up the phone.

Some Months Later

The sound of babies crying echoed in the room as Jay sat beside Jasmine. He cuddled one of the babies, while she cuddled the other. Their relationship wasn't what it was before, but it had improved slightly. Jasmine was determined to work out her marriage and keep her family together. Then the twins first birthday ruined everything. It changed their lives forever.

"Hello," Jasmine answered.

It was three in the morning, and she wondered who would disturb her sleep especially when she would have a busy day planning the twin's birthday.

"Hi, is Jay there?"

Jasmine sat up, she had to be sure that she wasn't dreaming. Three in the morning and James was sound asleep. To make sure she wasn't hearing things, she spoke once more.

"Hello!"

"Are you deaf?' The voice asked in an agitated tone. "Is Jay there? I'm in labor."

The accent was of someone with Caribbean descent, the voice was somewhat familiar.

"Excuse me...? I am James' wife. Anything you need to say comes through me."

"Tell your husband his son is about to be born and he needs to get down here. He knows where to find me."

The phone went dead on the other line.

"Wake up!"

Jasmine shook Jay aggressively. She didn't want to create a scene and wake the twins.

"Huh!" Jay groggily replied.

"Jay, get your ass up," she said leaning in closer and hitting him.

"What!" he answered irritated.

"One of your bitches called saying she is pregnant."

Jay looked at her, hissed his teeth fluffed his pillow, then he said, "Whatever, you are delusional and going through postpartum depression."

Then it dawned on her to check the caller ID. The caller listed was Jhonelle Henry. Jasmine rubbed her eyes once more, to make sure she was seeing right. Jhonelle was supposed to be Jay's cousin. What the hell, this made no sense. Her head spun, her stomach turned. The thought of James committing adultery and incest in her home was sickening.

Jasmine got out off bed, went to the mini bar and came to the bedroom with a wine bottle.

"You disgusting pig!" The wine bottle connected with his head. "Get the fuck out my house!"

James reached out to hit her, but thought against it.

"Your dick gonna fall off you sick bastard!" She yelled.

The sound of a crying baby interrupted their loud, heated argument.

"Consider yourself lucky," he responded, putting on his clothing. "At least it's not in your pussy."

"Get out !"

The crystal dish at the side table flew past his head.

The Following Day

"Jasmine...?" one of the two men said, walking into her office.

"Yes," she replied.

"You are under arrest."

"For what?" she asked resisting.

"Assault…"

"You have it all wrong. I'm calling my lawyer!"

The officer wouldn't allow her. Instead they threw her on the table and place her in handcuffs. The commotion brought everyone running from their desks. Friends, foes and fakers, they all had to see what was going on. Some whispered amongst each other. Others snickered while some looked on in shock.

"Get Laura on the phone," Jasmine said to her secretary.

"Yes, Ms. James."

The secretary wasted no time putting her fingers to work.

After being released from jail, Jasmine fell into a deep depression. Quickly, drinking became a major part of her life. At times she would pass out on the sofa. It wasn't long before the babies were removed from her care. Jasmine not only wound up in criminal court from James' charges of assault, but in the family court as well.

Five Years Later

Jasmine chuckled, as she drove her Benz through the streets of White Plains New York.

"Make sure my check is not late," she mimicked Jay.

Jasmine vowed he would never get away. She wondered who she was fooling, he already did. Not only was he disrespectful, but he brought embarrassment to her job. He had used her to obtain his green card, and lied that Jhonelle was his cousin.

All along, she was nothing more than his long time girlfriend and they both wanted to live in America. Jasmine heard stories about women marrying men from the Caribbean for green cards, never in a million years she thought she would be caught up in the scam. She laughed and cried at the same time because she lost the battle, Jay had won.

Months went by, and Jasmine complied with terms of the court. She visited with the twins, Mia and Tia on a regular basis. She brought toys and played with them. With each visit, things were not easy on her emotions. Jasmine and the girls would cry when the visit was over.

It was a hectic Friday afternoon, and Jasmine was headed to her supervised visit. Her phone rung, it was the caseworker calling to tell her that her husband didn't show and she was not sure what was going on. Jasmine hung up the phone and called Jay.

"You bastard, you think you're going to keep my kids from me? I pay child support. You better make sure I see my kids this weekend, or all hell's gonna break loose, Jay."

Jasmine huffed and called her attorney. Jasmine left a message for Laura letting her know she wanted this case in front of the judge's bench ASAP. Hours later, Jasmine received a phone call from Laura.

"Laura," she answered in a hasty voice. "I want this case in front the judge immediately. Jay did not show up with my kids. He thinks him and the heifer going to raise my children, and paint a bad image of me?" she cried.

"Jasmine calm down, please… Jay will not be going in front of the judge."

"Why not…?"

"He is dead."

There was a brief but tension-filled pause between them.

"Dead…?" she repeated with her voice cracking.

"Yes," Laura responded. "I am sorry honey."

"How?" she wailed in the phone. "How…?"

"Jhonelle and him were heading on their to get the kids for the visits when they swerved to avoid a car, their brakes failed and the car headed off the road and landed in the bush. Their car was wrapped around a tree."

"Oh God…! My kids! My kids!" Jasmine screamed, sliding to the floor while crying her eyes out.

"Listen, we will be in court Monday and petition for the kids to go back to your care. Right now the agency is exploring to place the children with your mother."

Jasmine didn't answer. She placed the phone at her side. With her head hung, she wept.

In the courtroom, the judge listened while adjusting in his chair. Then he spoke.

"Given the extreme circumstances, I don't believe in putting the children through anymore suffering, so I will be granting custody to the mother."

After thanking the judge, Jasmine smiled and hugged her attorney. "I can't wait to go see my children."

Laura headed out the court with her. Pausing she stated, "Isn't it weird how you wound up with your children back in your custody?"

"Yea, faith I guess." Jasmine responded before walking down the halls to her car.

With the bright sun beating against her Jasmine smiled because she knew the truth. She paid someone to arrange the accident at the intersection. With the failure of his brakes, James had no chance to survive. My husband he had to go because, "Hell knows no fury like a woman scorned," she smiled wryly.

2 Birds in the Bush

GENEIVA BORNE

"Welcome home daddy" Trina seductively said laying across the bed spreading her legs unveiling what her red laced teddy vainly attempted to conceal, but didn't.

"How you want it daddy?" She asked, posing in the most seductive positions she could create in her kinky imagination.

Trina took pride in flexing. Dorel wanted her in the worst way, but didn't want to run up in her and throw the usual straight-out-of-prison fuck on her. After being locked up for four long years he wanted to show her that he was a master. No one could do it better, that was hard sneaking in and out of closets at the medium security prison.

He hadn't made love in a real bed in a long time. It was always in some closet or unattended office. He sneaked sex with a prison guard and had never made love without the pressure of being caught or rush quickie jobs. Now that he was home he wanted to make it special, for her. After all Trina was the mother of his child and the one he'd be sure to marry. Seeing her for the first time in her natural essence instead of prison guard blue uniform, left him stunned by her beauty.

"Damn Bird," he affectionaltely whispered. "You look so good, I'm almost afraid of what I'm going to do to you". He'd never loved anyone or been moved by anyone like her. This woman shut all his defenses down.

"Dorel come here, I want you to do all the things you dreamt of doing to me. Please daddy, make love to me."

"Bird, I want to make love to you. It's just that I've been away so long…"

"Shhh… hush!" Trina reassured him. "Less talk baby, and more loving daddy."

Dorel felt like a high school kid. He wanted to please this woman so much that it made him feel insecure, a feeling he'd never entertained especially when it came to pleasing a woman.

"Don't move while I'm in the bathroom. Your man will be right back. When I do, you're going to get what you've been waiting for, for so long. Daddy loves you Bird."

Dorel's wink left Trina thinking it would be on and popping. She placed one finger in her mouth, sucking like it was a lollipop.

"Oh daddy, I can't wait," she purred like a starved sex kitten. "Don't keep this pussy waiting too long, you hear?"

Dorel had never felt his dick so hard before. He stroked his dick, inch by inch thinking of the beautiful woman in the bed waiting. He thought about the time when she was a correctional officer at the prison. They'd snuck to secluded places and have ungodly sex. He didn't want that, he needed to perform like he loved her for the woman she was, and for taking care of his child alone while he finished his prison sentence. He needed to show her that she was more than a sexual release for him but he loved her in every way.

He released all of his built up tension and was prepared to show her more than just a beat-down, he wanted her to feel love-making that created a special bond. He left the bathroom feeling his confidence building.

"I'm going to put this on her like she's never had it before."

His manhood had already risen again to it's full glory. He opened the bathroom door with a confident swag.

"Bird, I don't know if you can handle this baby. I hope you ready for what I have in store for you."

He walked toward the bed and pulled the covers back hoping she hadn't fallen asleep. Instead of Trina it was a blood soaked pillow, he tore the blanket off the bed to find only blood soaked sheets. Dorel dropped the blanket on the floor in horror. Looking around the room, Trina was nowhere to be found. He ran to the next room. The crib was empty and drenched in blood.

"Bird, where are you?"

He called her by her nick named he'd given her in prison, because she was the only thing of beauty he had inside those cold concrete walls. She was known affectionately as his beautiful bird.

"Bird...!"

Dorel woke up in a strange place. One thing he did know was this place wasn't the prison cell he'd spent the last few years waking up in. He attempted to get out of bed to find out where he was and felt the restraints of iron cuffs holding him to the bed. Dorel felt a sharp pain in his side. He looked down to see what was causing the pain and saw the white guaze bandage covering his abdomen. He ripped the bandages off to see a red stain through the next layer of white bandages.

"Mr. Pippin, are you trying to pull your stitches out? You've lost enough blood already do you want another blood transfusion?"

Dorel heard the voice entering the room, and footsteps walking toward him checking his side.

"I'm glad to see you're awake but you have to be really careful not to disturb your wound. You're very lucky to be alive it took doctors hours of surgery to save your life. Those stitches you have in your side from the wound are itching I'm sure," the nurse said.

"How long have I been here?" Dorel asked, realizing he was in a hospital.

"Almost two weeks ago they brought you in here for stab wound injuries that punctured your kidney and caused excessive blood loss. You had to have a blood transfusion and have been here for eleven days."

"What happened to me?"

"You were stabbed within inches of your life, and suffered some blunt trauma. So far you've been unconscious, but recovering from your injuries pretty well. Other than the constant nightmares you seem to have, you appear to be doing okay. The doctor will be in to see you shortly if you need anything I mean anything at all just press the button on the wall and ask for Nurse Davis."

The doctor who entered the room shortly after, told Dorel that he was recovering as well as could be expected but because of the transfusion and the threat of infection, he had to be kept for observation. The fact that he'd woken out of his state was a positive indication that his health was improving.

As Dorel's thoughts drifted the memories came flowing. He strained to answer the questions picking at his brain. The last memory was being in the prison yard during reck-time and Hector rushing him with a shank. He'd never had beef with Hector. Why would Hector want to kill him? The mixture of high dosage pain killers and antibiotics was in full effect and made him drowsy and lethargic. Dorel struggled to keep his focus and dozed into a near comatose sleep state with no effort.

"Wake up Pipen, you no good shitface!" Dorel heard the voice growl at him.

Everything looked blury as he adjusted his eyes but his hearing was sharp. He knew that unmistakable voice of evil anywhere. Dorel could barely speak, but he muffled, "What the fuck you want Sweany?"

The more he focused the uglier the picture became. Standing beside him was C.O. Sweany. Under normal circumstances being that close to Dorel; Sweany's life would've been in imminent danger.

"Pipin, I made a special visit over here just to let you know that you are being charged with the murder of Hector Gonzalez."

"Hector is dead?" He asked, thinking aloud.

Dorel was so drugged up he couldn't comprehend the full extent of events that lead to this situation. He looked at Sweany trying to channel as much conscious hatred as possible through the cloud of drugs manipulating his brain.

"I promise you, you'll be next," Dorel said, wishing he could break the handcuffs restraining him from strangling Sweany to death.

Sweany laughed at the comment like Dorel was on stage at comedy hour.

"Pipin you's a fucking joke. Are you threating me? I'll have your head cut off and shoved so far up your asshole that it'll be back on your neck. Better yet, I'll have you cut up and used as bait for prison rats. You'll disappear into thin air just like she did. But I won't have to, because you're going to live and suffer slowly behind prison walls until you die miserably knowing you'll never have the smell of fresh air, a home cook meal, or the taste of fresh pussy, because you'll be in prison so long you'll forget why you came in the first place. You see this is what happens when you fuck with things that don't belong to you, especially what belongs to me."

"Where is Trina?" Dorel asked.

"You would love to know wouldn't you? Well it's too bad you'll never find out," Sweany said with a grimacing smile that stretched from ear to ear.

"I know you did something to her; and I know you had me set up. Hector had no reason to try and kill me. I owe you for that," Dorel said.

"I should've killed you myself. You so pathetic helpless and weak... I'm going to make you suffer with every breath of air you take."

Sweany walked towards Dorel and smacked the breath out of him, then he put his hands over his mouth and nose pressing down hard enough to stop all chances of him breathing. Just as Dorel's brain began fighting for oxygen to stay conscious, Sweany let go. Nurse Davis walked into the room and noticed Dorel gasping for air.

"Is everything alright, officer?"

"Yeah, I was just questioning the prisoner about the murder he was involved in."

Dorel motioned with his eyes toward the nurse.

"He tried to kill me." Dorel said barely audible and still struggling to speak.

The nurse looked a Sweany in shock.

"These low life criminals will do and say anything to get their ass out of trouble. He's upset because he just learned that he's being charged with first degree murder. Listen, nurse I've been in law enforcement for over twenty years, you can't trust these animals."

The nurse didn't know who to believe a lowlife murderer or the veteran officer.

"Listen, this is not the court for him to be tried in. He's in a hospital bed. Right now, his life is at stake. Your line of questioning is upsetting him to the point that it is compromising his recovery. I suggest you leave until Mr. Pipin is better. He'll have his day in court, but it won't be here or today."

"I'm finished questioning him anyway. Just remember nurse, he's a murderer and can't be trusted. If given the chance he'd try and kill you."

"That's enough, please leave."

The nurse walked Sweany to the door making sure he left the

room. She went to Dorel to check his vitals and make sure he wasn't hurt.

"Mr. Pippin, I don't know what you've got yourself into and I guess a murderer doesn't have a particular look. I have a son about your age and it would break my heart to see him lying here clinging to life and being charged with murder. Your mother must be very worried about you."

"She's dead," Dorel mumbled, barely audible.

"I'm sorry to hear that. Maybe that's why your life took such a wrong turn. No mother around to rear you. I'm a church going woman. I'm not suppose to judge; only God can judge you but, looking in your eyes I see a good man, and looking in Officer Sweany's eye I see evil. I think you need help, but the only one who can help you now is Jesus. I'm going to say a little prayer over you asking for God's help and for you to be healed and make a full recovery and keeping you safe from all evil, especially that of Mr. Sweany. I feel evil down in my bones from him."

The nurse said a long powerful prayer for Dorel, the kind his mother use to do. He hadn't had anyone lay hands on him and pray for him since his mother died. Somehow when she was finished he felt relieved, not really knowing why, but something inside told him it would be alright.

He hated nothing more than vulnerablility and weakness, and right now he was both. His memory was coming through as if it were mud coming through a strainer. He needed answers and he knew where to get them.

All his life he'd told Nayshawn every important event in his life from the time they met at age eleven and Dorel would steal cars and they would go joy ridding. He was the only other person on earth he trusted other than himself. He knew that he kept him informed on everything that took place in his life, so we needed speak to him to help him fill in the holes.

"Is everything okay Mr. Pipin? You buzzed me."

"I'm sorry nurse Davis, everything is okay, but you did tell me to buzz you if I needed anything."

"Well, what is it, son?"

"I really need a big favor."

"A favor…?"

She looked at him confused wondering what he wanted. Later that day when the floor was pretty quiet and there wasn't much staff moving about because most had left for lunch, she reluctantly came into Dorel's room to carryout the favor she promised. Nurse Davis was an honest, by-the-book-Christian woman. She valued her job but she also believed that the spirit led her to do God's work and what kind of Christian would she be if she didn't help someone in need, and this poor soul definitely was in need of help. She felt no one would help him if she didn't. She removed the cellphone concealed in her ample bosom and gave him a little speech before allowing him to dial.

"You get caught you're on your own I will deny giving it to you and say you must've stolen it from my pocket while I was checking your vitals. Do you hear me Mr. Pipin?"

She sounded so much like his mother when she used to give him responsibility and she would stress the importance of him not messing it up.

"Yes, ma'am," he nodded.

He needed to contact Nayshawn. When Nayshawn's phone rang it was from an unkown number. He was apprehensive to give an answer, but knew that his boy Dorel had passed his number on to Trina. He took a chance answering, hoping it was her. The voice on the other end spoke with urgency.

"I can't speak long so I need you to answer some questions." "Whose phone is this? Is it cool to talk?"

"Yeah, this is the nurse's cellphone. She was nice enough to let me use it, but if the guard outside my door catches me, it's a wrap, so speak fast."

"I came to see you about two weeks ago. On that visit you told me about you and this chick Trina, and how she was a parole officer at the prison and that you and her was getting it in, and she ended up pregnant, but then her fiancé, a nigga name Sweany found out and was threating to hurt her; you were worried so you asked me to help her. I made arrangements to have her move up to my girl's house in Canada. She owns a big ol' house that she rarely uses because her business has her traveling so much. She had agreed to allow your girl to come and stay with her and have the baby there until you got out. I had made all the travel arrangements and everything, but that's when the communication fell off. I never heard from her and haven't heard from you since. I've been worried. That's all I know man."

"I woke up in the hospital with a serious gut wound. Somebody tried to kill me in the courtyard. It was Sweany that set me up. I didn't have no beef with anybody, and from what I heard this nigga is dead. Now I got a body charge. I'm trying to make sense of this, but these drugs they got me on got me out of it. I think Sweany's did something to Trina, and now he's trying to get me killed."

"You got to get up out of this. This nigga Sweany has you running for your life. I'll do what I got to do to help. Let me make some phone calls. Just stay in touch with me."

Dorel saw the officer outside his door looking in. He disconnected his phone call with Nay, and slid it under his mattress, closed his eyes as if he were dosing off into another morphine stupor.

The next day Dorel's strength was returning. He'd asked the doctor to lower the dosage of painkillers he was on. He welcomed the pain, not having full function of his mind that was more painful than any wound. He sat in his bed eating his breakfast and a guard entered the room, telling him that he had a visitor. Dorel wasn't expecting anyone he was hoping it wasn't Sweany again. A white man whom appeared to be in his late forties entered the room. He extended his hand to him.

"Who are you?" Dorel asked, looking at the extended hand without touching it.

"I'm an attorney, Ernist Finestien is my name. Mr. Bradley didn't mention me to you?"

The name Bradley registered in his mind because it was Nayshawn's last name.

"You mean Nayshawn? He told me he was going to help but I hadn't spoken to him since yesterday."

"Help you he did, and from what I hear you got your ass in a pitbull's mouth Mr. Pipin. That's why I'm here. If you let me, I will help you. First allow me to tell you a little about myself. I've been a criminal attorney for 18 years. I've tried cases on every level including federal cases. I've fought cases against the toughest and best prosecutors in New York, and won. My record is exemplary. There's always a way around or through everything. Do you understand me, Mr. Pipin? You're in good hands."

"How much does your exemplary service cost?"

"Trust me whatever the fee is, you don't have to worry about that. Mr. Bradley has already secured my fee, and has commited to handling futher charges. All I need you to do is tell me everything that is going on without withholding any details. Then concentrate on getting better so you can get out of here. You leave the rest to me."

Dorel concentrated as much as he could and told him how he was in the courtyard and someone came toward him and he couldn't remember the rest. All he knew was that he woke up in the hospital.

"Sounds like you were defending yourself. We can take the self defense angle. Mr. Pipin rest and remember as much as you can. I'll be in contact with you. Here's my card if you remember anything else please call me immediately. Collect calls are no problem."

Dorel, wanted to feel relief but he knew he had to start from the beginning to see what lead him here. Thinking about the conversation he had with Nayshawn his memory began to connect slowly with his last encounter with Trina.

"Trina where are you?"

The question played out in his head and tried hard to remember the last time he saw her. She'd pulled him from his cell and took him to somewhere private. She was not herself and was acting very nervous. She told him that she was pregnant, and that she wanted to leave Sweany and be with him. She looked so vulnerable and afraid, as if she was terrified of what Sweany might do to her. She told him that Sweany was suspicious and was behaving strange. He remembered feeling her in his arms clinging to him like a child holding on to a safety blanket, while telling her that everything would be okay. He sincerely wanted it to be, but unfortunately it didn't play out that way.

Dorel was always a man of his word and if everything wasn't okay, he always knew how to fix it, but he couldn't do anything from prison. He knew Sweany was behind his getting stabbed and Trina's disappearance. He was out to ruin my life. His memory began to fill in the missing pieces as he thought about his Bird, the nickname he affectionately called her. She was a rare and beautiful thing inside those prison walls, waking him every morning. He remembered how they fell in love, and every detail of the time they spent together. He remembered Sweany came in his cell and searched for no reason in the middle of the night. That was the night Trina disappeared and never returned to work. He never saw or heard from her again. He'd made arrangements for her to leave Sweany and move in with Nayshawn's girl, safe away from Sweany, but she never contacted Nayshawn. She disappeared into thin air.

His day in court

In court Finestien was like an animal in his natural environment. He knew every loophole like a good attorney should, but even better, he knew how to make it work for him even when it wasn't on the side of his client. He was thorough and cunning. He presented the court with evidence that Dorel was acitng only in self defense. He had witnesses lined up to state that Dorel had not done anything to provoke the attack but they weren't considered credible being as though they were criminals sitting in prison, but he did manage to get the prison tape of what happened in the courtyard.

It was all caught on tape, and showed Hector attacking Dorel from behind and Dorel killing him only in defense of his own life. Watching the tape Dorel saw how he passed out following the confrontation. Hector first walked up from behind and stabbed Dorel, and Dorel then took the knife from Hector and stabbed Hector in the heart right before he passed out from excessive bleeding. Hector didn't survive.

Finestien was an outstanding attorney, and Dorel was set free of those charges. He now only had to finish the last six months of his sentence for his original charge, which he would serve in another prison. Finestien was able to get him moved saying that he feared for his life under the circumstances. This meant he didn't have to serve time under Sweany's reign.

Release Date

Dorel couldn't believe how much had changed in four and a half years, and then again he couldn't believe how much had stayed the same. Riding with Nayshawn through his old territory in the South Bronx, brought back a lot of memories. Nay caught him up on all the juicy details on who was who, and who was doing what, since he had been away. He promised to play it smart this time and not get caught up in trap like he did the last time. He already had a legitimate job waiting for him as a detailer at a car dealership in Totawa New Jersery. One of his old partners had gotten out of the game years ago and started his own car dealership now he had one of the largest dealerships in the area. He knew Dorel needed a job to keep his nose clean and would do anything for his boy.

Once he went to see Rob about his job, Nayshawn took him on a shopping spree. Dorel was no slack when it came to dressing. Dorel wasn't much of a jeans and sneakers man. He adored dressing in fine silks, and wools and occasionally you would find him in jeans and Timbs, but usually on a day when he was making rounds in the hood or looking to play some ball. He also liked suits. He could hang a suit off of his sexy body like he was Tyson Beckford. No tie, just his shirt slightly unbuttoned and his jacket fully open, like he was walking down the runway.

After shopping, Dorel told Nay to drop him off at parole so he could report. He pulled up in front of the dingy brown building across from the courthouse on 161st in the Bronx in the wine colored CL3 with cream leather interior. It hadn't changed much in four years. Dope-fiends were still standing outside, thanks to the methadone clinic across the street. He got off the elevator on the tenth floor and went inside. It was packed. Dorel wasn't feeling like waiting all day. When Dorel entered the waiting area in his Gucci suit all eyes shifted on him.

He stuck out like a sore thumb. Dorel wanted to make his presence understood by those wanting to control his life for the next year. Dorel sat in the parole office in his Gucci suit and suede shoes no socks looking like he was a model. Everyone looked at him trying to figure out who he was and where did he come from. He had already been waiting half an hour, and hated to be kept waiting. He was getting agitated. He pictured what this clown was going to look like and prayed that he wasn't an asshole. He hated anyone one having any level of control over him.

"Who's Pipin?" He heard a female voice ask.

"Right here," he answered jumping from his seat.

"Follow me to my office," she said, barely turning around.

She walked past him and made her way back to her office. He followed her round ass and long legs. That's the only view he had of her aside from the back of her head, but the lower view was much more interesting. He thought to himself. This will be a piece of cake. Once I get her eating out of the palm of my hand then I will be free to do what ever I want without her sweating me. Dorel sat in the chair as she fumbled around with some papers. I'll be right back she said as soon as he sat down. She came back with a file with his name on it.

"Sorry I kept you waiting. It's been a hectic day. Where's your client?"

Dorel looked puzzled.

"I don't know of many attorneys to come to parole with their clients. He must be special or either paying you a whole lot of money. So where is he?"

Dorel played along, leaning back in his chair and folding his arms.

"Oh, he's in the bathroom, and he is paying me a lot of money."

She turned around and sat at her desk then took her glasses off. Dorel caught a better glimpse of her face and it made him freeze in a stare like he had seen a ghost.

"Wha-aaa-at are you doing here?" The question trembled out of his mouth.

"I'm sorry do you know me from somewhere?"

He couldn't believe his eyes. The beautiful face belonged to his angel. Trina.

"What happened to you, I thought you were...?" He couldn't speak.

"I don't know you. You've got me mixed up with someone else."

He snapped out of his state of shock and came back to reality. He looked across the desk at her name plate and it read Tara Evans. Damn, he was seeing a ghost.

"So, whoever she is must have had you shook," she said, smiling. "What did she do to you? Whatever it is, it must have stolen your heart because the look on your face is as if you had just found your lost love."

"She was my heart, and she was the most beautiful woman I've ever layed my eyes on, and you look just like her."

She blushed at the complement.

"I had a twin sister, but you couldn't have known her. Trust me, she would've told me if she was dating a fine attorney, but she was engaged before she disappeared anyway."

Dorel realized this was Trina's twin sister. He couldn't believe fate had led him to her.

"What do you mean you had a twin? What happened to her?" He asked still playing along.

"About a year and a half ago, she disappeared." Tara paused, and couldn't speak because tears began welling up in her eyes.

"I apologize for asking you about something so painful. I had no idea."

Dorel gently wiped the tears from her cheeks, the way he used to do Trina's. He became momentarily confused. The next thing he knew, he was looking at how beautiful Trina looked with her hair down. He felt like kissing her, but knew he had to exercise self control.

"It's okay… What's your name?"

"It's Pipin," he answered reluctantly, but felt no need to keep up the game that was no longer humorous.

"What? You mean you're Pipin my client? You were sitting here playing me all this time pretending like you were some attorney, and all along it was you, my client…?"

She was pissed. Dorel felt foolish to piss his PO off on the first visit. The last thing he wanted was to create an enemy especially with Trina's sister.

"Let me tell you something this is the last game you will ever play with me. I may look soft but I'm the toughest bitch in here and I can make your life a living hell if I really want to. Mr. Pipin you're already getting off to a bad start."

"Allow me to apologize. I didn't mean to take it this far, but when you mistook me for an attorney, I was going to play it out for a minute and have a laugh with you. I'm sorry I didn't mean to get you upset."

She fell for the words but refused to let him know it. She gave Dorel the bitch treatment for the whole intake appointment, and then reminded him that she would be watching him, so he better not fuck up. No client had ever gotten past her defenses and on top of that touched her.

Dorel didn't know how, but some way he had to get on her good side and find out more about what happened to Trina, more importantly how to get at Sweany. He couldn't help but think of how different Trina and Tara were. Even though they were completely identical twins Trina was sweet, and kind Tara was a real bitch.

She hated him because deep down she wanted him, and that bothered her more than anything. Her wanting a client was unreal. His sexy ass had to stroll in her office and played her emotions like a violin.

Now she couldn't get him off of her mind. What kind of man was he? She wondered. Damn, too bad he's a convicted criminal. Tara was also mad at him for being one of those black men that would've been a good catch had he not been such a fuck-up in society.

Why couldn't he have just gone to college and become an attorney like he lied about being, and been a good man to some deserving woman, even if it wasn't to her. Damn, just a waste of a man. She was going to do her little part to make him see that he made the wrong choices in life and how it affected the whole community. She was going to make him pay for his mistakes.

2 AM Visit

Trina was like a hound on Dorel's trail, even though he gave her no reason to be in the six months under her supervision. She continued to pursue him in search of any violation no matter how small. He always turned up clean.

Buzz-bzzZ!

It was 2 am in the morning. Who the hell is ringing my bell at 2 am?

Dorel jumped out of his bed with nothing on but his boxers. His bare muscular chest was still pumped from his workout before bed.

"Who the fuck is it?"

"It's parole. Open up!"

"No, this bitch didn't..." he mumbled.

He checked the peep hole. Damn! It was that bitch Ms. Evans. He opened the door and looked around to see if she had anyone with her. There was no one but her.

"Ms. Evans, isn't this a little late for a visit? I've been home for six months and I've never done anything to violate my parole, and you know I do have to work in the morning. Couldn't you have picked a better time to visit? Besides isn't it dangerous for you to be traveling out this time alone?"

"Pipin this is a routine visit. I visit my other clients at this time. What makes you so damn special that I can't come to your house when I see fit? Just know that we are licensed to carry guns, and believe me I'm not afraid to use it. Let me ask you a question. Do you open the door for everyone in your boxers?"

"You came here at early morning and you lucky I didn't answer the door buck naked with my dick swinging and all…"

"It's my job to know that you are not out there breaking the law or violating your parole. I see that you are doing what you are supposed to, so I can leave now."

"Before you go, can you say why you such a bitch?"

The question hung for a tension filled minute.

"You've been trying to bust me and put me back in prison for the last six months. I apologized for what happened on the first visit. I wasn't trying to play you. You're the one who assumed I was an attorney. I just played along to see if you would get a laugh out of it."

"Did you call me a bitch, Pipin? I don't play games with my clients."

"You think you're too good. Know what? You are a bitch you are nothing like you sister."

"Excuse me what did you say?"

"Wanna know what I think? I think you liked me, and I think you've thought about it ever since and that's what made you so obsessed with me. You wanted me all this time, and I think you want me now. That's why you're here."

"You've lost your damn mind. I don't want convicted criminals' dirty hands on me. I don't have to settle for no criminal when I can have a real man."

"But you don't. That's your problem. You're beautiful but very bitter, and no man wants that. You wish you had a man and because you don't, you go around taking out all your frustration on your clients. Well you won't be stalking me and harassing me much longer. My parole is up in six months. You have no reason to try and violate me, so you can go to hell you evil sick witch."

"I can still recommend extension. I can say that you violated tonight. If I really wanted to I could lock your ass up right now."

"What bitch?"

Dorel grabbed her neck and began choking her. As he choked the breath out of her he snapped out of his rage seeing Bird's sweet kind face, instead of Tara's. He loosened his grip and removed his hands from her neck. In a daze, Dorel didn't notice Tara reaching for the gun in her holster and putting it to his forehead.

"Oh, now you're going to shoot me?"

"Put your hands behind your head Pipin."

"What?"

"You just tried to strangle me."

"You were going to violate me for no reason. How could you do something like that? This my life dam it, that you're playing with! And now you're going to shoot me?"

Dorel put his hands behind his head. The minute she let her guard down Dorel knocked the gun out of her hand and wrestled her to the ground. They struggled and tussled on the floor. She proved to be stronger than he thought. Eventually Dorel pinned her to the floor. He sat on her to keep her from wiggling. She began to scream uncontrollably to wake his neighbors so he covered her mouth. He held his hands on her mouth for a few minutes.

"You know what I'm going to let your mouth go, and I'm going to give you what you really came here for. If you don't want me then you'll scream."

Dorel slowly moved his hand from her mouth. He was right all this time, she wanted him. Dorel wondered if her and Bird had the same erogenous zones. He knew there was a place on Bird's neck that would bring water to her eyes every time he kissed her there. He bet money that Tara had the same spot. He used his tongue to circle that electrifying spot on Tara's neck. And sure as money is green, Tara melted like chocolate on a hot summer's day. She didn't protest one bit or even flinch, but squirmed, inviting the pleasure he was giving her. He moved south and unbuttoned her pants. She accepted this with no resistance. He slid them off along with her silk hot pink thongs and noticed that she had a peach just a pretty as his Bird's. He kissed it like his long love had just returned. He parted her sacred space and searched for the little man on the boat. He found her pearl sitting there ripe, and ready. Her right leg began to quiver as he began eating here entré like she was filet minion. Tara was speechless and elated with ecstasy, she remained totally helpless.

Dorel didn't stop until she exploded, and all her love juice flowed in his mouth. Yes, they even tasted alike. Dorel smiled, lifting her legs and began licking her from front to back like he was giving her a Brazilian wax. He covered every spot from front to back and all that was in between. His long voracious tongue went deep inside her.

Tara hadn't had any one in between her special place in three years since her last relationship. She was well overdue for an orgasm that would make her forget all others and Dorel was just the man for the job, and he did just that. He found spots on her body that no other man had bothered to explore and he brought them to complete ecstasy. He impressed her completely by making her feel orgasmic heights that she never knew existed. He licked her kitty until she purred, than he sank his super snake deep into kitty.

Falling for a Client

All day at work Tara couldn't stop thinking about Dorel. Sitting at her desk typing her notes about her clients that she had seen that afternoon, thoughts of Dorrel sent tingling sensations down her spine, leaving moisture in her panties. She crossed her legs and kept typing. The phone rang.

"Parole, Ms. Evans speaking?"

A deep sexy voice came across the phone, "I'm waiting Ms. Evans, don't be late. Just be ready for what I'm going to put on you." The caller then hung up.

That annoying Dorel! She thought. It was already hard for Tara to concentrate now she couldn't get any work done. Shutting down her computer, she decided to leave the office early. She was going to put in some work on that big, brown love machine, Dorel. Just as she was about to leave the phone rang again.

"Hello, Ms. Evans speaking."

"Hello, Ms. Evans."

"Listen, I'm not going to keep you waiting any longer, I'm on my way."

"You're not keeping me waiting for anything."

"Who is this?"

"Oh, you don't know me anymore. You know I was almost your brother in law."

"Oh, Rodney, I'm sorry. I thought you were someone else. How have you been?"

"I'm not doing as well as can be expected right now. You know tomorrow is the two year anniversary of her disappearance. I still miss Trina. In fact, I'm calling to say goodbye. Tomorrow, I'm leaving and I'll send for my things later. I'm moving I can't stay in that house any longer. It brings back too many memories."

Trina had forgotten the date trying to erase all the tragic echoing thoughts out of her mind.

"I still think about her everyday, too. They still haven't found anything. Have you heard of anything, or is there anything you can remember about that day she disappeared that you hadn't thought of?"

"No Tara, I've wrecked my brain everyday trying to relive that day. I keep thinking if only, I hadn't gone to that security convention in California, I could've been there for her. I asked her to go with me, but she said she wasn't feeling well and wanted to stay here in New York to get some rest and feel better. I wanted to stay here and take care of her, but she wouldn't let me. She told me to go because I had already paid for the trip, but I shouldn't have listened to her. I should've been here with her, I don't know what happened."

"Don't blame yourself. It's not your fault. I blame myself too. I should've been there for her. She kept calling me telling me that something was going on in her life, but I had my phone off because I was out in the field that day doing my home visits to my clients, by the time I got to call her back it was about midnight but she never answered her phone after that, and I never heard from my sister again. How do you think that makes me feel? I feel like I let her down. I could've saved her, if I had kept my phone. I live with that guilt everyday."

"I still look at you like my sister, and you are the closest thing I have to Trina, so if you ever need anything just call."

"Take care of yourself Rodney and please send me your new address and stay in touch."

Tara hung up the phone and headed for the door. She arrived at Dorel's house, but not with the same enthusiasm as she had before the phone call she had reminded her of her past. Dorel had on Jahiem's cd, the aroma therapy candles burning, steak in the oven, his special butter and herb rice on the stove, and bread sticks and salad on the table. The lights dimmed and his tool was already hard. Tara walked inside and Dorel was uncorking a bottle. He kissed her on her cheek and took her coat.

"Wow, everything looks perfect." She paused looking at him in awe. "Especially you," she smiled.

"I want to have the perfect evening. Trust me this is only the beginning of what I have in store for tonight," he said pouring her a glass.

She removed her feet from the four inch heels while lying back on the sofa. He massaged her tired feet and she melted back into the pillows. Her mind drifted to the conversation she had prior to arriving at Dorel's. The more she thought about her missing or dead sister, she began to tense up. She didn't want Dorel to see her cry. She ran into the bathroom. He was confused and knew something had to be wrong. Dorel knocked on the bathroom door.

"Tara, are you alright?"

In a teary voice she answered, "Everything is okay. I just need a few minutes alone."

He stepped away from the door, and sat on the sofa pondering. After what seemed like an eternity, Dorel tried to convince her to open the door. She refused. Tara sounded really out of it.

"Tara, open the door now or I'm going to break it down."

Dorel stood about two feet away from the door and with one kick the door flung open tearing it from its hinges. He found Tara sitting on the toilet with his straight edged razor that he used for shaving placed at her wrist.

"Tara, what the fuck are you doing?"

Dorel grabbed her hand with the razor in it, and squeezed it until she dropped the razor on the floor. He checked her wrist. There were no deep cuts but she had scratched the surface of her skin with the blade.

"Tara, what is going on why are you trying to kill yourself?"

Her eyes welled up with tears. He placed her head on his shoulder.

"I can't tell you. Dorel, you wouldn't understand."

"Listen, you can trust me. Tara, I'm here for you."

Tara began to cry uncontrollably, "It's my fault that my sister is dead. I could've saved her."

Dorel knew she was speaking about Trina. This was the perfect opportunity for him to get information from her.

"Baby, tell me what happened?"

"I'm a bad sister."

"I'm sure what happened to your sister wasn't your fault. Why do you think it's your fault?"

"My sister and I looked exactly alike to the point our parents would've had a hard time telling us apart. My mother was Cuban and my father was black. When we were younger they would make Trina speak English and me Spanish in order to know the difference. Trina and I were always very close. She was always the sweet, soft spoken one, and I was always the feisty, outspoken one. I used to judge her all the time about the decisions she made in life, especially after our parents died. I felt like I had to protect her. When we were younger she used to always hook-up with the wrong guys. The bad ones, who were on the corner and headed for jail. When she was sixteen she got pregnant by one of them, and had an abortion. I was the one who told her to have the abortion. She listened to everything I told her to do. I thought that she needed me to control her life. I actually felt like she couldn't make smart decisions on her own. She finally met a good man, Rodney Sweany. He gave her the world. I told her to stick with him and marry him. He was the only man in her life that ever treated her right. They got engaged and everything was going well between them. One day she comes to me and tells me that she's pregnant by another man. I couldn't believe that she was messing up her life. I told her to have an abortion. She told me that she wasn't getting rid of her baby that she wanted to keep it. I told her that she was stupid. She was throwing her life away. I told her that I didn't want to speak to her anymore, because I was upset with her. The next day she was trying to call me but I wasn't answering my phone. I turned my phone off because I knew she was calling me and I was still upset with her. Later on after work when I got home, I saw that she had called me over twenty times. I felt like she was just calling me to make me see things her way. Me being stubborn and wanting to remain in control I waited to call her the next day, and when I did she never answered. No one has ever heard from or seen my sister since. I never found out who the man she was having an affair with. In my mind he was the one who killed my sister, but who is he? I don't know. Tomorrow makes two years since her disappearance."

Dorel thought back to two years ago. The last time he spoke to Trina he held her in his arms and promised to protect her. He had failed. His child would've been born and they could've been living the perfect lives right now, if she was still alive. As Tara spoke about Trina with great guilt, he knew exactly how she felt because he felt his own burden of guilt, and a tear rolled down his cheek.

"Who else knows that she was having an affair?"

"I told the police, but they never found evidence of her having an affair."

"Did her fiancé know?"

"No, I never told him. He doesn't know. I couldn't bring myself to tell him. It would break his heart. He really loved my sister and would do anything for her. He still loves her till this day. He called me today right before I left my office to tell me how much he still loves her and misses her. I feel so bad for him. He called to say goodbye and that he can't bear staying in his own house because it only brings back memories. He's leaving town. That's why I'm sitting in your bathroom with this razor, because I feel like it's my fault. I pushed her to be in a relationship that she didn't want to be in and that forced her to have an affair and now she's missing or dead, and I have to deal with the guilt. If I hadn't been stubborn and controlling I could've talked to her, and gotten more information about her situation, and helped her, and she wouldn't be missing today."

"Have you ever questioned the fiancé?"

"We've given all the information we could give. Her fiancé was in full cooperation with offering all that he knew. He wasn't even in town when she disappeared. He was in California at a Security specialist convention for his security company."

"Just because he wasn't around doesn't mean that he didn't have anything to do with it. Suppose he found out about the affair and didn't let anyone know he knew about it. Then he would've had reason to kill her. After all you said he has a security company. He knows all the right things to do to get away with something like this."

"I know Rodney, he's a good guy and would never do anything like that."

"What appears to be good on the surface isn't always good on the inside. How do you know that their relationship was in as good shape as you think? You said that you always judged her and maybe she was afraid to tell you some of the problems they were having knowing that you would blame her for messing things up."

"I'm such a controlling bitch!"

"No, you really wanted the best for her. C'mon stop blaming yourself. There are many things that could've happened that were outside of your control."

He held her as he comforted her fears. He began messaging her shoulders and telling her everything was going to be okay.

"I want you to take your mind off of all this stress and allow me to fix all your problems tonight."

"How are you going to fix all my problems in one night?"

"We're going to start by washing these tears away."

He turned on the bathroom sink, and took her hand and pulled her up from the toilet seat where she had been sitting, contemplating her death. He gave her a washcloth and she began washing her face. What would she have done if it weren't for Dorel? She thought. She washed her face in the sink she felt the heat of Dorel's body behind her and then she felt his long, hard tool rubbing on her lovely round cheeks right where her thong disappeared.

Dorel ruggedly ran his tongue down her neck and played with her ear lobes. She glared at the mirror as her lover molded her body like she was clay and he was the sculptor. Her mind left the bad place it had been earlier. Dorel let his hand run down her waist and unbuttoned her skirt. It slid down her legs with the greatest of ease. His finger played with her spot until her volcano erupted. She moaned in pleasure. Off went her black lace thongs. He opened the bathroom medicine cabinet and took out a bottle of Vaseline. He opened the top and ran his hand through it. He rubbed some on his tool and a little on in between the slit of her swollen backside. Nothing would hinder him from seeking his treasure. He gently bent her over the sink and with one swift move he was in.

Tara bit her lip for about one second to adjust to the initial discomfort. What have I gotten myself into? Just be a big girl, you can handle it. It had been three long years since the backyard had been lit, but once Dorel's ray of sun shined on it, it was pure ecstasy. It felt better than it had in her past. He always knew bitchy women were freaks and Tara was no different. Being inside of Tara reminded him of the times he made love to Trina.

"Oh Bird, you feel so good." He realized it was Tara he was making love to.

"What did you call me?"

Trying not to cause any alarm he put her thoughts at ease. He bent over and kissed her.

"Didn't you know that you are my little bird? So soft, so delicate, so beautiful…"

Tara was flattered by the nickname. She could live with it.

"It's okay if you want to call me Bird. I kind of like it."

Dorel smacked her on her ass.

"How do you like it baby?" Dorel uttered in her ear.

The sensuous moans and titillating mumbles Tara made him sure that she was more than satisfied. He loosened her hair from the bobby pins and let it flow freely. Dorel grabbed her hair like she was a horse and road her ass. The sink shook and the mirror vibrated as he thrusted in and out. Tara caught pieces of her reflection in the mirror in the mist of her moans. They peaked simultaneously and collapsed on the bathroom floor. He held her there on the tile floor for a few minutes and then he picked Tara's hundred forty-five pound frame off the floor with no effort and carried her to the bedroom like she was a baby.

He placed her on the bed and round two was about to take place. He had an insatiable appetite. Yeah, she had a monster on her hands. Tara loved every minute of it. It was worth sweating out her hair, loosing her voice, and getting rubbed to the point she felt raw. She had found the magic stick, and didn't want to ever let it go.

Somewhere in between passion they managed to have dinner. Dorel cut her steak up for her, he fed her buttered herb rice and he wiped her mouth. She hadn't felt so special in years. No man she had been with before had treated her like Dorel did, she felt like she had misjudged him and had mistreated him. She was hoping that she could have the next year or maybe the next lifetime to make it up to him. Dorel put Tara to bed for the rest of the night. He closed the door to the bedroom and took her purse. He found her address book and Sweany's address and phone number.

Dorel knew that there was no other explanation for Trina's disappearance, and he knew that Sweany was the one that tried to get him killed in prison. Now he was letting Tara bare the burden of Trina's death. He hated Sweany and knew that he had to kill him.

An eye opening morning

The next morning Tara awoke feeling like a new person. She got up and went into the bathroom and then looked all around the apartment and didn't see any signs of Dorel. To keep her mind occupied she turned on the television. Where could he have gone? She wondered and noticed her purse was not where she left it. Oh no, she thought. I couldn't have been wrong about him. She checked her wallet, nothing was taken. What could he have been looking for in my purse? She went through her purse thoroughly. She didn't carry credit cards when she was on duty all she carried was her ID, her gun, some petty cash and her phone book. She opened her phone book and noticed that one page was wrinkled and smeared, liked she had spilled water on it. She noticed Rodney Sweany was smeared.

Tara began to think about the conversation they had the night before and how much interest Dorel had in trying to make Sweany the key suspect in Trina's disappearance. It didn't make sense. Her mind led her back to the first day she met Dorel. He thought she was someone he had been with. Was it Trina? Could he have known her sister at one time?

There was only one woman that looked exactly like her, and that was her twin sister. Her mind was going crazy trying to piece her thoughts together. The door opened her heartbeat skipped. All of a sudden, she felt like she didn't know the person she was falling in love with. She picked her gun up, and hid it behind her back.

"Oh, you're awake. How did you sleep?"

"I slept okay, but I woke up to a surprise. Where were you?"

"I went to the store to get something to eat."

He walked over to give her a kiss. She pulled out the gun and shoved it in his face.

"What the fuck is going on Dorel?"

"Why the fuck are you pointing a gun at me?"

"You tell me what kind of game are you playing with my life and how do you know my sister?"

"What are you say…"

Before he could finish his sentence, he heard Tara's gun click.

"Speak now or I'm going to blow a hole through your lying fucking teeth."

"Okay, okay Tara let me explain. I knew Trina because when I was incarcerated at Coldwell she was a C.O. there, and I know that you are going to hate me for this but I was her lover. She was pregnant by me."

"What?"

Tara couldn't believe now it all made sense. She put the pieces together and now she saw why he tried to implement Sweany, and why he wanted Sweany's address.

"Did you have anything to do with my sister's disappearance?"

"No, I loved her. I wanted her to wait for me until I came home, but Sweany killed her, and he tried to kill me while I was in prison also, but I killed the guy he hired, and when I came home and saw you, I thought my angel had come back to me. I didn't mean to hurt you. You helped me deal with what happened to her. I love you Tara."

"You don't love me. You played a game with my life. How do I know that you didn't have Trina killed, and maybe you're trying to kill me?"

"Sweany had Trina killed, I was locked up remember. I would've been dead myself if I hadn't have killed first. Put the gun down Tara."

"What did you do to Sweany?"

"Bird, put the gun down and we can talk."

Tara paused for a minute confused about what to do. The news ticker on the television read loud and clear.

"News flash, a corrections officer from Coldwell prison upstate has just been found shot in his home in Queens. The officer has been identified as Ronald Sweeny. There has been no arrest yet..."

Her eyes quickly welled with tears.

"You did kill Sweany," she shouted.

Dorel eased his gun out from where he concealed it in the small of his back and pointed it at Tara. Now they both had pistols pointed at each other. Dorel knew that he was in no position to compromise. Tara was a scorned woman with a gun pointed at his face. She felt like Dorel was a man who had killed her loved ones, and was about to kill her. She had no reason not to kill Dorel. He didn't want to kill Tara, but knew it had to be either her or him.

Dorel pointed the gun at Tara and pulled back the trigger. Tara fired her gun hitting Dorel in the chest before Dorel's trigger released. He fell to the floor. Then she fired a second round that landed in his shoulder. Tara walked to Dorel's bleeding body, and stood over him. With his last breath he tried to tell her that she was wrong about him killing Trina. He told her that he loved Trina very much and that he would've never hurt her.

Tara turned and walked to the door she felt the slug hit her back and knocked her to the floor. She felt the burn of the bullet rip through her flesh. She tried to get up but couldn't move. She saw the red essence poured from her wound. She felt faint as the life evaporated out of her body. She could not hold her head up. Everything faded to black.

Dorel got up from the position he was in and removed the bullet proof vest he had on. It had caught one bullet and another missed the vest and pierced his right shoulder. He stood over Tara as she descended into another world.

"Sorry it had to end this way. I wished you would've just listen to me! It was either you or me..."

It hurt Dorel to have lost his bird once again, but at least he had taken care of Sweany. Dorel went to the living room where he had hidden the duffle bag that had $100, 000 that he had gotten out of Sweany's safe.

He called Nayshawn. "This place is a mess." Nayshawn knew what time it was.

When the clean-up crew arrived at Dorel's apartment, there was no body to take care of. Tara's body had disappeared. The apartment was completely empty. They put in a call to Dorel and let him know the status.

"What the fuck could've happened to her?"

Candy

BROOKE GREEN

"Candy!"

"What...?" I screamed back.

Granted, the home I shared with my boyfriend, Rome, and our three-year-old daughter, Kenya, was large, but there was no reason for him to scream my name like we were in the middle of the projects. I scooped the last of the scrambled eggs onto a plate and groaned loudly. I took my time getting to our bedroom because I knew he didn't want anything, as usual.

"Candy!"

My attitude kicked into high gear as I quickened my pace and prepared myself for a verbal battle.

"I know this mothafucka has lost his damn mind," I mumbled.

I reached the bedroom door with my mouth ready to rumble. "Why in the hell are you calling me like...?"

The look on Rome's face stopped me mid-sentence. I nearly choked on my words when I saw the maniacal look in his eyes.

"What the fuck is this candy?"

He sneered as he shook the prescription bottle he'd just found in my purse.

I took a deep breath and tried to play it off as if he was overreacting.

"Oh, I got them from my doctor the other day. You know I've been complaining about how I've been getting migraines lately."

I shrugged my shoulders and flagged the air like it was no big deal.

"Oh yeah, your doctor huh…? Well where is the script label?"

"Huh?"

"The label," he said, pointing at the bottle. "If your doctor gave these to you, then where is the label with your name?"

I was at a loss for words.

"Yeah, I thought so," he shook his head in disbelief. "What, you think I'm stupid or something Candy? First of all, you don't get 60 milligrams of Oxy-fuckin'-cotin for no goddamn migraines. Where did you get this shit from Candy, your trifling-ass-girlfriends, or some nigga…?"

I wanted to crawl into a hole and disappear. I closed my eyes tight and wished the whole scenario away. A few moments earlier, Rome and I were enjoying a relaxing Sunday morning, with me making breakfast and him settling in to watch a day's worth of football playoffs. One minute I was busy fluttering around the kitchen like the perfect homemaker I knew I wasn't, and the next minute Rome was standing in my face taunting me with my pill bottle.

"Answer the fucking question!"

I jumped as Rome's booming voice startled me out of my thoughts. I opened my mouth to speak but couldn't make up a name fast enough and, I knew better than to tell him that I stole them from his beloved grandmother who was dying from cancer.

"Oh, I see. Now you don't have nothing to say? I'm going to ask you one more time Candy. Where did you get these from?"

"I bought them from Buddy," I lied.

I felt bad for putting his young cousin in my lies, but shit, Rome already couldn't stand him so one more infraction wasn't going to change anything, right?

"I knew he had them," I continued rapidly, "but baby I swear I only got them to help with my migraines. And you know my neck is still bothering me and I can't get an appointment with my doctor until 3 weeks from now."

I stood rooted to my spot while I watched Rome watch me. After several seconds of silence, I squared my shoulders and opened my mouth to dismiss the entire subject once and for all but was silenced by Rome's next move.

He twisted the cap off the bottle and inspected its contents with a trained eye.

He frowned hard and emptied the pills into his hand. I swallowed hard as he picked one up and rolled it between his fingers. And another and then another.

Rome remained silent and, once again, I found myself praying for a do-over. Foolishly thinking he wouldn't notice that there were actually several types of pills in the bottle, I allowed myself to relax and sat on the bed.

"Bullshit!" Rome yelled as he hurled the bottle at my head.

I felt the sting of the pills against my skin before I had a chance to cover my face. "What the hell is wrong with you, Rome?" I whimpered. "I…"

"What the hell is wrong with me?" He yelled at the top of his lungs as he rushed over to pick up the empty pill bottle. "This is what the fuck is wrong with me!" He charged at me and mashed the bottle into my cheek.

Surprise, mixed with the force from his angry gesture caused me to lose my balance and tumble backwards. Before I could regain my balance on my own, Rome grabbed me by the arm and yanked me upright.

"What are you doing?" I struggled against his grip on my arm, which felt as though it would snap with one wrong move.

"Let me make myself clear since you think I'm playing with your silly ass. If I ever see this shit in my motherfucking house again, I'm a fuck you up for real. It's bad enough that you back to fucking around with this shit, but why'd you have to bring it in here? What if Kenya would have gotten hold to this and ate it?" He released my arm and backed away from me.

I drew in a sharp breath as he paused to let his last statement sink in. He definitely knew the mention of my daughter would get my attention.

"I…I'm sorry Rome. I promise, I really promise you that this is the last time. It's just that…" I said while massaging my newly formed bruises.

"Sorry won't cut it this time. You said sorry the last time remember? This is it. Last chance, Candy, you gotta make a choice. It's either me and Kenya or the damn pills."

My head snapped back and attitude crept into my voice, "Hold up. What do you mean you and Kenya? So what, you try'n a tell me that you are going to try to take my daughter away from me? She's not..." I stopped before I said something I'd soon regret.

Although Kenya was not Rome's biological daughter, he'd been more of a father to her than the bastard who helped me make her so rubbing that in his face would've crushed him. I decided to leave well enough alone because I knew that he would never make good on that threat. Shit, what man is going to willingly take on being a full-time dad when he doesn't have to?

Rome's eyes went dark as though he knew what I'd just stopped short of saying.

"Baby..." I began, but stopped when I saw Rome bending over to pick up the pills off the floor.

My heart began racing because I knew his next move would be to toss them out or worse, flush them down the toilet.

"Rome?" When he didn't answer, I rushed over to his side and pulled him up to meet my gaze.

"Baby, I'm sorry. Please believe me. I would never do anything to hurt our family. I just made a stupid mistake, that's all."

Rome remained quiet but he was at least listening. I let my head fall to my chest to allow myself a chance to see how many pills were left on the floor. I counted twelve on the floor and unless some rolled under the bed or furniture, Rome had 6 in his hand. Deep down I knew that my priorities were fucked up but my first concern was making sure that the $540 worth of pills did not go to waste. I needed to take Rome's mind off the issue at hand and focus on something more worthwhile, me.

I wrapped my arms around his waist and leaned up to kiss his lips, but he remained stiff as a board. I let my lips linger on his for a moment before moving to his neck. Knowing this would do the trick, I traced his collarbone with my tongue while my breath warmed his neck. I pulled him closer and reached for his zipper.

His breath caught in his throat as my tongue traveled to his earlobe and I began to nibble. I felt his body relax and I smiled to myself.

With his dick in my hand, I began to slowly massage him until I felt the tip getting wet.

"Do you forgive me?" I whispered throatily in his ear.

He grunted as I continued to massage his rock hard dick.

"Rome, do you forgive me, sweetheart?"

My other hand was tugging the button of his pants free and I reached in to cup his entire package. He answered by shoving his tongue generously down my throat. I sucked his bottom lip.

"Do you want to fuck my mouth?" I brazenly asked.

He groaned, nodding his head and moaned. I dropped to my knees and swallowed his extended dick. At this junction in time, I would normally play with my pussy in preparation of being fucked, but as much as I should've been enjoying the moment, I really wasn't.

Rome's long thick dick was grinding against my tongue. I began to feel the familiar longing as my mind worked a mile a minute to figure out a way to get just one of the pills next to me on the floor. His knees buckled a little as I performed like my life depended on it. And in a way, it did. As much as I loved my life with Rome, I loved Oxycontin, Percocet and Vicodin, *my candy*, much more. I knew for certain what would make me feel much better than even his hard dick would be my candy.

Addiction has a weird way of making you feel like all of the stupid shit you do just to get high, was perfectly normal. I had to focus on the task at hand which was taking Rome's mind off of my relationship with my candy.

Quickly I replaced my mouth with my hand and stroked Rome's dick while looking up at his expression my sucking had induced. I was in control.

"I want you to fuck my mouth good with your hard dick, for real. Fuck it like you miss it," I ordered.

He grunted as he forced the tip of his dick back in my mouth and grabbed two handfuls of my shoulder-length weave. A smile crossed my lips as I felt the pills he'd held in his hand fall around me. I stroked his balls with one hand and reached down to scoop up two pills without disturbing his pleasure-filled flow.

My heart raced and my wetness dripped down my thighs in anticipation of what was to come. Without breaking stride, I slid the candy on my tongue and allowed it to slide down my throat. With my mission accomplished, I jumped up and pushed Rome down on the bed to finish him off.

"I'm sorry baby." I sat on the tip of his dick and squeezed my walls as I slowly took him in inch by inch. "Do you forgive me?"

Grabbing both my ass cheeks, Rome began bucking up while vigorously nodding his head. It was my game now and I was already ahead. I threw my head back from the intense pleasure. He was hitting my spot and the candy I swallowed already was in effect. My body began to grow warm and I felt goose bumps all over. My body turned to jelly and Rome body shuddered as a climatic orgasm swept through me and my lover simultaneously like a hurricane coming inland. We screamed out in unison at the pleasure our grinding brought.

I lay still, sweaty and high as a kite. My pussy still leaking and my head resting comfortably on Rome's broad chest, I listened to him softly snoring. Closing my eyes, I waited for the implosion of euphoria to envelope me. An unavoidable smile of victory spread across my face when the familiar wave of feel-good washed over my body. My nipples hardened and my pussy got wet all over again. The best part of my candy was it made me feel all was right in my world.

The hair on my arms stood and goose bumps covered me. The feeling was orgasmic and I felt as though I could walk on air. I knew it would take a little longer to get the full effect of my high because of the time-release element of Oxycontin. If not for Rome's dick being in my mouth at the time, I would've chewed the pill and gotten an immediate rush. But since he wouldn't have taken too kindly to me gnawing on his dick, I had to take my candy however I could get it. When I felt sad, I took my candy. When I felt happy, I took candy. Sure 'nuff, when I felt anything other than high, I took my candy.

Rome stirred a little in his sleep and it shook me out of my reverie. I sat up and quietly slid off the bed, taking care not to disturb Rome. The last thing I wanted was for him to wake up and remember what brought on the argument in the first place. Even though I knew what I was doing was all wrong, I got down on all fours and began crawling around, gathering up the pills scattered about the room.

Volunteering to help care for Rome's sick grandmother was one way to ensure that I had access to her cancer medication. The scheme was entirely scandalous, but there was no way she would miss it. Besides, it was better than me having to spend money for bills, or worse, sell ass. I admit there were times when I really wanted to quit. Mainly when I ran out of candy and began going through withdrawal.

There are those who say that Oxycontin was hillbilly heroin. I wouldn't disagree. As good as it made me feel when I was high, it was ten times worse when I wasn't. That shit was no joke.

Picture Diana Ross in *Mahogany*, complete with the shakes, sweating up a storm, vomiting and having the runs. That was me. I had tried many times to quit but just like any other drug, it kept calling my name. And I kept going back.

I got on my hands and knees, gathering and counting fourteen pieces of candy. Then I sat at the foot of the bed trying to remember how many I had counted before. Just then another wave of euphoria cruised through my veins. Frozen in the enjoyment of my high, I smiled. Rome was asleep less than five feet away from me, and not wanting that feeling to end anytime soon, I quickly chewed another sixty milligrams of my favorite candy. With my flexible tongue, I tried my best to get all residue stuck between my teeth without drinking water. I frowned hard because the taste was unpleasant and my tongue became numb.

I heard Rome shifting on the bed and jumped to my feet. I had to catch my balance because my legs were like jelly. My eyes swept the floor one last time for any remaining pills. There was no more. With an unsteady gait, I made my way to the bathroom in search of a good hiding place for my candy. I spotted my box of tampons under the sink and knew it was perfect because Rome would never go digging around in there.

Tearing the plastic wrapper on the tampon, I dropped the pills inside the hollow end of the applicator. When I was satisfied that they were secure, I put everything back in its place before returning to the bedroom. All I needed was an excuse to give Rome when he awoke to find the pills were no longer on the floor. The pill bottle was still lying in the corner of the room where it landed after bouncing off of my head. I took it to the bathroom, threw it in the wastebasket and flushed the toilet thrice. The noise awoke Rome. He was staring up at me when I entered the room.

"What are you doing?" He asked with a hint of suspicion.

"Just taking care of the problem, baby," I smiled reassuringly.

Taking care to say the words slower than normal, I did not

want to alarm him with my thick tongue and sing-song voice that always accompanied my high.

"Huh?" he grunted.

"I'm truly sorry, Rome. And I want you to know that you'll never have to worry about my can-, I mean those pills again. And to prove it, I flushed them all down the toilet, baby."

Rome sat up, moved to the edge of bed and looked on the floor and around the room. For a moment, doubt crept into his eyes. Then he said, "Flushed them...? For all I know, you went in there and hid them," he said scrutinizing me.

My eyes widened and I shuffled my feet while trying to think of a plausible comeback.

"Rome?" I said walking over to the bed. "Baby, I told you that you wouldn't have to worry about this anymore. I understand why you're mad and I'm so sorry. I don't want to lose you or our family. That's why I got rid of them. Nothing is worth me losing you, or what we have built together," I said with as much sincerity as I could muster, even managing to squeeze out a few tears.

He looked as though he was struggling with the bullshit I just fed him but I knew I'd won him over when his shoulders slumped and he nodded his head.

"Okay, that's the right thing to do."

I smiled and leaned in for a kiss but was stopped short by Rome's hand in my face.

"Don't think this is over because we still have a lot to talk about, Candy. I can't have you thinking that you bringing this shit in my house is all cool and shit. Sucking my dick won't make me forget, and neither will you dropping a few crocodile tears."

I nearly choked. Was I really that obvious? My high was slowly dying. I knew the longer I stood there, the harder it would be to not respond and my high would die a horrible death. Suddenly an urge overtook me, and my mind drifted to the tampon box. I wasn't sure if going back so soon after flushing the contraband was such a good idea. I decided to tell Rome whatever he wanted to hear to cut the conversation short.

I sat on the bed and looked him in the eye. "Babe, I know you probably don't understand what I am going through but, I only took those pills because they're the only thing that takes away the pain I have in my neck."

"What pain?" The expression on his face showed nothing but disdain. "You haven't mentioned anything to me about being in no damn pain. In fact, you go to the gym damn-near everyday with no complaints. And now all of a sudden you're in enough pain for you to start taking 60 milligrams of Oxycontin? That's some shit they give to cancer patients."

Stopping short, he gave me a hard sidelong glare. I wonder if he could hear my heart racing. Fear replaced my already diminished high. I just knew Rome was connecting the dots in his head and I braced myself for another one of his attacks. Rome shook his head as if he was erasing any thoughts of me stooping so low as to steal from his cancer-stricken grandmother.

"We went through this shit before Candy," he continued, "and I told you then that I wasn't going to tolerate no junkie."

I flinched at the word 'junkie', and wanted to defend myself, but couldn't. It was true. A year earlier, I was in a car accident that caused a serious neck injury. I was prescribed Vicodin and Percocet while going through therapy. Truth be told, my injury was minor and I could've managed the pain with Ibuprofin. I started taking the pills as prescribed but it didn't take long for me to discover why people abused them. When I realized how Percocet took, not only my physical pain away, but my emotional and mental pain as well, I was hooked. I began calling it my candy because it made me as happy and giddy as a child with real candy.

When my therapy ended, so did my prescriptions, and that's when my trouble began. Rome started noticing money that was missing from our accounts and I was soon introduced to Oxycontin by a friend. I lost 30 pounds because one of the major effects it had on me was loss of appetite and vomiting. I began to have wild mood swings where one minute I was loving and affectionate and the next I was violently crying from withdrawal.

The final straw came when I used the money for the mortgage to buy an entire prescription from a coworker. I'd planned on paying the bill before Rome got wind of it. But as luck would have it, he intercepted the mail and saw the late notice.

Rome stayed away for a few days and was prepared to leave for good unless I agreed to go to an out-patient treatment facility. I stayed clean and away from all prescription medication until recently. I'd been given the task of looking after Rome's sick grand-mother two evenings a week.

"So now you don't have nothing to say," Rome said in a raised voice. "Oh no, not Miss I-always-have-to-have-the-last-word!"

I sat there in silence trying to find the right things to say and make everything better. To my relief, the door bell rang loudly, startling us both. Rome and I both sighed deeply, but for very different reasons. He looked as though he wanted to finish tearing me a new asshole and I, needed a much deserved break from his berating.

"That must be my sister with Kenya," he said, rising from his seat on the bed.

Even though I was thankful for the interruption, I didn't want to leave our discussion on an angry note. "Babe," I said, standing to block his hasty exit, "I don't want to argue with you anymore," I pleaded, "You're right, plain and simple. I promise we can talk about this later and clear the air. I was wrong again, and I have to live with that. But let's not let this ruin the rest of our day. Please," I begged with a meek expression.

"I have to get the door," he answered gruffly without meeting my gaze.

Rome pushed past me and headed toward the front door. I stood there for a moment trying to digest what I'd done. Hearing the patter of Kenya running toward the stairs suddenly made me conscious of my appearance. I hurried to the bathroom to fix myself.

Between the crying and Rome pulling my hair, I looked a hot ass mess. I pulled a brush through my hair and patted my face with a damp washcloth before returning to greet my baby.

"Mommy!" Kenya squealed, running to me.

"Hi, baby girl," I said, giving her a kiss on the forehead. "Did you have fun with Auntie?"

"Yes mommy. I missed you." She smiled the cutest smile and wrapped her short arms around my neck.

"Come on, let's go say thank you to your auntie." I put her down and patted her head. "Go back downstairs and tell Daddy and Auntie that I will be right there. I have to use the bathroom, okay?"

Kenya nodded her head and skipped out of the room. I waited until I heard her relay my message in her squeaky voice, and hurried straight to the bathroom.

Guilt tugged at my heart as I reached into the tampon box to retrieve my relief. Though I was in no real physical pain, I needed my candy to ease the emotional pain. I shook one pill out and did a quick mental count of how many I'd already taken. Three pills were too many, but my cravings were becoming more intense and happening far too frequently.

I had to do something about my addiction but I wasn't sure what to do or even if I really wanted to stop. Sure it was wrong but at the same time, it made me feel so good, I thought popping the lone pill into my mouth. Quickly, I chewed it up, while promising myself that as soon as I finished the ones I had left, I would make moves to quit for good. I rinsed my mouth and I had to steady myself from falling as my heart beat a mile a minute. A wave of dizziness nearly knocked me over. It never occurred to me that I had overdone it by taking so many in such a short period of time.

The problem with addiction, all rationale goes out the window. Even through my dizziness and heart palpitations, all I could think about was the next high. The rest of the afternoon went by in a blur. Rome left soon after we said our goodbyes to his sister and still didn't return for dinner.

I played with Kenya, my mind kept returning to the tampon box in the bathroom. Between my worrying about Rome not returning home and Kenya running me ragged, I couldn't enjoy the high I craved. I contemplated taking just one more but decided against it because I needed them to last as long as possible and I wasn't totally sure Rome wasn't hip to me getting them from his grandmother. That meant I couldn't be sure the next time I would be invited to care for her. Anxiety began to set in as I thought about not having access to my candy anymore.

"Mommy…?"

I pushed the thoughts to the back of my mind and focused my attention back to Kenya.

"Yes Baby?"

"You wanna play Bratz with me?"

I checked my watch and breathed a sigh of relief when I saw it was her bedtime.

"Not tonight sweetie. It's bedtime."

"Aw man," she said, poking out her bottom lip.

I smiled at her imitating *Swiper The Fox,* a character from her favorite show *Dora The Explorer.*

"Come on silly girl. I'll tell you what, how about you sleep with mommy until daddy comes back home?"

"Yeah!"

After bathing Kenya and putting on her pajamas, I laid her on my bed and promptly stretched out next to her. I kissed her goodnight and tucked her in. As usual, Kenya fought going to sleep and played around in the bed. Though I would normally make her stop and go to sleep, I was too tired to fuss at her. I closed my eyes and waited for Kenya to quiet down.

"Mommy, I baked a cake. Do you want some of my cake?"

I turned to face her and was met by her outstretched hands offering me her pretend cake. I took the imaginary piece of cake, put my hand to my mouth and chewed air.

"Hmm, thank you baby. That was the best cake ever Kenya. Now go to sleep for mommy."

Kenya giggled. I turned comfortably on my back and closed my eyes, praying for her to go to sleep.

Kenya quietly shuffled around for several more minutes before finally whispering loudly, "Mommy? Do you want some of my candy?"

"No Kenya," I said my eyes firmly shut. "I said go to sleep."

Kenya quieted down and I finally felt my mind and body relax enough to sleep. I was startled awake by the sound of Kenya coughing loudly and violently while trying to call out to me.

I jumped up, grabbed her arms and held them above her head to help clear her lungs. The coughing subsided but was replaced by loud crying and vomiting.

"Dammit!" I jumped out of the way. "It's always something with this child," I sighed while I hurried to the bathroom to get some towels for the mess.

Kenya had finally quieted down and was lying in the small puddle of vomit when I returned to the bed. I gently removed her pajamas and wiped her face and hands before wrapping her in a clean towel. I rolled her to the side and began wiping the sheets. Then I noticed it. It was small but I would have recognized it from a mile away.

My heart fell out of my chest as if I picked up the half eaten red pill off of the bed. I looked from the pill, my *candy*, to Kenya who was lying very still and barely breathing. It hit me like a ton of bricks. The candy Kenya offered me was *my candy* and she must've found the extra pill I'd overlooked.

"Kenya! Oh my— what have I done?"

When I lifted her up, her head fell back against my arm. Her eyes, which were half-open, suddenly rolled back and her body went stiff and then into violent convulsions. I screamed, "Oh my God! Kenya!"

I tried holding her tightly but the convulsions caused her to fall from my arms. I grabbed the phone and shakily dialed 911 while praying for the life of my baby. "Kenya baby, it's going to be alright. Mommy is so sorry. God please forgive me, please let my baby be ok!"

The dispatcher's voice called out to me through the phone, "Hello? Ma'am? Can you hear me?"

"Please, hurry please, send an ambulance! My baby is having a seizure and she needs help!" I cried.

"Okay ma'am."

I held my daughter tightly, rocking back and forth while bawling my lungs out.

What Goes Around

ARETHA TEMPLE

Standing in a house, ski mask on, pointing a 9 millimeter at Cheese, a big time money-getter, was Chatty. On both sides of her were CT alias Cutthroat, and his boy, Trif. Cutthroat had Chatty seduce Cheese, which helped him get to Cheese's stash. Catherine Staples AKA Chatty was twenty-eight years young, and the only child of Gail and Ronnie. Who would be shittin' bricks if they knew what there daughter was doing at the moment. They would die of heart attacks if they knew some of the other shit she'd done. A heart attack is what Chatty felt she was having, pointing a loaded gun in somebody's face.

Chatty was shaking under the black attire she wore. She was glad she was wearing a mask for two reasons. She did not want Cheese to know it was her, and she didn't want anyone seeing the fear in her eyes. The guys loaded up the duffle bags with money and Chatty looked over at CT.

CT, whose real name was Antonio Sanchez, was thirty-two years old, and a two-time felon. He had spent most of his childhood locked up. He didn't give a fuck about his life, or nobody else's. He was six feet-one inch, and his skin was the color of butterscotch. His hair was jet black and curly because he ain't had a haircut since who knew when. CT was very handsome, but insecure about his long slash he wore on the side of his face. He earned the buck-fifty when he was in juvie some years ago. CT was a Latino and Black mix.

His dad, big Cutthroat, was a pimp. His mother, Jennifer was the bottom bitch. CT's parents, if they were alive wouldn't give a fuck about him because they both were crack-heads. CT was also the only child, and the rest of the family all treated him like dirt. So he grew up in jail. His mantra was 'fuck the world', and right now he didn't give a fuck about killing Cheese.

"Hurry the fuck up!" CT yelled.

"Damn nigga, I'm going as fast as I can!" Cheese said, slowly stuffing the bags.

"Shut the fuck up!" CT said, walking up to Cheese and putting the gun in his mouth. "Nigga, I got chocolate bullets in here that will melt in yo mouth. Want some?"

Cheese wore a smirk as he shook his head.

"Shut the fuck up and bag that money!" CT ordered.

Cheese gathered all the money, but he knew he had other money under Killer's doghouse in the back. Cheese did not give a fuck about the little change they was getting. The real money was in the ground. If he got out of this alive, Cheese knew that he was gonna find out who the three were who had ran up in his shit. CT looked over at Trif. Trif went outside and returned carrying a shovel. Cheese expression became wide-eyed horror, like what the fuck?

CT smiled and said, "You thought I was stupid, huh? I know about the other hiding place you ain't looking at a first-timer nigga. I does this shit for a living."

Trif took the duct tape that he brought in and taped Cheese's mouth. Then he set him in a chair, and handcuffed him. They all left to get the money buried outside.

Later on that night, Chatty was standing in her full mirror looking at her self. She was not looking the same. CT was draining her. Her once big brown eyes were now dull looking, and had bags under them. She was missing patches of her long black hair from the pulls she received from CT whenever he got mad at her about something. Chatty was a little over five feet tall and well stacked. She was the color of penny. People always said she looked like Bucky, from *Flavor of Love*.

Chatty turned around in the mirror admiring her fat ass. It was upright and was the reason she caught CT's eyes. Chatty wished she never met CT. She loved him and did anything he asked. If she didn't, she knew he would kill her because she knew too much, plus his dick game was good.

CT was the first to hit her G-spot correctly. Looking in the mirror, Chatty was craving his dick. She touched her body, thinking about CT. Pinching her hard nipples with one hand and rubbing her clit with the other. Her pussy was so hot and ready where was CT? She wondered. Chatty walked over to her dresser, opened the drawer, and pulled out her little friend. She needed a little quickie until she could get the real thing when CT returned.

Lying on the bed with her legs spread, Chatty took her vibrating friend and rubbed her clit. Her eyes were closed as she sucked on her bottom lip. She was in ecstasy as the silver bullet vibrated against her clit. Chatty was wet and the silver bullet was drowning in her juices but she inserted it inside then took it out she kept doing this with one hand while the other was rubbing her tits.

"Chatty!" she heard in the other room but she didn't pay it no mind.

"Chatty, what the fuck you doing…?" CT asked, stopping in his tracks, and watching Chatty.

"You couldn't wait for daddy to come home?" he asked standing there looking at her nude, voluptuous body.

His dick became hard as a pipe instantly. He loved watching Chatty play with herself. It turned him on. Releasing his ten inch dick from its cotton cocoon, he stood there long stroking it, continuing to watch her work her swollen clit with the vibrator.

He crossed to the bed and grabbed a hand full of her pussy.

"Damn Chatty that pussy's wet," he said as one finger slipped inside and then the next. Her hot walls were already throbbing.

CT couldn't take it any more he had to have her. Quickly escaping out of his clothes, his dick was fully at attention and ready to bang. Climbing into the bed, he started down at her manicured feet. He licked and sucked her toes before running his tongue along the base of her foot and gently biting her heel.

Biting her diamond-shaped calves and the inside of her thick thighs, he worked his way up between Chatty's juicy legs until he found himself at her wet pussy. The moist lips spread apart slightly. She shook her ass from side to side and his dick throbbed with every movement. He parted her pussy lips the rest of the way with his hot tongue and began lapping up her sweet juices like it was honey.

He pulled her fleshy hood back and her enlarged clit stood out like a miniature dick. CT loved that shit, licking, biting, and sucking on it for dear life, rotating between hard and soft suction.

Chatty looked while her man sucked her pussy real good. She watched as he began slowly working his slick tongue. Back and forth it ran over and around her throbbing clit. He stopped every now and then only to give her clit a few forceful sucks. Each time, she'd grabbed the back of his head, moaning in lustful satisfaction.

CT slid two fingers in her wet pussy and began rubbing her G-spot at the roof of her vagina. He continued sucking on her swollen clit. Working both spots simultaneously, he sent continuous shockwaves of pleasure through her body.

Head thrown back and eyes behind her head she was in la la land, and was about to explode.

"I'm about to cum!" She yelled, clawing at the sheets.

Squeezing her juicy thighs together, she locked his head in place forcing him to keep licking and sucking as she erupted. Hearing that, CT took her bullet and inserted it in her pussy as he sucked on her clit even harder.

"Yeahhhhh, right there, baby!" she squealed, tossing her head back into the pillows.

Seconds later Chatty sprayed his face with her warm juices. Lapping it all up, CT's nasty ass loved that shit. He ran his wet tongue down along the ridge to her asshole, flicking his hot tongue in and out, and around her brown hole before working his way back up to her throbbing pussy.

After the intense climax, Chatty was out of breath but CT wasn't. He kissed her body until he got to her lips. Welcoming his hungry tongue into her mouth, her tongue eagerly greeted his. Tasting her sweet nectar on his lips only made Chatty hornier.

She grabbed his hard dick and rubbed the mushroom head on her wet pussy. Feeling her hot stick juices on his flesh, he knew Chatty was definitely ready. CT pushed making his dick go in just a little, teasing Chatty. He could feel his throbbing head, stretching her tight, pulsating walls. Damn! The intense heat and wetness had him open. Chatty hated when he teased her so she wrapped her legs around him and pushed him in all the way.

"Shit!" she yelled as the head hit her spot.

CT fucked her slow going all the way in and then pulling out causing her juices to run down pass her asshole onto the sheets. Chatty squeezed her pussy muscles every time he pulled out driving CT crazy. He started fucking her hard, trying to hit the bottom with long, fast strokes. Chatty grabbed her toes and made her legs touch the headboard giving CT all her pussy. Licking the back of her knee, CT slid his thumb into her tight ass. He continued drilling way, throwing his body weight into each stroke.

CT's nut was right there at the tip and he couldn't hold it so he rose up and pumped her hard over and repeatedly until he came.

"F-u-u-uck!" he yelled as he shot his nut all up inside her.

However, CT wasn't done. His throbbing dick was still rock hard. He flipped her over onto her knees and smiled at the sight of round juicy ass spreading wide. He pulled her back to the edge of the bed and stood on the floor. Spreading her cheeks even farther apart for maximum access, he shoved all ten inches into Chatty's soaking pussy with one hard thrust, and smacked her ass cheek hard with his free hand. Chatty shivered with pain and pleasure as CT pounded away. Leaning over, CT planted kisses all over her neck and back and licked up and down her spine without missing a stroke.

Chatty pushed back hard and fast on his hard dick, meeting every stroke. Together they built a steady rhythm, until they both were in a lust-filled zone. The creamy wetness building up around the base of his dick, and her loud moaning only fueled him. He grabbed her hair, pulling her head back as he drilled away.

A few moments later, Chatty was coming all over his rock hard pipe. Her toes curled, and she snatched the sheets halfway off the bed. Her juices ran down his shaft and dripped onto the wrinkled linen.

When Chatty woke up from the pussy beating CT gave her. She found that he wasn't there. She looked around the room she and CT shared then climbed out the bed. Legs sore and weak she walked gingerly into the hallway then went into the bathroom. She had to urinate badly. Where the fuck is he? She wondered after looking at her watch. It was almost midnight. Chatty wiped her sore puss then washed her hands. She went back into the room, getting back in the bed after grabbing the telephone. Dialing CT's number, it rang five times before he answered

"Why the fuck you keep calling me?" he barked.

"Because I woke up and you weren't here!"

"Chatty you calling like the house on fire or some shit!"

"Shit, I wouldn't know I was up in this bitch by myself!"

"Bye Chatty, I'll be home!" he barked and hung up.

Chatty threw the phone and it landed on the other side of the room. She looked at where it landed. There was a bag tucked nicely under the dresser it looked like it was being hid, but Chatty seen it and was curious.

At 3 a.m., CT slipped into the house trying not to make a sound. Little did he know Chatty was sitting up waiting for him. He took off his shoes at the door and started stripping out of the rest of his clothes as he got closer and closer to the bedroom. When he got into the bedroom, he found Chatty sitting on the bed with the bag he had hidden.

"You killed him, didn't you?"

"What the fuck you doing going through my shit," he barked looking like a crazed man.

"You said you wasn't gone kill him, CT!"

"How the hell you know I killed him?" he asked.

"Because these are the guns, I remember these guns were loaded and all the bullets were in them. You do remember I watched you and Trif load these muthafucka's, now one gun has two bullets missing!"

"Why the fuck you care that I killed him, huh?" he asked, choking up Chatty.

"You said you weren't!" Chatty cried.

CT saw her tears and his anger turned to rage.

"Cut the bullshit I ain't on the crying shit! Yeah I killed that fucka!" he yelled. "And you better shut the fuck up about it!" he said grabbing Chatty by her hair. "You hear me?"

Chatty shook her head up and down. CT let her hair go then took the rest of his clothes off leaving just his black wife beater, boxers and socks on. Chatty crawled up in the bed putting her knees to her chest as she watched CT put the bag in the closet. She watched his expression on his face as he did it. CT did not have a care in the world about killing somebody, and she just didn't understand it. CT grabbed his peach flavored Dutch out his pants pocket, and left the room.

Chatty got up and went into the living room. The air was full with weed smoke and it smelled good. Chatty wasn't a smoker, but this morning she wanted more than a contact. She saw CT sitting in the chair in front of the TV but it wasn't on. She looked at him from his feet to his eyeballs. They stared each other down. CT look had such a bad boy swag as he puffed, and blew smoke, it turned her on.

Chatty walked over to his chair and straddled him as he puffed again, but this time before blowing his smoke out, Chatty put her mouth against his making him blow the smoke in her mouth as they kissed. CT smiled then took the Dutch and put it in his mouth backwards, and met Chatty's lips again giving her a shotgun. Chatty instantly felt high and horny. She climbed off CT and set in front of him planting kisses on his legs working her way up to his stomach while rubbing his dick threw his boxers. CT was enjoying the pleasure he was getting while puffing the L.

He looked down at Chatty, her head bobbing and weaving on his dick getting it sloppy wet as she played with his balls. Chatty was slurping and sucking something vicious like dick was going out of style. She looked up into CT's eyes while sucking him off.

"I love yo ass!" he announced rubbing his hand through her hair, while still holding the L in the other.

"I love you too baby," Chatty said then stood halfway up dick still in her mouth then gave it a deep throat. Then she came back up, her mouth was sloppy, wet.

"Why the fuck you stop?" he asked.

"I ain't done, baby..."

"Fuck nah, you ain't done!" CT said, getting up from the chair, and putting his spliff in the ashtray.

CT's dick was hard, and Chatty was stroking it as he stood in front of her. Then she set back on the floor with her legs open.

"Damn, look at that shit," CT said, rubbing his hands all in her wet pussy. "My pussy, that's why I killed that nigga," he said passionately biting Chatty's neck and still rubbing her pussy.

"But you told me to fuck him, baby," she moaned.

"I know I did, and you did right, this pussy made him talk."

Chatty and CT was on the floor kissing and rubbing each other.

"Lay on yo side," he whispered in her ear.

Chatty turned as CT grabbed her ass, and rubbed her ass crease to her pussy hole. Then he pulled the left ass cheek to the side and stuck his dick in her pussy.

"Damn baby that feels good," Chatty moaned as CT went in and out of her, slowly rubbing her clit

"Don't it…?" he whispered pounding her from the side while grabbing her throat. They stayed in that position for a while until they fell asleep on the floor.

Later on that day, Chatty found herself thinking about Cheese. He was an alright dude, and she loved his gentle touch the couple months she fucked with him were fun. He showed her a lot of shit that CT never did. Cheese stayed wining and dining Chatty. He treated her like a queen, and she liked him for that even though it was a job. She found herself catching feelings. Chatty was getting dressed when CT told her, "Call that bitch you met through Cheese so you can see what's been going on."

The bitch he was talking about was Tay. Tay was a cool, ghetto-fabulous bitch who was in the game, and Chatty did miss her ass so she called her up.

"Bitch, where the hell you been hiding?" Tay yelled.

"I miss you too heifer!" Chatty laughed.

"I was getting worried about you. I thought maybe you left the earth after what happen with Cheese."

"No, I didn't leave the earth just out the way. I'm real fucked up about what happen," Chatty said walking through the house. "Do they have any leads or anything?" Chatty asked worried.

"Nah girl, but they know it was a set up. Scotty says it was an inside job."

Scotty was Tay's brother. "I can believe it was an inside job, but who?" Chatty asked

"Who knows, shit you know they ain't even found Cheese," Tay said, popping gum. Tay was always chewing and popping gum. "Scotty said his boy went over Cheese house and seen it fucked up and the dog dead."

"Girl I'm so glad I wasn't there that day," Chatty said.

"Scotty said you had something to do with it!"

Chatty's heart skipped a beat "Why he think that?"

"Because Cheese always had his cameras on outside the house and this night the tape is missing, and nobody knew he kept his stash under the dog house, but a couple people."

"And me…?"

"Exactly…!" Tay yelled into the phone.

"Wow. Hold on a minute Tay."

"Did you know that Cheese body was missing? Thought you killed him?" Chatty whispered to CT whose eyes were the size of baseballs.

"Alright girl, I'm back," Chatty told Tay.

"So what's good with you? You wanna step out with me?" Tay asked.

Chatty did step out with Tay, but not without CT, they both were looking good that night. Chatty had put on her blue and red Apple Bottom jumper and wore her red stilettos. The jumper hugged her hips and thighs so tight that CT kept staring.

"Don't get fucked-up tonight!" he yelled while walking away, looking at her.

"Boy shut up!" she yelled back at him.

Chatty shook her head and laughed because she heard when he said, "Boy played on Tarzan!"

Chatty and Tay met up at a place called Jackson's that was owned by basketball player Jim Jackson. It was First Friday, and everybody was looking their best up in there. Tay greeted Chatty with a hug. Tay looked cute with her skin-tight, green Baby Phat dress, matching her green eyes. Tay always kept her hair in a blond fade that looked good on her. She made many niggas hate on her because she had more waves than they did.

CT walked in way before Chatty and Tay. He was sporting a brown and beige Polo shirt with matching shorts. On his feet was a fresh pair of ostrich brown sandals. CT was looking better than he ever looked before with his fresh haircut that was a tapered fade and two diamonds gleaming in both ears.

Tay and Chatty mingled around the room, but Chatty felt uneasy when she was in front of Scotty. Scotty spoke but she still felt uneasy and felt like she needed to throw up. Take it easy girl, she kept telling herself.

"I'm out," Scotty said to Tay.

"Damn you just got here," Tay said, still popping her gum.

"I got things ta do," he said, walking away.

"My brother, my brother," Tay said popping her gum, and shaking her head but Chatty was glad he left.

Chatty and Tay found a seat, and talked about people. Chatty missed having somebody other than CT to talk to. She didn't have any friends and all her girl cousins were older than her.

"Damn who is that sexy muthafucka right there!" Tay yelled over the music.

Chatty turned to where Tay was looking and almost fell out her chair when she seen that it was CT who Tay was lusting over.

"I don't know girl, but I gotta pee!" Chatty said running off.

When Chatty got in the bathroom she looked in the mirror at herself, thinking as she fixed her hair. Then Chatty just stood there looking at herself, wondering how she got herself into the shit she was involved with. She never forgot the warning. "Dick will have you doing some crazy things," her mama used to say to her.

When Chatty stepped out the bathroom, a tall muscular body with dreads was standing in front of her. He turned around and Chatty bit her bottom lip. The guy smiled showing his pearly whites and walked away. Chatty felt her panties getting wet. Damn! She smiled, walking back to Tay who was in a deep conversation. Chatty wanted to turn and go the other way when she seen it was CT who she was talkin to.

"Chatty you alright, babe…?" Tay asked as Chatty was walking up.

"This is Chatty," Tay said to CT.

"Chatty this CT, he won't tell me what it stands for though."

Chatty smiled, and sat back down, trying not to pay them any attention. She focused her attention on the chocolate dread she bumped into a little while ago. Chatty noticed he was sitting up at the bar talking to a couple of people, and she got away from CT and Tay. She headed for the bar.

Walking over to the bar, all eyes were on her. She looked good in a white jumper that hugged her curves the right way. Chatty ordered a Long Island ice tea and waited. When her drink came, she heard somebody say, "I got this."

Chatty turned and Mr. Dreadlocks was smiling.

"Thanks," she said nodding to him.

"No problem, but um are you going to be able to drink all that?"

"I'll try," Chatty said.

She was about to walk away, but Dreads pulled her back.

"Wait, you ain't just gone get a drink and not give me a conversation, what's your name?"

The night at Jackson's was over. Chatty and Tay were walking out. CT had left, and didn't see dude give her his card. She was tired of hearing Tay tell her how good CT looked and how he made her panties wet. Tay told Chatty to call her and they went there separate ways, before Chatty could get in the car good enough CT called.

"Where you at?" he questioned.

"In the car…"

"Alright, hurry home!"

Chatty looked at her cellphone, and threw it back in her purse. When Chatty stepped in the house, CT was sitting in his favorite chair smoking. He looked good, but she walked past by him, and went to the bedroom, stripping out her clothes. She couldn't wait to take her shoes off. Her feet were killing her. CT came in the room.

"You think you slick, huh?"

"Huh? What the fuck are you talking 'bout?" Chatty asked, looking clueless.

"I'm talking about you all up in that nigga face. Yeah, I seen you," CT said hitting his Dutch and blowing it in Chatty's face.

"You got a lot of damn nerve. The way you was all up in Tay's face, nigga!"

CT chuckled and hit the weed again, "That was the plan stupid!" he yelled with smoke coming out his nose and mouth.

Chatty knew it was work but watching it made her stomach hurt, just like it disgusted CT to watch her with Cheese those few months they were together.

"You remember the work you did, right?" he asked her shaking his head up and down "Well it's my turn," he said taking off his shirt.

"So you gon fuck her, CT?" Chatty asked holding her stomach.

"If that's what it takes. Fa'sho I am," CT answered, leaving the bedroom.

Chatty stood there belly hurting. She couldn't take it, knowing CT's plans were to fuck Tay. She had to go along with him cheating on her, and not knowing was one thing, but knowing the shit was going down, made her wanna shit.

A couple days went by. It was Tuesday and Tay called Chatty to see if she wanted to go to GQ's, a hole in the wall bar, for two dollar Tuesday. Chatty agreed to go since CT wasn't home half the time now anyways. She didn't question his coming and goings. She didn't wanna hear shit about him and Tay, but she was quite sure she would hear it from Tay tonight.

Chatty linked up with Tay in the parking lot of GQ's. It was only 11:30 p.m., the club wasn't packed yet. Tay was sitting in her Cadillac, talking on the phone. When Chatty pulled up, she just knew in her heart that CT was on the other end of the conversation.

Tay got out the car and fixed her shorts with one hand, and telling Chatty to hold up with the other hand. Chatty stood there listening to Tay saying, "Okay baby this, and yes baby that."

She turned her head and rolled her eyes. After standing there for five minutes, Tay put her phone on her hip, popping gum.

"Gu-url, I don't know what I'm gon' do with that boy-ee!"

Chatty didn't ask her who and what she was talking about, so Tay didn't say anything else about it.

They were walking by a big garage, and Chatty jumped when she heard a dog barking.

"Girl, that dog you know he's always barking!" Tay laughed as Chatty kept looking back to see if it was gone run up on them.

"Sup Tay?" the big guy standing at the door said.

Two uniformed cops were out front. One was a big dude that was turned the opposite way so Chatty couldn't see him but the other one was facing them and looked sneaky.

"Whassup Big man!" Tay greeted.

Tay and Chatty walked through the lounge. Tay stopped and spoke to everyone she knew then they went to the bar and sat down. A caramel colored chick with spiked short hair, asked, "Y'all wanna order something?"

Chatty told the girl she wanted a bud light lime for right now and Tay said she didn't want anything yet. The girl went and got Chatty's beer than came back.

"Four dollars!" she told Chatty.

Tay and Chatty talked about everybody who came in the bar. Women acted comical. When summer hit they put on anything, and think it was cute.

It was 12:15 a.m., and the place was getting packed. Tay and Chatty got up and mingled around. Chatty didn't dare wear heels tonight. She wanted to be comfortable so she wore her orange and yellow Baby Phat sandals that matched her Baby Phat short outfit. She was rocking tonight.

Tay had on a money-green, gold, jacket-pants outfit by Rocawear, with matching green and gold stilettos. Both the girls were dimes. They had all the niggas' eyes on them, even the women stared with their lips turned up.

The girls got on the dance floor when lil Wayne's *Lollipop* came on, and got down. As they danced, Chatty felt nothing but breath on her neck.

"Why haven't you called me?"

Chatty didn't have a reason to turn around because she already knew who it was so she just kept dancing, and dude kept dancing with her.

"I'm hot. I gotta get out of here!" she yelled.

Chatty walked fast to the exit with her newfound friend on her heels yelling, "Yo!"

Chatty was ignoring him and bust through the door to get outside, where the two officers was still standing. The sneaky one looked and smiled and said, "Well, well, well look who I see. Ain't seen you in awhile boy, where you been?" sneaky cop asked Chatty's friend.

Chatty stood back and listened. The dude told the sneaky cop, "Well you know I been laying low and shit nahmean?"

"Yeah, I know what'cha mean," the sneaky cop snickered. "I didn't think you'd come back here after that robbery. But I see you did. Hmm what brings you back here?"

Dreadlocks smiled and said, "I'm visiting." Then he turned to Chatty. "Let's go back in," he said to Chatty and opened the door. He walked inside, leaving Chatty staring over at the cop who winked at her.

"There's a patio in the back," he told her as they walked to the patio that was full of smoke from weed and cancer sticks.

He pulled a Newport short out his ear and lit up. Chatty looked around the crowded patio. She spotted CT walking with Tay, but mean-mugging her. Chatty looked up at her new friend who was talking to another cat. She looked over at Tay and CT who was hugged all up, and that was it.

Chatty ran out the patio and bumped into all kinds of people but didn't care. She wanted out that club. When she reached the outside, everybody looked at her like she had monkeys on her head. What the fuck, she pondered, staring back.

"What's wrong sweetness?" the sneaky looking cop asked Chatty.

Chatty s shook her head and said, "Nothing, it's just hot in there and I'm very irritated."

"You sure it has nothing to do with the company you keeping?" he asked with his eyebrow up.

"What do you mean?" Chatty asked.

"Step in my office. Let's talk," the sneaky cop said.

He started walking and Chatty followed.

The next morning, Chatty tossed and turned in her bed. She was tired of CT not being there. Is this how CT felt when I was with Cheese? She wondered. She looked at the time. It was 12:00 p.m. so she decided to call Tay just to see if he was there with her. Tay didn't answer.

"Fuck this shit!" Chatty yelled and threw the phone.

She got up, slipped on some shorts and shoes, grabbed her keys, and stormed out the door. Chatty pulled up and parked a couple houses down from Tay's. Nobody was outside so that made it easier for her to stalk.

Chatty walked up to the house then froze when she heard a door slam. She looked around but didn't see anyone. Tip toeing in the back, Chatty heard voices and recognized Tay's, now on her knees Chatty crawled near the talking. Tay was sitting on her patio in the back, having a conversation.

"She still ain't answering. I wonder what she wanted."

"She doesn't want shit she just lonely!" Chatty heard CT saying.

"Well I wonder why she so lonely?" Chatty heard Tay saying, followed by what sounded like kisses.

"I need to call that nigga, Trif."

"I ain't talked to him in a couple days, but you know him he always pops up when you need him," CT said.

"True dat true dat... So CT, what you gon do with Chatty now?" Scotty asked.

"I don't know yet, but I'm thinking. I got that tape from the cameras in that nigga's house. It's fucked up that his body missing and I'm sure I murked dude."

"Well he gotta be dead because he would've came looking for me. That fo'sho. That was my nigga," Scotty said.

"Ya nigga, huh...?" Tay asked. "Ya'll some no-good niggas!" Chatty heard Tay shouting followed by a door slamming.

"You just as dirty...!" Scotty yelled.

Chatty sat there a little while longer when she heard CT say, "Hmm..."

It took everything in her not to jump out and catch them in the act and spazz out on them both. She did sneak a peak and did not believe what she was seeing. They didn't see her. Chatty covered her mouth and ran off.

Chatty got to the car, and threw up before getting in. She drove off, her mind racing. Chatty didn't know her next move, but she been played the fool too long, and it was time to do something about it.

Pulling up at a gas station, she purchased some Dutches. She was planning on getting lifted after what she had heard and seen. It was necessary. Reaching in her back pocket to get the money to pay, she came across a card given to her the other night when she was out with Tay. Chatty kissed it and smiled.

Once Chatty reached home, her whole attitude changed. She wasn't taking anymore shit from nobody. She kicked the bedroom door open went to CT's weed stash grabbed a hand full and got her smoke on.

After her weed session, Chatty took a shower, got dressed, and was out. She was now on her way to go meet the one person who could help her get some payback.

Later on that night, CT walked in and Chatty was sitting in his chair smoking.

"What the fuck you doing?" he asked with his face all screwed up.

Chatty didn't budge. She just kept smoking as if she didn't hear him, and that burned CT up. He walked up to her like he was about to hit her but Chatty still didn't budge. She did stand up showing that she didn't have any panties on and her big brown ass was jiggling as she walked around CT and went into the kitchen, this made CT grab his dick.

Chatty walked back into the living room. CT bit his bottom lip and said, "Why you walking around like that?"

Chatty turned, looked down at his hard dick and back at his bewildered face, then said, "Shit, I was about to play with my pussy. You wanna watch?" she smiled, pulling out her rabbit. "But!" she said rubbing her nipples. "No touching."

"Why the fuck not…!" CT yelled.

Chatty didn't pay him any attention. She just sat on the couch. Her legs were spread wide, showing CT her thick lips and swollen clit. Chatty was already soaking wet and it was driving CT crazy just watching.

"See, this is what I've been doing since you're gone all the time now over there fucking Tay," Chatty said, letting the rabbit roam.

Her pussy was soaked that CT could hear the wetness. He took off his shirt, pants, and boxers with the quickness, not giving a fuck about her saying no touching. Shit he was gonna fuck. Fuck what she talking about!

"Let me ask you something daddy, do Tay's pussy do this?"

Before CT knew it, he was sprayed. Chatty let her juices spurt out. She knew CT loved that. CT could not take it anymore and got on his knees and slurped the rest of the pussy juice streaming down her juicy thighs.

"Didn't I tell you, no touching? I don't know where that mouth been," Chatty said closing her legs.

CT grabbed her legs and spread them wide open but before he was able to stick his dick in Chatty hit him with.

"I found us another hit."

"What?"

"This dude they call Nigel, he from Brooklyn and he been on me like fly's on shit."

"How the fuck he manage to do that?" CT asked, standing up dick still hard.

"Well, he's the guy that you seen talking to me that night in Jackson's."

"So you have been talking to this nigga on the low?"

"No," Chatty lied. "One day I seen him again at the gas station and he stopped and talked to me and he asked can he kidnap me and take me back home with him."

"How the fuck you know this nigga got dough?"

Chatty didn't answer that question she just smiled.

"So how that shit going with you and Tay?" she asked.

"I tell you, she ain't easy like that nigga, Cheese was, and her brother keeps shit on lock."

"I bet," Chatty whispered under her breath.

"What you say?" CT asked with a screw face.

"Nothing…" Chatty chuckled.

A couple weeks went by and Chatty was in New York laying up in Nigel's king size bed. She had just hit him off with some good wet pussy, and they were just chilling there. All of a sudden they both jumped up because they heard something in the front room. He sat up, getting his heater from out the drawer. Before he could walk to the door, two masked men were standing with guns in both he and Chatty's face.

"Get the fuck out the bed!" one of them yelled at Chatty.

She grabbed the sheet and wrapped it around her body, but fell as she was getting out the bed.

"Now I want you two in the living room while I get what I came for."

Two days went by, both CT and Scotty were lounging over Tay's house when the front door was kicked in. It scared the shit out of them. Three masked men where pointing guns at them. One of them took off the mask.

"You fucking bitch!" CT yelled.

"You dick sucker!" Chatty yelled back, slapping him with the gun.

She held the gun on him and she didn't even feel scared. Chatty no loger cared if they knew it was her.

"Look at you two flaming muthafucka's! Yeah, I know about y'all two. One day I was sitting right there on the other side, listening. Listening to all the shit y'all was cooking and how stupid I was. You used me you gay bitch!" Chatty yelled, smacking CT with her open hand. "You should not have let me in on all this shit because now you gotta pay for all the shit you took me through, you, you dick-in-the-booty-nigga!" she said, spitting in CT's face. "Well as you see I gotta new crew, and we want all the money, bicthes!"

"Bitch, you ain't getting shit!" Scotty yelled.

Chatty turned and looked at him as if he was crazy and said, "I think you should keep your dick suckers closed. You were so jealous of Cheese weren't you? He didn't want to be your butt buddy, that's why you had CT kill him so he wouldn't tell that you tried to suck his dick."

There was so much anger in Scotty's eyes, they turned purple. He wanted to kill her but that shit wasn't happening not with the two goons she had holding her down. Their guns were squarely in his mug.

"Yeah, I know what happen that night Scotty," Chatty laughed, walking over to one of the masked men.

He went outside and a couple minutes came back with a bag. The bag CT knew so well and probably shitted on himself after seeing it in Chatty's hands.

"You should have gotten rid of these guns dummy, but nah. You wanted to pin all that shit on me didn't you? It was meant for me to find the bag of guns and get my fingerprints all on them. But what's so fucked up, I didn't even realize that this was the surveillance tape from Cheese's crib and I'm all up on this bitch too," Chatty said, shaking her head.

"Somebody is missing up in here. Where's Tay?" Chatty asked then laughed. "Oh I forgot, she's in the trunk of the car. Go get her."

One of the guys ran outside to the car.

"It's funny how people run their mouths when their life's on the line. Little Miss Ghetto Princess had diarrhea of the mouth. She told everything. And guess what?" Chatty asked, laughing like a crazed person. "I got a surprise for all y'all."

The guy returned with Tay. She was looking a hot mess. She sat on the couch with the rest of the assholes. Chatty took out her cellphone and dialed. Then she put the cellphone back in her pocket.

Couple of minute's later three more masked men came in the house. Chatty sat down to watch the show.

"Where my money?" one asked.

Then the other said, "Yeah, fuck boys where the fuck is our money?"

Now CT and Scotty were looking confused, and CT was the one to speak up.

"Y'all money… What the fuck?"

"Yeah, our money dick-boy!" the masked man said, removing the mask.

CT's eyes got big as flying saucers while Scotty's head fell to his chest.

"Thought you killed me huh?" Cheese asked. "But you did kill my dog!" Cheese said, followed by a blow to CT's head with the gun.

"Should a shot me in the head, stupid…! I had on a vest!" he yelled, bitch smacking Scotty.

The other masked man pulled off his mask, and Chatty stood up. She kissed him on the lips.

"Y'all remember Nigel?" Chatty asked then laughed.

"Yeah, Nigel was the one who found Cheese in his crib handcuffed and duct taped. He was on to you two fuckas, and he knew just how to get you. Yep through me, but see we needed each other huh, baby?" Chatty asked him followed by another kiss. "See CT, I was using you just like you used me. I guess what goes around comes around huh?" Chatty said, standing in front of him. "I'm about to go get me something to eat I'm hungry! I'm pretty sure I'll be seeing all that money later. I deserve it, and oh y'all all get one more surprise!" Chatty announced, leaving the house laughing, and nodding her head at the S.W.A.T. vehicle sitting in front.

The sneaky cop known as Dust was there. A couple years ago his son was killed in a robbery set up by Cheese and Nigel, but they couldn't really pin anything on them so now it was time for payback for Dust thanks to Chatty. Dust promised to split the money with her. I'm leaving this shitty city, Chatty was thinking going outside.

She jumped in Nigel's Hummer and watched. As Dust and his crew ran up in Tay's house, her eyes caught someone in a car further down the street, but it was dusk and she couldn't see who it was. The person was smoking because she saw the red flare every time they took a pull.

Chatty peeled off, and turned up the radio feeling good about what was going down. She drove, bobbing her head to that nigga Fifty as he sang, "*I get mines the fast way the ski mask way...*"

All of a sudden the window of the hummer came crashing in. Chatty couldn't move. She was numb and her face was wet and thick, crimson liquid dripped from her eyes. Shit became blurry in a hot second. She could see the familiar looking man opening the door, and raising his gun to her face.

"No-o-o Trif!" Chatty screamed.

A Hoe is a Garden Tool

JADA T. ROBERTS

I always knew I had dark clouds surrounding me everywhere I went. At age eight, Mommy took me and Randall, my now defunct lawyer brother to South Carolina. We visited our cousins and my blind great-grandmother, Cora Jean. I expected down south to be sunny and bright with clear blue skies, but seeing Grandma Cora was a frightening sight for a kid. Her skin reflected the color of soot, but her fake teeth were pearly white just like the long braid of hair snaked down her back.

Mommy told us that Grandma Cora could see things. Randall and I snickered when she said that, knowing good and damn well that Grandma Cora was blind as a bat and damn near dead as a doorknob. Mommy ushered Randall towards Grandma Cora. She touched Randall's russet colored face and rubbed his head full of soft, tight curls. At age nine, he was smart, but was beginning to lurk into the gritty streets of Brooklyn, NY where we lived.

She told him, "Boy, you gonna do good thangs. You smart." She then waved her crooked finger at him, her closed eye sockets fixated on his baffled face. "You never complete thangs though."

Randall, the petrified one, shook a little and looked over at me. He ran off like a little bitch, and I rolled my eyes, knowing the blind woman couldn't see me. Mommy caught me though, and she scowled. I wasn't the least bit fazed when it was my turn to go over to see what Grandma Cora had to say about me.

She rocked a little in this old, rickety, rocking chair that looked older than her. Making a creaking sound, she kept a steady pace. The closer I approached her up the porch stairs, the faster she rocked in her chair. A crow came out of nowhere, perched on the side of Grandma Cora's foot.

I stood there in front of her, the bold relative from NY with my arms folded and waited for the old woman to tell me my future. When I was face to face with her, she fell backwards in her chair, her patent leather colored legs sticking straight up.

My mother came out of the house, helping her up from the dull wood porch. After Mommy cautiously sat her upright in the chair, Grandma Cora hissed, "The clouds are all around her." She circled her hands in a halo formation. "Dark, can't you see them?"

Grandma Cora didn't wave her finger in my face like she did Randall's. She didn't pet my head either. "You come back next summer, bring the boy, not the girl," she murmured to Mommy. She felt around for her cane on the floor, holding her hand out to Mommy so she could help her inside. The big and bad in me didn't let her words linger as I tugged at my cut off Lee jeans shorts and ran off to go find Randall.

Next summer never came. We attended Grandma Cora's funeral that same year right before school started. And at the funeral, I could've sworn I heard Grandma Cora's words thick as the clouds she claimed were all around me. I covered my hands over my dark cherub face, pretending to be crying, trying to drown out Grandma Cora's last words to me.

Back in Brooklyn, all the boys called me Angel, but my real name is Sinclair. Sinclair Peters. When I turned fifteen, I can remember Mommy being mega strict with me. Maybe she was trying to make sure those dark clouds didn't follow me out in those mean dark streets. I wouldn't listen though. I wanted to hang with my friends, but she wasn't having that.

"Where're you going?" She had yelled.

"Out!" I'd yell right back, slamming the door, and leaving her to throw her Holy water, oils and scriptures after me.

By the time I turned seventeen, Randall had gone off to college to study Pre-Law in NJ. Me? I didn't give a fuck about school. I wanted the fast money, clothes, cars and of course guys. Shit, I was already fucking at thirteen. Good thing I had a chill friend named Jeena who would co-sign for my ass every time I came up pregnant. At least three times.

She would act like she was my mother at the abortion clinic so my real mother wouldn't know anything and the pay off was I'd strip for her later. I didn't mind. Shit, that was better than raising babies. Besides, Jeena always let me stay at her house after Mommy would throw me out occasionally. I was able to smoke weed, drink and she even got her kicks from watching me suck off one of my many boyfriends' dick.

Everybody was outside one burning, hot, summer day in '94. Listening to music, shooting dice, kids jumping rope, and two chicks were fighting. I ignored all of that, walking down Franklin Avenue sporting new Air Jordans and no socks, tight cut off Daisy Dukes which revealed my dark firm ass cheeks and a bright red halter, revealing a washboard flat stomach. I had recently cut my hair in a feathered bob.

I had a couple bucks in my pocket, enough to buy a fifty cent soda and a beef patty. I was horny as hell and my nipples stayed hard as I hauled ass to my destination. I was on my way to see this guy named Skill, who lived near Empire Boulevard, not too far from me on Union Street. I was on a high to suck Skill's eight inch dick when I came face to face with the flyest dude I'd ever seen.

He stepped out of his burgundy Suburban sporting a dark brown linen suit and alligator shoes to match. I sized the suit up to be Armani or Prada. He had skin the color of melted butter and his eyes were blue. I mean really blue. I knew they weren't no contacts because he stared straight at me. Shit he stared straight through me.

I waited for the light to change, humming a tune to a rap this new rapper named Notorious B.I.G. just dropped and who I really liked because he was very dark skinned like me. I tried to play cool when I crossed the street and kept on walking. Blue Eyes turned away from me, chatting with another dude standing by the side of the truck. That guy was short and stocky with long matted dreadlocks. He had this skank looking light skinned bitch with him. Her long hair was pulled back in a ponytail and she wore played out suede Pumas and cut off shorts which revealed her flat ass.

"Dark Skin," he called out to me. "Come, me want to talk to yuh."

By the time I spun around, Blue Eyes was so close up on me I had to blink twice to make sure he was real. Standing at around six feet two, two hundred twenty pounds to my five feet five one hundred twenty pounds,

I felt like we were the perfect combination. His innocent look was met with clean shaven head and face, along with a perfect set of teeth. He half-smiled at me and looked right through me again with eyes that said, "I want to fuck you," and I looked right back at him with my deep set brown eyes that said, "When?"

He slipped me his number. "Call me, my name is Olu. I'll take you out tonight."

I watched as he strode over to his truck and drove off with Flat Ass and Fat Boy. I took that number and made an about face right back to Jeena's to tell her my good news. She was a slim vanilla wafer colored chick, with long, silky hair and dark cat shaped eyes complete with a killer smile that would make you drop your drawers or panties. Whichever way she wanted it.

"Yeah, I heard of Olu. He wants to take you out, huh? I heard that dude's got a Mandingo on his ass." She burst out laughing, knowing that was my specialty.

She was truly right as I was now getting stroked by Olu's ten inch dick at his Midtown Manhattan apartment. It was a no-brainer when I met him in front of Jeena's building on the corner of Eastern Parkway and Rogers Avenue, hopping in the backseat, making sure that the other ho from earlier wasn't in the back. She wasn't and neither was Fat Boy. I was glad, because all the way to 47th Street, I gave Olu the best hand job and he had to stifle me a couple of times so he wouldn't hit anyone's car as we whizzed through the city like we owned the night.

His place was laid the fuck out. Blue walls painted like the Atlantic ocean, just like his eyes. He had exotic gold, African figures of people and animals, carefully locked away in showcases throughout the living room and dining room. His white furniture with white shag rugs was custom made he told me when I asked.

"Made in Italy," he said as he pushed me down on his round bed.

My red mini Christian Dior silk dress rose up a little revealing the black lace thong I had on. I commenced to take off the black Gucci stilettos that I borrowed from Jeena. He stopped me though, "Leave them on. Take the dress off."

I stood up and seductively took the dress off as he grabbed my breasts flicking them with his hot tongue, making me moan just from that light touch. I gyrated my hips against his clothes and felt his rock, hard dick begin to curve like a banana. I couldn't wait to release my cream to complete the banana split desert.

He unloosened his black linen pants, unbuttoning his matching shirt, leaving the pants hanging around his ankles. I scooted my ass towards the edge of the circle on the bed and he pushed two fingers in my hot box. I moaned loudly.

"Olu! Shit, I wanna taste you!" I screamed out, shocking even myself.

He ignored me though, teasing me with his fingers as I played with my nipples. They were harder than they were earlier when I was speed balling to Skill's house earlier. I couldn't hold out anymore as I arched my back and came all over his fingers and hands. He took his fingers out and seductively licked my juices, all the while staring at me with those sexy blue eyes.

He turned me over, sliding my thong to the side and entered me from behind. I didn't even give a fuck that he wasn't wearing a condom. I wanted to feel all of him. He pumped long and hard in my tight pussy, teasing me with the head. I wanted to suck him off so bad, but he also felt so good, I couldn't stop. I felt sweat dripping from his face as he pumped harder, then slow, then harder again. He didn't grunt and didn't moan. He was quiet. Then he asked, "Do you like it?"

"Hell yeah... Give it to me Olu!"

"Do you *love* it?" he asked, holding a steady pace.

I knew he was teasing me, but part of me never felt like this before. Shit, was this love for real?

"Yes, I love it!" I yelled out.

I held onto the blue velvet spread, trying to keep my knees from bucking under me. The heels I wore helped me stand my ground as the spikes sunk in his white carpet. He pumped faster and faster, stroking long and hard. I was wide open. Spreading my ass cheeks, I finally gave in bursting a huge one all over his long ass pipe. He spanked me, softly across my ass cheeks and said, "I'm not finished."

He continued on in every position. Each time I came first. He went on and on for about two hours until finally, he released. Long and hard, sweet and sexy, in me—Fuck! he came in me.

He directed me to his oasis style bathroom and helped me shower. I was in heaven at his touch, the way he looked at me.

"By the way, what's your name Shorty?" he asked.

Damn, I was so horny for this dude that I didn't even remember to tell him my name.

"It's Sinclair, but my street name is Angel," I said, drying off with his navy blue Ralph Lauren terry cloth towel.

He looked over at me and said, "Okay, but I like Sinclair better. I'll be back to bring you something to eat."

"Yeah do that, because I'm real hungry," I laughed and fell across his bed.

He left me alone in his room and I slowly drifted off to sleep, dreaming about our night together. I was so into him—he so into me.

I woke up and someone was really in me. It wasn't Olu. Dammit! It was Fat Boy. That dirty, sweaty dude who was in the passenger seat of Olu's Suburban was doing my ass. I began screaming, but Olu held a burner to my face.

"Now you said you wanted to eat, so this is what you're gonna eat. My man Ink is gonna give you all the food you wanna eat," Olu seethed.

It was like he hated me and I had just met this motherfucker. So I had no choice but to allow Ink to fuck me, inside and out. He slurped on my pussy and made me suck his dick. Tears of anger stung my eyes, but they weren't really towards Ink. They were for Olu because this crazy motherfucker was on the other side of the bed watching us the entire time, stroking that Mandingo dick of his.

The next morning, I woke up in Olu's bed. My vision was strained and I didn't have any clothes on. My neck was sore, probably from Ink grabbing my head back towards him as he tongued me down and hit me with his short dick doggy-style. I was starting to remember and immediately woke all the way up.

No one was in the bedroom. I heard voices coming from the living room. A couple of female's voices. The same flat ass ho from yesterday. She was on the phone and looked me up and down then hung up the phone. She said, "Well, you gonna work with us or not?"

I was puzzled, but quickly shook that shit off. I now understood that Olu and Ink were pimps. And whoever this bitch was, she had to be the main ho. Damn, what the fuck am I gonna do?

"Yeah, I guess so, when do I start?" I asked her.

There was no turning back now. I was too humiliated to go back on my block. The bitch looked my naked body up and down again. My head was throbbing and I wiped the side of my face and felt crusty saliva. I hoped. I didn't want to know what that shit was on my face. The chick must've read my mind because she gave me some other clothes to put on. Tight white spandex and a royal blue striped blue tank top. I left my dress behind. I still had my shoes to put on. I put on the clothes she gave me while the other chick, a Puerto Rican shorty with long dark hair, big eyes and wore a hot pink mini dress and white stilettos asked me, "So what's your name Mami?"

I smoothed my hair and replied, "Angel."

"Oh, okay, my name is Maribel. This is my homie Joelle. We work for Olu and I guess you'll be working for us now," she said, sucking on a Charm's Blowpop, and rotating her thin lips around it.

"Okay, not a problem, which *us* are you referring to?" I asked her, putting my hands on my hips.

"Chill mami, no disrespect. You'll be working with me and Joelle. Olu has us working over on South Road in Jamaica, Queens. You know where that's at?" She waited for my answer as Joelle grilled me. I couldn't read her mind, so I turned away and answered Maribel.

"Look, I know where that's at. I just wanna know what I gotta do so I can go back to my block," I said.

Joelle laughed, getting up from the couch. "Girl, you ain't going home no time soon. Olu owns you now. He has a place for us in a burned out building right around where we'll be working at. But don't worry, the rewards are plenty."

She laughed again, tugging at her ponytail and straightening out her orange cream colored short set. "So now let's go."

I went to wash my face in the bathroom and gave myself a long look in the floor length mirror. "Damn girl, you wanted to be a grown up, now you got it."

I tried to beef myself up to make it seem like I was going to work at an office or something. We hopped in a cab, didn't have to pay the cabbie since Maribel sat in the front and gave him a blowjob while he drove us to Queens.

Arriving in Jamaica, Queens on what Joelle deemed, 'The ho stroll', was a different world for me. Burned out buildings on 150th and South Road took up an entire block. Nearby South Jamaica projects was where the hustlers came out like vampires in the night, on a prowl for crackheads so they could sell them their next rock. Or bust a nut.

There were a few other older chicks out on the stroll looking for work. Cars stopped for us as we spread out on the block. The only thing Joelle and Maribel taught me was the blowjobs were fifty bucks, and a quick screw was seventy-five. I was sold, but that was short-lived when Joelle warned me, "But you know Olu gets to keep most of that money, right?" I wasn't the least bit upset, I had been on the streets long enough to know that a pimp keeps most of his money if not all of it. And still I wouldn't make a break for it and go home.

She turned her back on me before I could answer and I went to work. After about five customers, including quickies and blowjobs, within three hours at my new residence, I was hungry for food. I spotted Joelle bending her flat ass over in a window of a souped up Chevy Caprice and let her know I was hungry.

"Yeah, me, too…Let's go get something to eat. We waited for Maribel to finish fucking this African motherfucker, around the corner from the building we were to be staying at and decided to get something from one of the many stores on Jamaica Avenue.

I was so tired from everything. Olu had played me and I didn't know what to do. As we sat down in the Chinese restaurant, I told Joelle I was going to use the payphone.

"Bitch, no you ain't. You wanna use the phone, wait until tonight!" she yelled. I sucked my teeth at her and she got in my face. "Look, you chose this shit when you took Olu's number, right? So cough that shit up. Be lucky your ass ain't home sucking dudes' dicks for two dollars. Wait till Olu hits us all off tonight. You'll see."

I couldn't believe I let this bitch punk me. I looked over at Maribel, who in turn grabbed the bags of food and walked out the door. Who the hell did these bitches think I was?

At the end of the hot, stale day, after fucking in and out different cars, working all day and night on the stroll, I came up with at least five hundred dollars. Not bad for my first day. We went inside our building, a walkup with three floors and a stale smell to it. The building was dark and we had to step over a man who had nodded off on the floor sitting in front of the door. Joelle kicked him and he looked up at her bug eyed and scrammed out of the way.

The place was small, with a wood table and two old chairs. Tattered shades were drawn shut on the dirty windows, and a small TV sat on a coffee table with a wire hanger sticking out of it. There was another bedroom down the small hallway and the bathroom was across the hall. I opted to go sit at the table so I could dig in my chicken wings and beef fried rice ignoring the smell of musty heat.

"Bitch, you gotta earn that seat, that's my seat and the other one is for Maribel. You just started working," Joelle said punking me.

I said nothing, shrugged my shoulders and sat on the floor. My view was the dingy kitchen and when I blinked, I saw a mouse on the counter. I clammed up, but then began to eat. Joelle and Maribel talked amongst themselves as I sat there drowning them out. I wanted to shower, change my clothes and sleep in my bed. I didn't forget my phone call.

"Yo Joelle, I need to use the phone," I called out to her.

She looked over at me, "Sure, go right ahead, it's in the kitchen."

They both giggled like shit was funny. I peered inside the kitchen and came face to face with a flock of roaches crawling all over the gold speckled dull counter. Didn't matter to me, I just wanted the phone. I reached for the beige receiver on the wall and began to dial when I heard two male voices.

"Who the fuck told y'all to stop working and be up in here eating…? Get the fuck back out there and go back to getting me my money!"

Recognizing Olu's voice, I hung up the phone and came out the kitchen. His once beautiful eyes were like igloos as he stormed over to me and slapped the shit out of me. I tasted blood in my mouth when I came to. "Who the fuck are you on the phone with? Better not be no five-oh. Bitch, put them shoes on and go back outside and start getting me my money!" He spat at me. His clean shaven face made him look like a devil in disguise.

"Daddy, please, we was just leaving, right Joelle? Here's your money from today," Maribel chimed trying to get Olu's attention.

She gave him a stack of bills. Ink went and sat on Joelle's lap and started thumbing his hands across her breasts.

"Yes Daddy, we was just leaving, come on Angel. Let's go," Joelle quivered as Ink licked her on the side of her face.

She gave Olu the money that we both made for the day. I grabbed my shoes and ran out the door with Joelle and Maribel, wiping away at the blood that ran down the side of my face. Olu called me back, "Sinclair, get back in here. I need you to do something." He rubbed on his bulging nutsack. Joelle and Maribel looked up at me from the view through the staircase and kept trotting down the stairs.

I went back to Olu and he grabbed at my hair and slammed the door behind me. He dropped his navy blue silk pants to the floor and rubbed on his big throbbing penis. I didn't think this shit was love anymore. In fact I knew it wasn't when Ink came behind me and pulled down his funky jean shorts, pushed me down on the floor and entered me. I had no choice but to stroke Olu's dick while Ink humped on me with no rhythm. Why'd they have to do this to me? Shit, I already had enough of fucking niggas that I didn't know. As much as I hated to admit, I wanted to go home.

They continued to rape me as I blocked the entire thing out. Between the noises in the building from the druggies, Ink's tired ass moans, and Olu's firm grip on my hair, I was totally out of it. I heard the whispers of Grandma Cora Jean's words from long ago tickle my eardrums and then heard sirens.

"Oh shit, that's the cops, yo we gotta break out!" Olu hissed, pushing me away from him. Ink scrambled for his shorts.

"Bloodclaat, me was just about to nut again. You nuh have nuting here do yuh?" he asked Olu as I struggled with bewilderment to pull up my spandex.

"No, I moved all that shit out of this shit-hole the other day, so if they come in here, ain't shit they can do to nobody. And bitch," he said, directing his finger at me. "Don't you say nothing to them either."

Before I could shake my head yes, I heard a kick on the door. It was a herd of cops yelling and screaming for us to get on the floor. One of them, a tall red headed man with a thick moustache wearing a tight black jacket and jeans waved a piece of paper in our faces. He had to be the lead detective as he flashed his badge of deceit.

"I have a warrant for Herman Higgins and Dexter Wills. We were told you've got some narcotics stashed in here," he smirked at Olu and Ink.

"Man we ain't got nuting! We was just buying us some pussy here from the gal here, see?" Ink pointed at me.

My hands trembled above my head. This shit was becoming knee deep.

"Well pussy or not, she's here and so is this," he said grabbing a plastic bag of what I knew was cocaine from his rookie officer who came out of the bedroom.

The rookie beamed with iron as he slapped cuffs on all three of us and read us our rights.

"Wait a fucking minute man, that shit ain't mine. I came here to meet this ho right here and she bought us both here," Olu dimed on me, grunting up from the floor and was led away.

I couldn't fucking believe this shit, but I kept quiet. I had to set a plan in motion, but I didn't know what. I didn't know what the fuck just happened to me in a matter of twenty-four hours. As I was thrust in the backseat one of the cop's cars and we drove off, I caught a glimpse of Maribel in front of the same Chinese restaurant that we had bought food from earlier. Joelle was leaning against the payphone that she didn't want me to use.

The red headed detective interrogated me at the 103rd Precinct in a dim room and I had the slightest fucking idea of what to say. I knew one thing, I wasn't gonna say shit. The red head and another woman cop got in my face.

"I'm Detective O'Mallow and this is Detective Ricco. We wanna know one thing and one thing only. Where'd you get those drugs from? You'd better talk, because Mr. Higgins is ratting you out like the piece of shit he is," Detective O'Mallow happily admitted to me.

"Yeah Ms. Thing," Detective Ricco started. She brushed her thin white fingers through her dark curly hair and leaned in closer to me where I sat. "Why won't you talk?" she asked.

"You don't look like a drug dealer, you're a ho, just like Mr. Higgins said you was. 'A ho is a garden tool. Used to rake the weeds' is what he told us, so that means you don't mean shit to him if you go down with him, so where did those drugs come from? Where did you come from? We never saw you on the stroll before."

I sucked my teeth and folded my arms, ashamed of the funk from my mouth and underarms. "Look, don't I get a lawyer or sump'n? I ain't saying shit unless I got my lawyer!" I leaned back and closed my eyes devouring the sick things Olu said about me.

The two detectives glanced at each other. "Okay, she won't talk, lock her ass up."

I was led to a cell with other mangled looking whores. Shit, I was one to talk. I found a spot, sat on the cold floor and waited for someone to come and get me. This was some petty shit.

The wait turned into six months and a transfer to the Rose M. Singer House for Women at Riker's Island. My pimpled face public defender, Mr. Jenkins, was no good. He couldn't get me out of the situation and bail money was out of the question. Told me I had resisted arrest, and that they needed me as a witness to the drugs that they found at that sleazy hole from before.

"But I keep trying to tell you, they weren't mine!" I hissed at him when he came to visit me. He clutched a folder full of papers and wiped at his big forehead although it was brick in the visiting hall.

"Ms. Peters, you keep saying that, but you won't say why you were there. Yes, you did confess to being a prostitute, but do you think the judge is going to believe you when you tell him that you were soliciting for the first time? The prosecutor has a slew of witnesses from your old neighborhood who are going to testify that you, um, well, prost-, I mean solicited your body for money." He cleared his throat then said, "Then you get caught with two pimps with drugs. Looks like you all were in on this, but Mr. Higgins is probably not going to do any time for this." His voice lowered three octaves.

My eyes bugged the fuck out of my head. I pulled on my jumpsuit's collar. "What do you mean? He'll probably get off on this? What the fuck about me?" I ranted.

Mr. Jenkins cleared his throat again. Then he peered over his shoulder at the big black guard standing three feet away from us. Mr. Jenkins' gray eyes settled on my tired ones.

"He comes from money dear, that's why. This may be a losing battle for you, the best I can do for you is to cop a plea, five to seven the most. I'll try to get you maybe three. I wish I could help you, but even the fact that you don't have any prior offenses, may or may not work in our favor. You…"

His words trailed off as I watched part of my future go down the drain. I couldn't believe motherfuckers wanted to rat me out—over what? What was in it for them? I also couldn't believe this limp dick motherfucker couldn't get me off this shit. And I couldn't believe that Olu's real name was Herman fucking Higgins.

I was screwed. I didn't need Mr. Jenkins to tell me. I damn sure didn't need my mother to tell me shit since she refused my collect calls anyway and then blocked them altogether after the first month. Randall was the only one who looked out for me, putting money in my commissary.

"Don't worry sister, I'll be there for you all the way," he said on a visit before my court appearance that following week. The day before my court appearance, I called Jeena.

"Girl, it's so good to hear your voice, you just don't know," she whispered in the phone.

I began to tear up, but sucked it up. "Yo Jeena, this is some bogus shit, why the fuck are they doing this to me?" I cried.

"Because baby, when you don't snitch for the cops, they give you a one way ticket to hell. I'm sorry, Sinclair, but you may have to ride this one out. Worse they could do is give you a coupla years and then you'll still be young."

I began to whimper again. I didn't want to hear Jeena anymore, so I hung up. I went back to my cell and wandered off to sleep.

Next day in court, the trial began. The case against me was that I was an accessory to a drug ring. Sure enough, I sat at the table with my lawyer and listened as every nigga from my hood testified that I did solicit my body for sex and would do just about anything for money.

"Would Ms. Peters sell drugs for money?" the pale thin prosecutor asked. She had long blonde hair and wore a black pantsuit.

Skill looked over at me and smirked. "Yes, I believe so. She was always hard up for money and sold her body for it, so yes, I believe she would."

He leaned back in the hard wooden chair and grinned rubbing his dark hands over his low cut fade. I looked him dead in the eye then. I didn't care what anyone said about me. The fucked up part, I didn't have anyone say any good shit about me except for Randall. My brother always had my back. Jeena couldn't testify because of an old charge she had.

"But how is it that you went away to college, Mr. Peters, and your sister dropped out of Sarah J. Hale High School in the tenth grade?" the bitchy prosecutor asked.

Randall sighed, "I don't know, but I do know that my sister is not a drug lord, like you all claiming her to be." He stood up. "But that other nigga, he is. You need to lock his ass up! He set my sister up, that motherfucker! You cock sucking bitch! You wait—you'll pay for what you're doing to my sister!" Randall was flailing his arms on the witness stand sending a message to Olu.

The judge, an old bitch who wore her hair in a mushroom shaped bob, banged her gavel. "Bailiff, take him away, this witness is banned from my courtroom. Let the court rest, I've heard enough." Banging her gavel again, she got up to leave, her robe wickedly flowing behind her.

So I chalked it up when the jury found me guilty for possession of narcotics in the third degree. I took my fate like a soldier facing an enemy in the Persian Gulf War. And although I was seven months pregnant with Olu's baby, I went back to the Don't-give-a-fuck attitude, and listened as the judge decided to sentence me to four years. Four years at the Upstate New York Albion Correctional Facility for Women.

As I was led away by the bailiff, I turned around to see if Randall was let back inside the courtroom. He wasn't, but I saw Jeena disguised in Muslim garment in the back row. Her eyes told me not to worry. I knew she would always look out for me.

Two months later, I gave birth to a beautiful baby boy in a cold hospital. I named him Randall after my brother, the savior who dropped out of college to become a private investigator for the hood. He was living back in Brooklyn. Mommy moved to South Carolina and never spoke to me.

Just as I had finished nursing my baby a week after I had him, there were two social workers who approached me in the hospital room, where we were still housed.

"My name is Lauren Barnett and this is my colleague Tracy Hill. We've come to take the baby to his guardian. You do understand that, right?"

I began to shake with fear as Baby Randall's blue eyes drifted closed. I knew he was full. I also knew they were coming to take the baby to Randall.

"Yes, I understand, can my brother come here to see me before the baby leaves? I just want to tell him how to hold him and to please bring him here to see me every month and…"

The other social worker named Tracy who was a plump black

chick and wore her hair in Goddess braids said, "Ms. Peters, your brother's petition to be legal guardian over the baby has been reversed. The baby's father's family has agreed to take care of him while you are, um, away," she explained with the quickness.

"After your brother's outburst at the court, it was discovered that the baby would be better off with his grandparents. They can make arrangements for the baby to come and see you. Don't worry. He'll be in good hands," she said, folding her sausage sized fingers, obviously not fazed by what she just told me.

The other social worker was smoothing her sandy brown bangs from her face as I slowly got up from my chair and placed the baby in her arms. This fat bitch in front of me reminded me of that other bitch Joelle, so I hooked off on her dead in her pie shaped face. Blood and teeth splattered across the room. The correctional officers burst in the room, one of them a well built female who wrestled me to the ground.

"Give me my baby!" I screamed. "Take him and keep him in my family! Please Ms. Barnett! Please, don't do this to me!" My voice grew hoarse and I wrestled with the C.O.'s. They held their knees in my back to keep me from getting up.

"I just want to kiss my baby, please!" I yelled in agony.

Ms. Barnett bent down to me with tears in her eyes with my son. I looked up in defeat and leaned my lips to Randall's pale face and brushed him with two kisses before she quickly got up and put the sky blue blanket over his face. She looked back at me squirming on the floor and hurried out of the room. The other bitch Ms. Hill was led away to get treated for her busted grill. The C.O. with her knee in my back took her club and hit me in the back of my head. I blacked out.

In my dreams, I saw Olu wearing a black judge's robe. I heard my baby Randall crying in the shadows. I saw me and Jeena pushing Olu off of a cliff and laughing at his screams as they turned to silence. I saw my brother Randall graduating from law school and being the best defense attorney there was, and then I saw me again, a different person. Not the whore or drug dealer everyone claimed I was. I was happy. Then I heard Grandma Cora Jean's thick hissing telling me I had dark clouds around me, but those whispers were tamed with Mommy's trail of oil and Holy water she was throwing at me. Maybe it was time to tame my dark clouds and give it some sunshine. That sunshine was my son.

Months turned into years, three to be exact and I was a changed woman. It didn't happen overnight. I had a few fights with some of the bitches who wanted to test me. After my fourth year of lockup, I came across this chick I knew from my twenty-four hour ho stroll, Maribel. She couldn't run from me as I came face to face with her in her cell. She was pregnant like I was when I first came to Albion. Her hair was now dyed a white blonde and she had dark rings under her eyes. Wonder who had pimped her out? I looked at her arms and noticed track marks— Dope.

"Angel, what's up girl? You still look the same," she nervously said.

I wasted no time with the chit chat. "What the fuck happened that day? I want to know!" I grabbed at her throat.

"Look Angel, it was all her, you know that. I would never dime you out like that, shit I was just as scared of Olu and Ink as you were. Please believe, I would never snitch! You gotta believe me, mami!" She rambled and sniffed snot through her small nose.

I put her down, realizing she was carrying a seed.

"I want to know everything that happened, from the time you all ran downstairs and left me there to get raped then jailed for some shit I still don't fucking understand," I demanded. I grabbed the steel chair that was on the other side of the small cell and sat down waiting for her to tell me. She calmed down and went to her sink to splash some water on her face.

"Okay, this is what I remember," she started.

I waited. She leaned against the metal bunk bed as she told me what I already knew.

"That bitch, Joelle, is a snitch and she was afraid you was gonna take her place. She knew those drugs were in that house. She put them back in there the night you got, well, you know." She stared down at her swollen feet.

"The night I was raped you mean, right?" Fury shone in my eyes and Maribel's watery eyes could not clear the fire out of mine.

"Yes, but I didn't think you would go down like this. She wanted to get away from Olu and Ink. She also didn't want you on top. She wanted you and me out of the picture so she could get into her own game, the drug game."

I wasn't satisfied with Maribel's story, but it helped me to know that Joelle was still out on the streets. I tried not to worry about nothing, since I still had a year to go.

"Look, no hard feelings aight?" I stood and faced her, rubbing her shoulders in a friendly sisterly kind of way and left her room. I poked my head back in. "What you in here for anyway?"

She smiled, "Petty larceny, some ole bullshit, Adios mios!" She laughed and shook her head.

"Yeah, me too, petty bullshit," I said and watched the stupid smile disappear from Maribel's face.

Maribel gave birth to a baby girl and her father came to take the baby and raise her.

The next month, he came to claim Maribel's body. I received some powdered donuts Jeena sent me through the mail along with other food items to enjoy. How clever was she to disguise them in an Entenmanns's box! The donuts were laced with strychnine poison. Enough for stupid ass Maribel to eat to the very last crumb, licking her fingers and then break out in convulsions, pulling her throat in a tight jam and eventually stopping her heart altogether. Her daughter would be better off without a dope head such as Maribel was anyway.

At the age of twenty-one, I had gained a little weight, mainly muscle. I had a host of letters from Randall and Jeena, the only two to still have my back. I finally went to class to get my GED, read several books, hundreds to be exact and earned an Associate's degree in Criminal Justice.

I never did receive a visit from my son or his grandparents. In the new millennium, I went before the parole board, and to my amazement, they let me out. Even with the extra year they tacked on for whipping that fat bitch's ass who took my son, they still looked at me as a decent person. Yeah, the fuck right! But I was out and there was work to do.

As soon as I went to Jeena's place on Grand Avenue in Williamsburg, she hugged me and grabbed my hand, leading me to a bedroom.

"Look inside the chest," she said gleefully.

I did and what I saw in there gave me the biggest smile I had had in years. I mouthed thank you to her and closed the chest. Later on that night, my radical brother Randall came to pick me up in a black Nissan Maxima.

"Sis, you still look the same. Beautiful," he said as we whizzed away towards the Bronx.

His once curly hair was replaced with shoulder length cornrows. I knew I was due for curfew at my halfway house at nine o'clock. I knew that Jeena really loved me and wanted to be with me. I also knew that when Randall came to get me, it was to see a nigga I had been waiting to see for a real long time— Ink. So fuck parole right about now.

When we pulled up to an old dark warehouse in the murky area of Hunts Point, Randall made sure I was safely inside. My heart thumped with rage as I approached this nigga who was surrounded by ten brawny guys who wore all black shades. I had on a matching outfit. I stared at Ink who was tied to a chair and naked, and then above him. There was a wooden box of rats held tight by a pulley and two guys holding each end of the rope.

"Long time no see motherfucker, where's my son?" I spat at him.

This nigga who still looked the same minus the swollen eyes and busted lips, had the nerve to say, "Fuck you bloodclaat ho!"

"With what…?" I asked.

And with that, I pulled out the sharpened garden hoe blade from under my coat that Jeena had tucked safely in her cedar chest and came down on Ink's shriveled up dick and chopped it off. I turned away from him and drowned out his piercing screams and the squeals from the rats when my brother's friends released the box and walked out of the warehouse with Randall. I still had work to do.

Experience is priceless too bad we have to pay for it with our youth…

Pit of Her Stomach

CAROLINE McGILL

Taj sat with her arm around Jill's shoulder. She was comforting her pregnant best friend at her time of loss. There was a woman standing at the front of the church, in the middle of a tear jerking solo, and Jill was crying uncontrollably. Taj's heart went out to her. Jill's fiancé, Jeff, was in an ivory, marble coffin a few feet in front of them. Poor Jill was eight months pregnant with their first child. She was having a boy.

Jill wasn't the only one crying. She was Jeff's third baby mother. The other two sat on the pew behind her. She and Taj sat on the front pew with Jeff's mother, grandmother, and two aunts. The church was pretty big, and it was packed. Jeff was a well loved dude. The place was decorated with so many flowers it looked like a floral shop.

But something just wasn't right. Taj just had a funny feeling. She kept on glancing around the church nervously. Her left eye was jumping. That meant something was going to happen. Taj was a little superstitious because she was raised by her superstitious southern grandmother.

Some folks in the south believed that your left eye jumping meant your luck would be bad. And they believed the right eye jumping was an indication of good luck. Taj tried to be easy and relax, but her gut told her that something was going to go down.

After the soloist was done, the preacher stood up at the front. Reverend Bixby followed that heartfelt solo with a sermon full of fervor. Midway through, he had half of the congregation in tears, and the other half up on their feet shouting. The reverend continued preaching and telling it like it was.

"Here lies a good man! He was a good son! A father of two, with another one on the way…And he will be missed. Can I get a Amen? Well, now! God wanted him home. I say, God wanted this young brother home. It wasn't his time, but God knows best. Jesus! I pray for the killing to stop. It's just so senseless. Lil' children growing up with no daddies and Mother's losing their sons. It don't make no kind a sense! Lord knows, sometimes we just don't understand. God, we need you! I say, Lord, we praise you! We trust that you will make a way! Out of no way! You did it for Job! And I know you'll do it for us! I know you will!"

He wiped the sweat from his brow with a navy blue silk handkerchief he took from the breast pocket of his suit, and continued.

"I heard a lot of people stand up and say how good this man was! He helped a lot of people, and touched a lot of lives! See, God judge us by the things we do. He say "let the works I've done speak for me-e. So to the family, I say don't worry! You see, it's alright…Don't you weep no mo'! Lord, don't you mourn. Let not your hearts be troubled, 'cause Brother Jeff don' gon' on to another place! A better place! A place where the thunder don't roll and the rain don't pour. Good God almighty! Where troubled winds no longer blow! Glory hallelujah! I'm talkin' 'bout heaven, ya'll. Do you wanna go? I say, do you wanna go? 'Cause *I* wanna go. And if you get there before me…When you get there… Tell my mother… And tell my father… That one day… I'm comin' home! I said I'm comin' home! Glory be to God! Hallelujah!"

Jeff's mother threw up her hands in the air, and cried out, "Rejoice! Hallelujah! Praise God! Rejoice!" Two of the church ushers dressed in white stood over her and fanned her.

There was a loud thud, the church doors flew open, and a crew of thugs entered menacingly with big guns drawn. They were all dressed in black, with matching black boots, hats, and ratchets. At the sight of the intimidating looking crew, parishioners began to panic and look for a way out. Everyone knew that there were slim chances of a happy ending in this situation. That posse's intent was clear, like they came to kill.

They walked down the church aisle and further intimidated everyone by ice grilling them threateningly, and pointing guns at their faces. Amidst the thugs was one female, dressed in black army fatigues, black Timbs, and a black hat just like the rest of them.

The last man of the bunch entered the church, and the others in the crew respectfully parted, allowing him to pass. They posted up along the aisle on both sides to make sure nobody made a move. The last man headed up to the front of the church with two men following close on his heels. His presence was that of authority. It was obvious that he was captain, and the other two were his lieutenants.

The captain gave the command, and his lieutenants sprang into action. Jeff had already been shot eight times when he was killed four days ago, but they walked up to his casket and coldly opened fire on him again, putting a brand new set of holes in his corpse. The lieutenants, Loc and Fuck-You-Phil, had been briefed and given orders earlier that day. No mercy was to be shown to anyone at Jeff's funeral, not even the preacher. Whoever didn't cooperate was to be gunned down. It was that simple.

People hovered cowardly down by the pews, and witnessed horror in the desecration of Jeff's corpse. To shoot a dead man in his casket was unheard of—and in the house of the Lord? They had to be out of their minds. The funeral attendees all realized that their lives were in danger. The crew of young criminals in their presence was bold and reckless.

The whole church got down, lurchig for cover, including the preacher. Everybody ducked except for Jeff's mother. She refused to let her son's memory be disrespected that way. She had to speak up in his honor.

"My God…! What have you done? What kind of people are you? Have you no hearts, and no souls? My child is already dead. You all are nothing but the children of Satan! Get outta here! I rebuke you in the name of Jesus. Get outta here! My son is dead! This is his home going ceremony. You killed him once, and you come to shoot him again? How can he rest in peace? My God, have you no shame?"

Jeff's mother was upset, and very emotional. She threw both hands up to the sky like she was looking to God for answers, and shook her head helplessly.

She was a woman of God, but her son's murderers were unmoved by her display of maternal bereavement and holiness. Loc, the shorter one wearing the black Yankee fitted cap, walked right up to her and shot her in the forehead at pointblank range.

The woman fell silent, and her blood splattered on Jeff's grandmother, who was seated right next to her. After witnessing her daughter's murder, the elderly woman's initial reaction was of one of protest. She called on the Lord, and stood up, as if there was something she could do—Even though she was powerless. Fuck-You-Phil responded with a slug to her chest. That shot knocked her back in the pew. The poor old lady clutched her chest in disbelief, clinging to her life. Two seconds later, she was dead.

The two lieutenants, Loc and Fuck-You-Phil, were a special pair. Neither of them played with a full deck. At the sight of the old woman's demise, Loc started laughing, hard as hell. That was the way he had earned his street name. He was just straight loco.

Fuck-You-Phil had his moniker because his name was Phil, and he was known to have told a few dudes who begged for their lives "fuck you" before he pulled the trigger, and took their heads off. Both of the lieutenants were honored they had been delegated the task of shooting up Jeff's corpse, and were delighted to take shit a step further. Fuck that nigga, and his whole family.

To shoot a dead man at his funeral was the highest form of disrespect. That nigga Jeff had fucked with the wrong person's money, so Jeff had to go. The captain, Butch, was so angry about the loss Jeff had caused, he wanted to kill him again. That was one of two reasons he had rounded up his troops and crashed the funeral. The other reason he was there was to find Jeff's partner, Bless, to retrieve his muthafucking' money, and kill him too.

Loc had been smoking a blunt laced with some powerful angel dust right before they came. He was out of his mind and in a straight I-don't-give-a-fuck mode. He was already crazy, so dust made him insane to the twelfth degree. Loc turned to the congregation, and pointed to Jeff's grandmother.

He yelled, "Yo, ya'll think that's disrespectful? I'll show you mothafuckas disrespectful! Ya'll wanna see disrespectful? Ahight!"

He unzipped his black fatigues and removed his flaccid penis. He waved it at the congregation with an evil smirk, and then he walked over and pissed on Jeff's corpse. Everyone gasped in horror, each half expecting God to strike him down right there for his despicable act.

After Loc relieved his bladder, he put his dick away, and just stared at everyone. He yelled, "Ya'll mothafuckas better act like ya'll know! Who else up in here want it? Who the fuck else want it? Nobody move, nobody get shot!"

He raised his gun, and fired twice up in the air. It looked like he was busting shots at God.

"T.B.G. mothafuckas! T.B.G. up in this bitch! Yeah, niggas!"

That was the name of their crew. T.B.G. simply stood for The Bad Guys. Butch was the captain, and he and his dudes didn't give a fuck. They were ruthless. They figured shooting up the funeral was appropriate. There was already slow singing and flower bringing, so it was nothing to body a few more mothafuckas.

Jeff's mother had asked for it, and his granny was old anyway. Fuck it! Butch's heart was stone cold. The person he had come for, Bless, wasn't in sight. Bless was Jeff's partner, and he was one lucky nigga. Fortunately for him, he had been smart enough not to show up to see his best homie laid to rest. Somebody must've been praying for his ass. But he was a marked man. He could run, but he couldn't hide. Butch had already decided that his days were numbered.

After learning that Bless wasn't there, he scanned the pews for someone he could get answers from. He zoomed in on Jill and Taj in the front. They were trying to hide, but he saw them. Butch knew that bitch, Jill was having a baby by Jeff, and Taj used to be Bless' girlfriend. He walked over and addressed them both with no nonsense.

"Where the fuck is that nigga Bless at?"

Taj and Jill both shook their heads, and shrugged. They really didn't know. Both of them were terrified. After seeing them niggas shoot Jeff's mother and grandmother, they knew they would kill them without a second thought.

Butch wasn't buying it. He ordered Loc to get the girls, so they could kidnap them. Those bitches were going to give up some mothafuckin' answers. He had lost a lot of money, and somebody was going to get his shit back.

Loc snatched Taj and Jill up outta the front pew. They were both scared to death, but Taj was more afraid for Jill because she was pregnant. Again, she told Butch they didn't know anything. Butch silenced her with a deadly look. He warned Taj that if they didn't tell him where Bless was, he would have bullets put in her, Jill, and her baby. That was the last opportunity he gave them to speak. Neither Taj nor Jill uttered a word.

Butch could see that these broads weren't going to assist him voluntarily. He was rapidly running out of patience with them. Butch was a real dangerous, but quiet dude. He wasn't much of a talker, but people listened when he spoke. And those bitches weren't going to be the exception to that rule. They were going to give him the information he needed. He would make sure of that. He ordered his lieutenants to march them out of the church. There were two bulletproof, gray vans with tinted windows waiting outside.

Butch had been the last man to enter the church, but he left out first. He and his two second in command exited the church with the girls next, and the rest of his troops moved out behind them.

On the way out, the last goon on the back of the line, named Lefty, noticed an old gray-haired man dialing on his cellphone. Lefty paused, and mercilessly put a bullet in grandpa's face. He did this as a warning to the others to think twice about calling the police. After a final steely glance around the church, he exited without a word.

Outside, Taj and Jill were seated in the back of one of the vans. They were surrounded by machine gun toting thugs. Taj glanced over at her homegirl. It was dark inside because the van windows were tinted real dark. She couldn't really see Jill, but she could feel her next to her shaking like a leaf. Jill must've been real nervous. The last words she mumbled to Taj were, "Yo Taj, if you know where Bless is, you need to tell these niggas. I'm about to have my baby."

The women were driven to what they would later learn was the T.B.G. headquarters, thrown into separate dark rooms, and bounded to chairs. They would find out soon that the rooms were for interrogation.

Butch decided that they would lean on Taj first, because he had a feeling she knew more. She had to because she was fucking Bless. He locked Jill in a room alone. Butch figured Taj needed a little persuasion. He sent for his resident down bitch, Cherry. After her psycho, got-somethin'-to-prove ass got a hold of Taj, she would realize the realness of the situation.

A short time later, Taj was sitting in the dark tied up when the room door opened. Her eyes squinted from the sudden light. She could make out a chick entering with two dudes behind her. Taj was approached by Cherry Coke, the self-proclaimed first lady of T.B.G. If a lady was what you could call her.

As soon as she came in the room, she placed her gun on Taj's temple and demanded to know where Bless was. Cherry Coke was skied up off cocaine and was mad hype. She wanted to show Butch and the rest of the team how much she repped for T.B.G. For those two reasons, she got real extra with Taj. She knew that bitch knew something. She was fucking that nigga.

"Taj, you funky-ass bitch…! You better give that nigga Bless up, 'fore you fuck around and be the guest of honor at a funeral, like the one we just left."

Taj didn't say anything. She wasn't talking to anybody, she didn't give a fuck. Not even Butch. It was hard to ignore Cherry because her breath was hot as a fire breathing dragon's, and stinking so bad it was nauseating.

Cherry Coke got fed up with Taj's silence, and hauled off and smacked her across her face. She hit her like she was trying to take her head off. Afterwards, she said, "Now do you hear me talkin' to you, *bitch*?"

Taj spat blood to her left. Cherry Coke had caught her good. She wanted to jump up and beat that coke-head bitch's ass, but she was tied up. A gun was also pointed in her face. Plus there was an armed man in the corner of the room. Taj knew the odds were stacked against her, but she was going to get Cherry back. She would make it a point. That crackhead bitch's ass was hers. Taj silently put that on her deceased mother.

Cherry Coke looked at Taj expecting to see fear, but that wasn't what she saw in her eyes. It was hatred and resistance. The bitch thought she was hard. Cherry wanted Taj to fear her. She was the first lady of T.B.G. They were the most feared crew in all of Brooklyn, and she demanded respect. Cherry Coke slapped the shit out of Taj again.

Taj had eaten one hit. She let that bitch rock. But after that second slap, she was vexed. Her first reaction was to hock spit in Cherry's fucking face. After Taj's spit splattered across her face, Cherry quickly wiped it off with the back of her hand. She said, "Bitch, I'm a fuckin' kill you! Do you know who the fuck I am?"

After that, she took the gun and busted Taj upside her head. Taj's hands were tied, but she leaned back and kicked that bitch Cherry in her midsection. She wished she was free so she could beat that bitch.

Cherry doubled over in pain. After a second, she came back up with the pistol and clocked Taj in the face. She hit her in the nose that time. Taj saw light for a minute, and excruciating pain spread across her face.

Cherry spat, "Bitch, you wanna fuckin' die today? Do sump'n else and you gon' get your death wish. I will kill you, stupid-ass bitch!" She glared at Taj. "I got sump'n for you, bitch."

She took a walkie-talkie from her hip, and called for the thirstiest hounds on the team.

There was lots of hoopla in the streets about T.B.G. Just about everyone feared them, but it was safe to say that Cherry had exaggerated her position in the organization somewhat. She wasn't actually a member of T.B.G. She was more like their property. They kept her around for their use, like the coke whore they had turned her into. She was passed around the crew to anyone who wanted to have his way with her. Cherry was T.B.G.'s property, and all the members had equal access to every hole in her body. She was really just a whore, who did all of her servicing in-house.

Cherry started out as a shorty Butch was dealing with, but he soon discovered she was weak. The day he turned her out, he had caught her stealing coke from his stash. That really pissed Butch off because he had already given her a nice fifty bag of snow to get right on. Butch realized then she had a nose like a vacuum cleaner. He had slapped her around a few times, called her names, and poured an ounce of powder on a tray on the table. It was a real mountain of snow.

Butch grabbed Cherry by her hair, and pushed her whole fucking face into the pile of coke. He made her snort as much as she could before he let her up for air, and started talking shit.

He said, "You up in here stealin' my shit? You want some more, ho?"

Then he shoved her face back down and yelled, "You had enough yet, huh bitch?" Since she was such a greedy bitch, he wanted to teach her ass a lesson.

The third time he did it, he said, "Your name is Cherry, right? Now that shit is *Cherry Coke*. How 'bout that? You want more, bitch? Have some more! You stinkin', filthy, rotten bitch…!"

Cherry shook her head vigorously. She couldn't take it. Her nose was burning so bad, she was crying. She felt like her heart was going to bust from the rush. She wasn't an idiot and knew snorting that much coke could kill her. She begged Butch to stop.

"No more, please…! I'm so s-s-sorry!" she squealed.

Just to show that bitch who the mothafuckin' boss was, Butch mercilessly slammed her face into the pile of coke one more time. He held the back of her head so she couldn't move. Cherry tried not to inhale, but she had no choice. She had to breathe. That last blast was so powerful, her tongue was numb, and she couldn't even speak anymore.

Butch yanked her hair hard and made her face him. He looked at her with pure disgust, and told her she was nothing but a sorry-ass coke whore. He then informed her that she owed him for all the coke she had just snorted up. Cherry was scared, and out of it. She didn't even protest.

Butch unzipped his jeans and let his dick loose. He demanded that she get down on her knees.

"Come on, bitch, and pay this bill. You in debt to me… Now get down and suck my joint. Hurry the fuck up!"

Cherry was high as hell, so she was out of it. A hard smack across the jaw by Butch put some sense in her head. Knowing the type of dude Butch was, she jumped down quickly, and did as she was told. He would not hesitate to use that big gun he kept on his hip, so she gave that blowjob all she had. Cherry was good, so she got Butch off pretty fast.

But he wasn't finished with her. After he shot off down her throat, he summoned all of his soldiers, and announced the opportunity for them to get right—all thirteen of them. Cherry was ordered to pleasure them one by one, two by two, and three by three. Butch stood watching the makeshift gangbang. He ignored her cries and protests when dudes were rough. Some of them strapped up, but some went raw, shooting their loads inside her.

A couple of hours later, he told Cherry's sore throat and pussy having ass to take a break and a shower. When she was cleaned up, he "suggested" she do a few more lines, to make herself feel better. Even though she had almost gone into cardiac arrest and overdosed barely two hours before, Cherry went for it. She got high all night, and before the sun came up, she had serviced six dudes again with no problem.

Butch wasn't stupid. He hadn't just been tricking coke for the hell of it. He knew what he was doing. His plan was to pump so much coke in her system that she would spend her days trying to reach that high again. She would probably die trying. He increased her addiction level by fifty. Butch was willing to keep her around and feed her habit, but that bitch would do as he said.

Cherry did everything he said too, from servicing his crew regularly, to even busting shots at niggas when he told her to. Cherry was gun happy, and had put many niggas who fucked up Butch's money in the wind. Niggas ran without firing back. The streets knew she was T.B.G. property. She was a bitch with a pass.

Cherry loved doing dirt with Butch. They only shared personal time together when he gave her one-on-one talks, to go over her assignments. Cherry was so dependent on Butch, and eager to please him, she never fucked up what he told her to do.

That's why she took this Taj situation very, very serious. If Butch wanted answers, he was gonna get answers. Cherry knew how to make that bitch start singing. If Taj could stand up to what she had in store for her, she was one bad bitch.

Taj was a stand-up chick. She wasn't going to talk. She was from Brooklyn. BK didn't raise no rats. That was the code of the streets and it was inbreded in her. But there was only so much a woman could take. Taj was stripped naked, and tied down horizontally, with her legs open. Her wrists and ankles were bound. Cherry kept hitting her, spitting on her, and inserting foreign objects into her vagina. She fucked her with a broom, a cordless phone, a big wax candle, and she even tried to stick a sneaker in her pussy. The sneaker didn't fit, so she stuck the candle back in. Cherry even went so far as to light the end of the candle that was sticking out. The men standing around whistled like wolves. Cherry had been violated by the dudes in that house so much, it was nothing for her to violate another bitch. She was putting on a real show for the gang.

She told the fellas she was about to have some birthday cake, and that nasty bitch bent down and started eating Taj's pussy. The men went wild, and that caused her to really go in. She spread Taj's vaginal lips so that her clit popped out, and she hungrily sucked on it.

Cherry, a bisexual, was enjoying herself. Fresh meat was tasty, especially with Taj bucking in protest. Meanwhile, the candle in her pussy still burned.

Taj vomitted from Cherry's stink mouth on her twat. She had never been with a girl before, and the fact that it was this coke-whore-bitch, she was planning on killing, made the act a turnoff. If she could've gotten loose from the ropes she was tied in, she would've killed the bitch right then.

Cherry could see that Taj didn't approve, but she was going to make her like it. She was going to turn that bitch out. She snatched that candle out of Taj's pussy, and walked around in front of her. She wrapped her arms around her thighs so she couldn't move, and pushed her face in Taj's pussy. She ate Taj out with fervor, in a way she knew was good to her. Cherry Coke looked up at Taj, and said, "Say you like it, bitch! Say you like the way I'm eatin' this pussy!"

Taj was so mad tears welled up in the corners of her eyes. She bit her lip in anger, and stared at that bitch coldly. She rolled her eyes, and hissed, "Fuck you bitch! Hell no! I don't like that shit! You fuckin' nasty dyke!"

Cherry bit down as hard as she could on Taj's inner thigh. Taj yelped in pain. Cherry laughed, and said, "Don't scream, bitch. You gonna like it. You gonna *love* it! Watch! And if you don't, I'm a blow your mothafuckin' head off."

Cherry parted Taj's pussy with two fingers, and she bent down and tongued it for a few more minutes. She slipped four fingers in and out, and stuck her thumb in her asshole.

Taj just laid there with her eyes closed. There was nothing else she could do. She felt like a filthy exhibit in a freak show. The gang members surrounding them rubbed their crotch in anticipation. Some of them were literally drooling.

Cherry was concentrating on Taj's clit. To Taj's dismay, it started feeling good—real good. She tried to fight it, but she felt an eruption mounting in her groin. Taj bit her lip to keep from crying out. Against her will, she came hard. She was shaking.

Cherry had eaten a few pussies in her time, and she knew when a chick was cumming. Taj's juices were flowing. She could taste them. Cherry continued to lick her clit rapidly, forcing her fist in her pussy. Taj squirmed and cried out in pain, but Cherry wouldn't stop. She fisted Taj's pussy deep. She had her whole hand inside of her.

Taj would never admit it, but she had never experienced such pleasurable pressure. Against her will, she came again. Cherry could feel her pussy walls contracting on her hand. After a few more seconds, she noisily extracted her fist from Taj's soaked tunnel.

Cherry stood up, and smiled at Taj coyly. She seductively licked two of her fingers.

"I told you, my little, slut bitch. I knew you'd like it. Now lick your cum off my fingers, and see how good you taste."

She walked over and smeared Taj's pussy juice all over her lips. Taj turned her head, but she couldn't escape the sticky film Cherry smeared on her face. Cherry wanted to eat that pussy again just to show that bitch, but the natives were restless. By now, the men were groping and pawing both of them, especially Taj.

That was where the pleasure stopped. The men pinched her nipples and roughly squeezed her breasts, and jammed their filthy fingers in her ass and pussy. When she resisted, Taj was beaten, and then raped repeatedly. They had their dicks all over her face and lips. One after the other, they shot semen all over her body, inside and out. Before it was over, one mothafucka even peed on her. Taj was humiliated so badly, she wanted to die.

Before Taj knew it, that bitch Cherry climbed up on the table. She stood over her and smirked. Then she squatted putting her ass on Taj's face. Taj turned her head and fought as hard as she could, but Cherry plopped her stinking, rotten, funk box right in her face. Taj spit, and gasped for air.

"Get the fuck off me! You stink-pussy, dyke bitch! I'm a kill you, hoe! That's my word!"

Cherry grabbed her hair, and said, "Bitch, you better shut the fuck up, and eat this pussy. Kenny, gimme that fuckin' gat…"

Kenny passed Cherry the .45. She cocked it, and stuck it right to Taj's temple. She stared down at her coldly.

"Bitch, I said eat. And you better do it good as I did you. You don't fuckin' stop until I get up and tell you to. You hear me?"

Against Taj's will, she had to lick Cherry's stinking slit. There was no way in the world she could pleasure her wholeheartedly. She just couldn't. But Cherry dug that steel gun barrel into the side of her head. Taj was afraid that crazy, coked-up bitch would make a mistake and pull the trigger, so she gave in.

"Alright, get that fuckin' gun out my face, bitch! Alright…!"

Cherry gave her a warning look, and hesitantly passed the gun to Face, another one of the goons.

"Face, do me a favor. If it don't look like I'm enjoying myself, put a bullet in this bitch's melon."

Face had a crazed look in his eyes like he would do it. Taj knew she was surrounded by stone cold murderers, and she believed he would. Cherry wrapped her fist in Taj's hair, and directed her face back to the place.

Taj was afraid for her life, so she swallowed the vomit that rose in her throat and started lapping Cherry's pussy like a kitten on a bowl of milk. She tried to hold back as much as she could, but Cherry commanded her to suck on her clit.

Taj closed her eyes and tried to use her imagination. She had to pretend she was doing something else—anything else. She would've rather eaten a bowl of hyena shit then Cherry's diseased bat cave. She almost threw up again, but took a deep breath and shook it off. She placed her lips on Cherry's clit and sucked it gently, pretending it was ice cream of her favorite flavor. It was hard though, because of the foul smell.

After a minute, she heard moaning. She guessed she was doing it right. She wanted to get it over with quick, so she started licking and sucking faster. Cherry was humping her face excitedly and moaning.

One of the dudes shouted out, "Hurry up and cum, hoe! I wanna put my dick in this bitch's mouth." That drew a few laughs from the others.

Cherry looked at him defiantly, and spat, "No, fuck that! Butch gave me the green light to do what I wanna do, and I wanna cum in this bitch's face. Nigga you fuckin' up my groove… Now just shut the fuck up, so I can cum."

The dude shook his head impatiently, but he didn't say another word. The sight of that girl-on-girl had him so turned-on, his dick was throbbing for release. He began unconsciously stroking his own member to please himself.

Cherry kept riding Taj's face, grinding her juices all over her nose and chin. She was taking advantage of the situation. Taj was seething underneath her, but she kept on licking the smelly pussy. She couldn't see with Cherry's ass plopped in her face, but she felt another guy mounting her. He pawed her breasts, and then he penetrated her and started stroking real deep. He was built large, which made it worse.

Taj was tied down to the table with her legs open, so she just laid there and said her millionth prayer that she didn't catch AIDS or something from those niggas.

More of the dudes wanted to participate, but there were limited holes for them to penetrate. One dude hopped up on the table too, and stuck his dick in Cherry's mouth. She just grabbed it and started sucking it like a lollipop, and kept fucking Taj's face.

Another dude yelled out, "Yo, I want that pregnant bitch!"

Cherry overheard him, and said, "Word, go get that bitch! I want her out here. She gon' taste this pussy too!" She went back to sucking the dick she had in her hand.

Two of the goons, Lefty and Rell, left to get Jill. She had been sitting in the dark for too long. Jill was relieved to see light when they opened her door. The men untied her, and told her to follow them. Jill didn't know where they were taking her, but she had one request.

She said, "Excuse me. I'm sorry, but I gotta pee."

The men just looked at each other. "Aight, ma", the taller one named Lefty said. They led her to the bathroom so she could relieve her bladder.

After Jill used the bathroom, they told her to take off her clothes. She looked at them puzzled, and shook her head. What the hell was wrong with them? Couldn't they see that she was pregnant?

Lefty made a face. He said, "I didn't *ask* you. I ain't never hit a pregnant chick before. I wanna try that pussy. So just listen to what I tell you. Don't gimme a reason, shorty." He showed her the gun in his waist.

Jill saw that he wasn't kidding. She searched the other guy's face for some sort of sympathy, but there was none there either. She didn't want these niggas to hurt her baby, so she had to do what they said. She took off her blouse, and then she hesitated.

Lefty nodded at her, encouraging her to finish undressing. Jill reluctantly removed her skirt next. The other goon, Rell, took the liberty of unfastening her bra himself. He was anxious to see those big, milk filled jugs. When he got Jill's bra unhooked and slipped it off, his tongue hung out like a panting dog. He palmed her tities and squeezed her nipples until they stiffened in his fingertips, and then he bent down and sucked on them one by one.

Jill recoiled in disgust, and tried to push him away. Rell laughed, and told her they were going to a party. He and Lefty forced Jill down the hall to the room where the action was going on. Jill was nervous before they opened the door, but she was in no way prepared for what she would see next.

In the room, there was a crowd of excited dudes standing around a table watching something. When the door opened, they all turned around and whistled at Jill, with her filled out pregnant hips and breasts. They all went wild like she was fresh meat.

Jill focused in on what they were watching on the table. Her jaw dropped in shock. She couldn't believe her eyes. Taj was tied up on the table, naked and spread-eagled, and there was a guy having sex with her. But worst of all, that nasty bitch Cherry Coke was sitting on Taj's face, moaning and bucking like she was cumming. The other thing Jill noticed was the crazy looking guy with the gun pointed at Taj, forcing her to do it. Jill was afraid—very afraid. Her heart went out to her friend, and she prayed she wouldn't be subjected to the same degradation.

Jill had the feeling her prayers would go unanswered. This was evident by the seven guys groping her tities and ass. She knew they were going to rape her. They had guns. There were four visible in the room, so she knew she didn't have any wins. Just like Taj, she knew she was doomed.

Cherry hollered out in bliss, as she came all over Taj's face. Taj had eaten her pussy real good, just like she ordered. The sound of Cherry yelling out in pleasure caused the guy who was stroking Taj to increase his rhythm. Now he was about to cum. He pulled out, and shot all over Taj's stomach. Jill watched in horror, and realized that they weren't using condoms. What the hell type of freak show was this? She wondered in fear.

Little did Jill know, a lot of the gang already had sex with Taj nine or ten times. And less than half of them had bothered using a condom, even though she had begged them all to.

Cherry got up off Taj's face with legs that trembled. She slapped Taj lightly across her face, and stroked her hair.

"Good girl. You made mommy's pussy feel so good. Now you get a treat. You get to get your pussy licked too…By her."

Cherry pointed at Jill, who just stood there looking at her like she was crazy. Cherry said, "Bitch, did you hear what I just said? Get down and lick her pussy!"

Jill said, "Hell no! That's like my sister!"

Cherry said, "Bitch, I don't give a fuck if she's ya' mama! I said get down there and eat that pussy. It got a sticky glaze on it for you too," Cherry smirked.

She was referring to the many different types of semen on Taj. She was covered in cum punch. Jill went wide-eyed with fear, backing up, and shaking her head. Taj pleaded with them too. She was embarrassed that Jill had seen her that way, especially with Cherry sitting on her face. But there was no way they could do each other. They were best friends, and as close as sisters. She hoped because Jill was pregnant, Cherry would just let it go.

Cherry wasn't letting anything go. She took the gun back from Face, and pointed it at Jill. She smiled wickedly, and walked over and placed it on her belly.

"Bitch, I said eat that pussy, or I'll blow your fuckin' baby head off! Get on your mothafuckin' knees now!"

Cherry knew what she was doing would destroy their friendship, and was just being spiteful. If those bitches didn't start coughing up some answers about Butch's money, they wouldn't live long enough to enjoy their friendship.

The dilemma Jill faced caused tears to flood her eyes. Cherry was trying to make her do some foul shit, especially with that semen all over Taj. The thought made Jill sick. She doubled over and threw up right there on the floor.

The sight of her barfing didn't stir any emotions in Cherry, a cold bitch with no heart. She told Jill pointblank that if she vomited again, she would kill her. Then she ordered her to get over there and lick that pussy clean.

The dudes were yelling, "Do it! Eat that pussy! Do it!"

Tears streamed down Jill's face. She realized she didn't have a choice. She stood in front of Taj, who she could see was crying too. She didn't want this anymore than Jill did. What type of shit were they caught up in? Those mothafuckas were sick.

Cherry Coke hit Jill upside the head with the gun to give her a final warning.

"Bitch, keep playin' with me…! You think I won't kill your fuckin' baby?" she said cocking the gun.

Jill took the hint. The knot Cherry just put on the back of her head was throbbing like crazy, and she didn't want to be subjected to anymore violence. She had to worry about her unborn child. Her baby had been through enough. That day was his father's funeral. Jill slowly bent down and looked at Taj's vagina. Cherry Coke pushed her head inside, smearing the semen all over her face.

Jill vowed not to swallow that disgusting stuff. She closed her eyes, and began to lick her best friend's pussy at gunpoint. Taj just laid there with here eyes closed. They both wondered if they were ever going to face each other and how.

Cherry leaned down and watched Jill closely, scrutinizing her every move. She coached her, and made sure she was doing it right.

"That's right, lick it. Hold that pussy open. Now suck on the clit. That's right, bitch! Suck it!"

When Cherry was finally satisfied that Jill was doing it right, she got down on her knees in front of her, and parted her pussy lips. Jill looked down and saw that Cherry was preparing to eat her out. That bitch was sick. She was a straight freak.

Cherry had never eaten out a pregnant girl, so she was curious to see what flavor that milk was. She spread Jill's pussy open and stuck her tongue all the way inside. She didn't come up for air until Jill's legs started trembling. Her pussy had a distinct flavor to it. Cherry wanted more. She tongued it for a few more minutes, before she stood back up on her feet.

She noticed that Jill wasn't making Taj squirm yet, so she spread Taj's pussy lips for her, and showed her how it should be done. Cherry sucked on Taj's pussy for about thirty seconds, and then she made Jill do it again the way she showed her. Jill just wanted to get it over with, so she did what Cherry said. It must've felt good to Taj because now she was breathing real heavy. This dude walked over, and started rubbing his dick across her lips while he was jerking off.

Jill kept her eyes closed, and kept on licking Taj the way Cherry instructed her too. Taj moaned softly a time or two, and the flavor down there suddenly changed. Jill realized she must've made Taj cum.

Cherry noticed Taj's body twitching too. She liked to see that. Now it was her turn. She jumped on top of Taj and spread her legs open, so that her pussy was right in Jill's face too.

Jill looked real hesitant, but Cherry pointed the gun right at her head.

"Eat me, bitch! Don't worry, this shit's good for your baby. Pussy is full of vitamins and minerals."

A few of the men laughed, and tugged on their dicks. They were anxious for the opportunity to fuck Jill. They had all heard about how good pregnant pussy was.

Cherry grabbed the back of Jill's head, and forced her face in her pussy. Jill gagged and choked, but Cherry wouldn't let her up for air. She traced the gun along her ear. Jill got the picture, and went to work. She fought the bile that kept rising in her throat. She sucked on Cherry's clit, which caused her to moan loudly. Taj just laid there underneath Cherry while Jill licked her pussy. She was still tied up, and very helpless.

Lefty watched Jill's peanut butter colored ass up in the air while she was bent over eating Cherry out. He wanted to be the first to fuck her. He walked up behind her, and slid his dick inside of her. She was already wet and slippery from Cherry eating her out. His entry was a breeze. He palmed her tities, and stroked that pussy deep.

Jill started crying again while she was raped and forced to lick Cherry's smelly box at the same time. Her name should've been Rotten

Cherry, Jill was thinking, feeling like she'd lost all her dignity. All of her self-respect was gone.

And more alarming, she and Taj were in a situation where they could easily be killed. These mothafuckas were crazy. They had killed Jeff's mother at his funeral, and his grandmother too. And they would kill them too, without a second thought. This wasn't a game.

The men had a field day molesting, degrading, and sodomizing Jill the way they had done Taj. After having an outright orgy with all three of the women, they began to disperse and retreat to their beds. Most of them were weak and sleepy from all the freaky sex they had participated in.

The horrendous torture had lasted over three hours. After it was over, Jill was escorted back to the other room she was in, and retied. They left her alone, filthy and naked.

Butch didn't have anything against Jill and Taj. His only concern was that three-hundred grand that Bless and that dead nigga Jeff burned him for. Those girls just messed with the wrong dudes. But those bitches still hadn't given up Bless' whereabouts. As far as he was concerned, the team could have their way with them.

Butch ran a tight ship. Anyone who crossed him got it in the worse way. His team of goons was loyal, and they followed his orders. He treated them all well in exchange.

An hour later, Butch gave Taj another opportunity to give her man up. They tried calling that nigga, but his calls were going straight to voicemail. Taj was allowed to speak again. She was desperate to save her and Jill's lives, so she looked at him earnestly and lied.

She and Jill's lives depended on it, so she promised Butch that she would get his money. Taj convinced him that she needed to be let go, so she could go set Bless up.

In her heart she didn't really believe she could pull it off. She didn't even know where he was, but had to do something. She hadn't seen Bless since the day after Jeff was killed. They had argued about his decision not to attend the funeral. She had thought that was fucked up, and a real sucker move. Now Taj wished she and Jill hadn't attended either.

After much deliberation, Butch decided to let Taj go. He didn't have many other options to get at Bless. He had already sent a team of goons to his mother's house, but the apartment was empty when they had arrived. The occupants had vacated the premises in a hurry. They had waited hours, but no one returned. Butch guessed that nigga Bless was smart enough to get his moms out of harm's way. That nigga knew how he got down. Butch warned Taj that if she didn't come through for him, he would be sure to kill Jill and the unborn fetus.

Taj begged him to let her take a shower. Though his eyes remained cold and expressionless, he gave her permission. He had cameras hidden in the interrogation rooms, and had seen the inhumane way in which she and her pregnant friend had been treated.

He was turned off by the display of unsafe group sex, and not the least bit interested in participating. But Butch wouldn't have participated in such festivities because he wasn't that hard up. He was just cold. The type of nigga to pimp on a bitch stone cold in chilly blood, that was who he was. Calling him icy was a real understatement. The only reason he was allowing Taj a shower was because he couldn't stand looking at her cum-drenched body.

Taj was grateful and scrubbed her skin so hard, she almost took a layer off. She tried to put it behind her, but knew she would wear the scars from that brutal rape the rest of her life. Taj cried her heart out in the shower. The tears streaming down her face was immediately washed away by the rapid running water.

After Taj got cleaned up, Butch ordered his driver to take her home. Before releasing her, he again warned her not to try anything funny. He was letting her call it, and a bad choice would end in Jill and her baby's murder. Taj could tell from the steeled look in eyes, he meant it.

He walked her over to the room Jill was in and told Jill what it was. He said, "I'm letting your homegirl go, so she could get my fuckin' money. She has to point me to that nigga. If she doesn't, you and your baby is dead."

He grabbed Taj and hurried her along. Taj would never forget the look on Jill's face watching her leave. Her eyes had pleaded with her to save her and her child.

After Taj got away, she was torn. She wanted to go back and save Jill but she knew that if she returned they would both be dead. Taj's heart ached for her dear friend and what she knew was to become of her. The thought was sad but it was something she would have to live with if she couldn't come through. Damn, what could be done?

She vowed to kill that bitch Cherry one day for violating her like that.

An hour later, after making twenty seven unsuccessful attempts to contact Bless, Taj sat in her bedroom crying. She tried to be strong, but knew what a fucked up predicament she had left Jill in. She couldn't go back. She couldn't get a hold of Butch's money. She had to get out of town. There was no sense in both of them being killed. Taj shook her head in disbelief and disgust. What she had just been through was crazy.

At the same time, she had to hurry and make moves. She figured it was only a matter of time before Butch sent his goons over to collect his package. Jill's life was in danger.

Taj packed as many clothes as she could stuff into an overnight bag and small suitcase, and hopped in her jeep and pulled off into the night. She hated to leave, but she knew that her days were numbered if she stayed.

It didn't take Butch long to figure out that he had been burned. He was totally remorseless in his decision to do away with the pregnant Jill. Jeff had fucked him, and this was his way of making him pay for generations. He would kill this unborn seed that he hoped was a boy. Butch had to send a message that he would take out nigga's namesakes, if they crossed and violated him.

He glanced at his watch for the umpteenth time. Time was up. Taking a deep silent breath, Butch mentally counted to ten. That was it. Taj hadn't called him or named any contact. That bitch must have thought he was joking or something, taking his threats idle. She must have been out of her mothafuckin' mind! He mused, scratching his chin and staring out the window with his arms folded.

Anyone who had dealt wrongly with Butch knew that wasn't a good sign. Pondering, crossed arm stance, and the chin scratch, meant that he was contemplating the way a person was going to die. This particular time it was Jill's fate he was sealing. He already knew she had to go, but it was just a matter of how. Butch decided to make it quick. From what he had seen on the cameras, she had been tortured enough.

Jill was untied and taken from the room. She began to panic because she knew where they were taking her. It became harder and harder for her to breathe with each step. Her stomach was cramping. She could feel her baby balling up inside of her. It was as if the fetus sensed danger and it was trying to find a corner to hide.

Jill stared down at her belly in horror. She placed her hand over the gunshot wound, like she was trying to stop her baby's life from draining through it. She kept praying that God was with her. Standing there frozen in fear for a minute, she didn't feel her baby moving anymore.

For nearly nine months Jill had carried the fetus inside her. She had a real connection. Jill didn't feel it anymore and knew. Her eyes watered up at the thought. Her heart was broken.

Jill looked in the eyes of her baby's killer and begged for her life. Her pleas were in vain. Loco grinned at her coldly, and squeezed his hammer, nailing her in the forehead, right between the eyes. Her lifeless, naked body slumped to the ground. She was taken to a dark alley, and her naked corpse was dumped in a garbage dumpster.

It was if an angel flew over her. She could actually feel the breeze from the flapping of wings. God had smiled down on her, and by his grace, she was still alive. But Jill was fighting for her life. She had taken a bullet in her forehead.

She arrived at the hospital, stark naked, battered, covered in semen specimens, fighting for her life. Samples were taken and the perpetrators were identified, but Jill never made it to court. She couldn't face the T.B.G., so they walked. Years later she became a full-fledged crackhead. She was abducted by the same niggas who kidnapped and raped her. Alone in a room and being fed crack by the T.B.G. that familiar feeling once again began rising in the pit of her stomach…

RUSH
The Sweetest Sin

Zoë Woods

I

Chrisette Rowan laid in her king size bed at her home in Manassas, Virginia, skin against the silk sheets. She rubbed her fingertips up and down the middle of her stomach. The clock read 4:53 a.m., and for some reason she had awoken well before the alarm was supposed to go off at 6:45 a.m. This morning felt a little different. She had an unfamiliar surge of energy and was restless the night before.

Her mind was intent on figuring out who was the man that she saw at work last Wednesday. She knew he didn't work there, but she didn't want to ask around. Chrisette was a very private person when it came to separating business from pleasure. Something about this man made Chrisette wet the moment she saw him walking out of the conference room.

That day Chrisette had her back against the wall, talking with a co-worker but couldn't remember anything of the conversation. Yet she remembered what this man was wearing from head to toe.

He had the sexiest lips, a light skin complexion, wavy hair, and his suit fitted like no other. She caught him staring back a few times in between her glances at him. If only she weren't at her place of employment,

Chrisette would have approached him. I've got to find out who that was. Damn... He was so gorgeous, she thought, reminiscing. Her hands gradually made it down her stomach to her lace panties. Her newly waxed pussy made it easier for her fingers to glide over her lips. It felt so good. Her left hand ran circles around her nipples, making them hard. Her other hand was busy inside her panties, rubbing her clit and fingering her pussy. It became even more moistened by the second.

Before long she had cum, thinking about a stranger who plagued her mind. She imagined his tongue doing work. "O-o-oh fuck...!" Chrisette bit her lip, moaning as her thoughts leaked and her whole body shook from an orgasm. Her hand was soaked from her juices and only slightly satisfied; she played with her clit until she came twice.

"I could have slept a little later this morning but I guess I'll get an early start to my day. There is so much to do. Oh, I almost forgot, I have to get my dress for Alicia's wedding. Should I bring a date? Hmm, I think I'll go solo and see what all of the groomsmen look like. I may find something tasty," she smiled.

Getting up and heading for the shower, Ms. Rowan mentally put together her whole day. After about twenty minutes in the shower, washing her hair, brushing her teeth, she stepped into her walk in closet, and picked out a crème colored skirt suit with matching shoes that had a three inch heel.

Chrisette was strongly confident, but not conceited. She loved life, loved herself, and treated people the way she in turn wanted to be treated. Three years after graduating from college, her confidence had helped land her a nice, six figure job. Surprisingly she worked for Miranda Merris, a woman who was just as confident as Chrisette and who saw the potential that Chrisette possessed. Her boss was always on top of things at the company, and didn't cut anyone a break. If you screwed up, you got a letter of dismissal. She was a perfectionist and very aggressive. Miranda lived for her multi-billion dollar company and had no personal life. She was all business and never discussed her personal life with any of the employees in nineteen years that she worked there after her husband's passing.

Chrisette was one of the few that Miranda had complete faith in, and entrusted her with a lot of responsibilities that she wouldn't allow others to have. Chrisette kept a close, small circle of friends. Miranda was never harsh with her, but she'd witnessed her fury. Chrisette kept their relationship strictly professional. With the exception of her best friend since grade school, Alicia, Chrisette didn't have too many female friends. They were so much alike and lived similar lifestyles until Alicia met her fiancé, Mark three years ago. Chrisette never really thought of settling down, just making that money and having fun. She purchased her own home at the age of twenty five, took care of her parents, and would do anything to help those in need.

Chrisette was admired by many and hated by some as well. Standing 5'7" with a golden bronze complexion, thick thighs, voluptuous breasts, she walked with her head held high at all times. She always had a bright smile, always natural and never wore make up. Her light brown hair sat at the middle of her back. She pinned it up daily, giving her a classy, professional, yet sexy look.

At 7:30 a.m. she was ready to head out the door, grabbing her purse, brief case, keys, and three files off of her desk in the living room. She entered the garage and settled into her Phantom Black Pearl Audi A8. Within an hour she had arrived at work and drove through the parking garage.

"Hey Jamal," she yelled out the window to a maintenance man, talking with one of the parking lot attendants.

"What's up princess? How are you feeling this morning?" he asked as Chrisette slowly drove by him.

She stopped the car, and backed it up to speak with Jamal for a minute.

"I'm feeling good, ready to get upstairs and start work so I get out of here on time today. How have you been?"

During the time she spoke, Jamal's eyes were looking into the car at her legs and being his usual flirty self. Jamal had a thing for Chrisette but never got the time of day the entire year he had been working there.

"I'm alright, you know just doing me. I'm surprised you stopped today, any other time you fly passed here like someone is chasing you."

"That's because they are Jamal, it's you," she said laughing.

"Oh you got jokes today huh? I see how you playing. I'm saying though, when can I get a chance to talk to you outside of work. You know I've been trying to get at you for a minute right?"

"Yeah, I hear you. I don't think you're ready to chill with me though."

"What's that supposed to mean?"

"Just what I said, Mr. Jumpsuit… You're not ready," Chrisette repeated, making fun of his blue jumpsuit that the maintenance people were required to wear.

"Let me be the judge of that. Are you going to give me your number or do I have to jump on your hood on the way out of here today?"

"No, no, you don't have to do all that. Here," she said handing him her business card that included her cell number, and told him to reach her that evening.

Jamal's face lit up like a kid in a room full of candy. Chrisette thought he was attractive, he had a nice dark brown complexion, bald head, labeled thuggish by some people, but that didn't bother her. He kind of reminded her of Tyrese. Jamal just wasn't someone she'd normally date or fuck. It could have been that she knew he was too easy for her to get. But hey, today was a good day and giving Jamal her number could be just what she needed.

II

In the crowded elevator, Chrisette stood in the front near the doors. She didn't get a chance to see everyone behind her, and wasn't interested until she noticed someone staring in her direction. With a slight turn of her head she saw the man who made her cum hours earlier without even being there. A quick smile followed, and she turned her head forward, blushing excitedly that she had an opportunity to see him again.

Was he new here? Maybe I should get off on the same floor he does, and see where he goes? That might be too obvious. I'll just introduce myself after some of these people get off of the elevator. Her mind raced upward with the elevator. The beeping sound announcing the seventh floor jarred her. The doors opened, and all but two other people besides them remained.

Now was the time for Chrisette to speak up, but suddenly she was speechless and that wasn't like her. At the eighth floor the remaining two people got off and then it was just her and this mysterious man who had her full attention.

"Are you a new employee here?" she said abruptly.

"Actually, no I'm not. I'm meeting with someone upstairs," he replied.

His voice made Chrisette lose all common sense. She just stood there, nothing to say but feeling weak from his presence, and that deep, sexy voice. She glanced quickly at his hands and didn't see a ring on either one. Her eyes came back up to his face, again she smiled, and began to ask his name just as the door opened on the twelfth floor.

"This is my stop, enjoy your day, beautiful," he said, strutting easily out of the elevator.

As he glided by her, Chrisette took a whiff of his cologne. It was so intoxicating she became hot instantly. Her face turned red. She immediately realized that she was against the grain this time. She was normally the one who made men weak—not the other way around.

The elevator door closed and Chrisette realized that he got off on the same floor that she was supposed to get off. In an effort to not make herself look stupid, she rode it up two more floors and briefly visited with an acquaintance before getting to her office back down on the twelfth floor. This was going to be an even better day for Chrisette as she thought about the possibility of running into this man again through out the day.

With all the work she had to get completed, the odds of that happening, was going to be slim. Three hours into the day, she was able to take a quick break and stepped out to confirm appointments with her secretary, Linda. Linda was a fifty-two year old, very pleasant, white woman. She was always willing to go the extra mile for Chrisette.

They got along well, and chatted from time to time about non-work related things, but nothing really personal. Chrisette decided that it might be okay to ask Linda if she had seen the man from the elevator. She described him as best as she could but Linda hadn't seen the person she was talking about.

"Thanks for getting these typed up for me Linda, and if you happen to see anyone that looks like that please buzz me okay?"

"No problem Ms. Rowan, I sure will," Linda said with a wink.

Chrisette took the papers she'd received from Linda into her office and placed them on her desk. She then headed to one of the break rooms to get something to drink. A quick walk down the hall and she turned left into the empty room. Counting her change to get bottled water, she dropped one of her quarters under the machine, and bent down to see if she could reach it. The coin was too far back.

"I guess I'll settle for tap water, for the time being," she said to her self, not wanting to walk back to the office for more change. In the cabinet, she reached for a paper cup and headed to the sink.

Chrisette turned on the faucet. She smelled the cologne from the elevator and turned to look around. She saw her mystery man standing in the doorway with a cup of his own.

"I guess you're waiting for the lovely tap water?" Chrisette asked jokingly.

He laughed and replied, "Not really, but that machine is broken so it'll do."

"I'm glad you told me, I was going to get something out of it. I'm Chrisette, and you are?"

"Nice to meet you Chrisette, I'm Robert."

The two shook hands and Chrisette felt something that she hadn't felt before, it was nothing that could be identified but she liked it.

"So, you said you were meeting someone here, are you finished with that now?"

"Yes, I am. I was actually heading out in a few moments. I take it you work here, right?"

"Yes I do, for a few years now."

"So, do you spend your entire day in this building or do you break free and go out to lunch?" Robert asked, eyeing Chrisette's body like she was a Goddess.

"Of course, I go out. Although I have to admit I have spent many days here without even leaving the office. I try to make it out as often as I can though. There's a really nice restaurant about fifteen minutes from here that I like to go to."

"Hmm, I could go for something new. Would you mind joining me for lunch sometime?"

"Yes sure!" Chrisette said excitedly and after a moment feeling a little embarrassed by how quickly she replied. "Well how about today, if that's not too soon?" she continued.

"Chrisette, it would be fine. Let's meet in the garage first floor in about fifteen minutes."

They both exited the break room and went in different directions. The whole time Chrisette had the biggest smile on her face with a racing heart that was interested in finding out more about this man that had her captivated.

She met with Robert as planned, and they left the garage in their own cars with him following Chrisette to the restaurant. She had an hour for lunch but ended up getting back to work forty five minutes late. Lucky for her, Miranda was at meeting in Baltimore that day. The time that she spent with Robert didn't seem to last long but Chrisette found that she desperately wanted to spend more time with him. They exchanged numbers and Robert told her that he'd be in touch that evening.

There was no question that the rest of the day was spent thinking about him more than it was completing her work. During one of her meetings she fumbled her words giving her presentation on several occasions. Excusing herself early, she thought nothing of it. Her main concern was getting finished with the work day and heading home in hopes of getting to speak with him again. She felt like a high school girl with a major crush but this time she was a grown woman and needed that rush!

III

That night, Chrisette didn't receive a call from Robert but Jamal did call around 10:30 pm. "Hello?"

"What's good ma?"

"Is that how you talk to all women, Jamal?"

"I see you know my voice already!"

"Caller ID and I don't know anyone else who would call me ma," she laughed.

"Yeah, well I'm one of a kind," he responded.

"I believe that. So why are you calling me at this hour? What's up with you?"

"I'm sorry, is it too late?"

"No it's okay…just wondering why it took so long. The way you were acting I'd have thought you would call as soon as I got off of work."

"Aw, here we go with the jokes again. Nah, I had to take care of something but you knew I was going to hit you up."

"Yeah I did. So lets get to the point…what do you want from me?" Chrisette asked in a low and sexy tone.

"I'm saying, I'm trying to get to know you better, maybe chill and do whatever."

"Whatever?"

"Yeah, I've been watching you for a minute ma. I'm trying to see you outside work. How you feel about that?"

"Where do you live, Jamal?"

"In Alexandria. Where you at?"

"Manassas. So you can make it over to my way. What're you doing right now?"

"That's what's up, nothing. You want me to come through?"

"Yeah, you can say that," he laughed, and coyly slipped in his address.

"I'm on my way," she said.

"I'll see you in an hour," he said.

Chrisette didn't know what she was going to do with Jamal when he got there. He was a bit young for her taste, but tonight she could work with that. During the hour that she waited for him to arrive she'd gone downstairs to the living room wearing nothing but a black tank top, and a pair of pink panties. She'd let her hair down, feeling freaky, hot and ready to find out what Jamal was really after. Chrisette wasn't shy when it came to sex. She knew what her body could do and what it desired.

The door bell rang a few minutes after she'd sat down on the sofa. She got up and walked to the door and checked the security camera to be sure it was Jamal before opening one of the double doors to the main entrance.

"Well, it took you long enough."

"D-a-m-n girl! Is this special treatment for me? Please tell me it is. I'd be upset if you come to the door like this for everybody."

"You're silly. You act like you haven't seen a woman in a tank top and panties before."

"Not when I first come to the crib! And damn sure not this fly, but I ain't complaining."

"I know you're not," Chrisette said, walking toward Jamal as she closed the door. "So, you've been chasing me for a while. Now you're here and you've got me, what are you going to do?"

"This is crazy, are you playing?"

"Why would I be playing Jamal? Do I look like a kid to you?"

"Not at all, I'm just shocked that after all this time you're finally coming around... And like this."

Chrisette grabbed his belt and started to undo it as she kissed his neck. Jamal took off his hat and threw it on the floor, receiving her kisses, and planting a few of his own as he lifted her tank top over her head and tossed it in the same direction of the hat.

"Get on your knees," Chrisette demanded.

Jamal didn't hesitate. He kissed her stomach and bit her panties, pulling them down with his teeth then with his hands the rest of the way.

Chrisette was backed against a wall and placed one of her legs on his shoulder as he planted his face between her legs and began to taste the sweetness of her pussy. He was giving it to her so good that she ended up sliding down onto the floor for him to be able to spread her legs wide open, and get a good taste of paradise.

He spread open her pussy lips with his fingers, and licked every inch of her mound before putting his tongue as deep as he could into her pussy. Returning to her clit, Jamal licked and sucked on it until moans escaped her throat. She got even hotter, grabbing the back of his head and pulling him closer. He gently bit her thigh and went back to eating her pussy, making sure that she came in his mouth.

Jamal couldn't wait to get inside of her. He just wanted to fuck the hell out of her and have her craving him the way he craved her for the past year. Jamal begun undressing when she pointd and said, "Grab those over there."

He reached and picked up three condoms on the shelf.

"Oh so I can have you in my mouth but now I have to be the one to wear a rubber right?"

"That's right!" she smiled.

Jamal put it on quickly and got back down to finish what he started but to his surprise they quickly switched positions. Chrisette got on top of him, riding him backwards with her ass facing him.

"Oooohh shit," Jamal hissed as she sat on his dick, sliding it in and he felt the tightness of her pussy.

He held both of her ass cheeks, squeezing them and loving the sight of her entire body, feeling like he was dreaming. Quickly he knew that it was real as she started riding him, rocking her hips like a pro.

"You like this pussy?"

"Hell yeah… Take all this dick!" he answered moving with her as she fucked him good.

Although she'd had better, Chrisette was pleasantly surprised at Jamal's dick size. She knew she had him where she wanted him and made him cum three times before backing up and making him eat her pussy again. She sat on his face, riding like she did on his dick.

The suction noise could be heard as he went to work on her pussy, his face full of her juice. Jamal was hoping that Chrisette would return the favor but didn't ask and she didn't offer. Her pussy was so good that he was satisfied with having fucked her and got the woman he had been wanting for so long.

Jamal wanted badly to take off the constricting rubber and feel Chrisette's moist pussy, but would have to hold out and hope for it next time. Their sex session lasted for over an hour and Jamal left Chrisette's house a very happy man. Chrisette on the other hand, was content for the moment having met the needs of her rush— for now.

IV

Four days went by and Chrisette sat on her bed talking with her best friend Alicia about her upcoming wedding.

"Chrisette…there's something I want to talk with you about and it's really important. You know I love you like a sister and under any other circumstances I would not ask you this…"

"What's wrong? Is everything okay?"

"Yeah, yeah…it's just, well do you remember Tiffany? The girl I introduced you to at my party a few summer's back?"

"You mean Tiffany, the video vixen?"

"Yeah that's her. Well, I'm going to tell you this because I know that I can trust you, and it'll explain why I'm asking you this other question. Tiffany's been going through a lot. She's got some health issues that are pretty serious. I wanted to make her feel good and let her know how important she is. I was wondering if you wouldn't mind if I asked her to be my Maid of Honor in your place. Now before you say anything, Chrisette believe me, it's really important that I do this for her…I think this would lift her spirits."

"Alicia, that's big of you and I guess… I guess I understand. So this means I don't have to wear that ugly dress after all, right?" Chrisette laughed.

"Yeah girl, you don't have to wear it but you're still going to be in the wedding, I love you and I can't wait to see you."

"Me too, I'll give you a call in a few days."

After they hung up, Chrisette decided that she would give Robert a call since he had not yet called her. Maybe he lost my number? She mused pressing *231 on her speed dial and the phone rang four times and then the voicemail came on.

"*Hello, you've reached Robert, I am currently unavailable to take your call but if you would like to leave a message I will get back to you as soon as possible.*"

Chrisette hung up the phone without leaving a message, knowing that her number probably showed up on his phone anyway and tossed her cell phone over on the bed. It rang within a couple of minutes and she looked over wondering who it could be. She looked at the caller ID and it was Robert. Smiling, she answered, "Hello, how are you?"

"I'm doing good… Sorry I missed you a moment ago. I was just getting out of the shower."

"That's alright, I'm glad you were able to give me a call back," she stated, wondering what his body looked liked dripping wet.

"I was going to give you a call this weekend. It's good you reached out to me. What're your plans for tonight, you have any?"

"Hmm…no, I don't have anything going on tonight. What did you have in mind?"

"How would like to come see me? I'm about thirty minutes away from you."

"Oh really... How do you know where I live to estimate the time from your place to mine?"

"I know a lot of things, beautiful. So what do you say, can I see you tonight?"

"Can I trust you? I mean, how do I know you're not a serial killer or something, just inviting me over to chop me up?"

Chrisette couldn't help but to laugh along with Robert but she was very serious.

"Do you think I'd hurt someone as beautiful as you? Come see me, I'll text you the address. Bring yourself and not too much else."

"Alright, I guess I can come. Do you live alone? Hello, hello?"

Chrisette could only hear dial tone on the other end. That's strange. He just hung up like that? I guess he found being mysterious was intriguing but I'm taking my knife just in case, she thought.

By that evening, she was standing in front of nine dresses that she laid on the bed, trying to decide what to wear. Then she re-entered the closet and thought that maybe some nice fitting jeans and a blouse would be sufficient for the night. After all he didn't say that they'd be leaving his house and going anywhere.

Turning back to look at the dresses, she saw one that wasn't too fancy and selected it. The dress was black with an open back, long sleeves, and a few inches above the knees. She picked out a pair of open toed heels to go with it, added an ankle bracelet for a little pizzazz, and got ready to head out the door. Chrisette took a look at herself in a full length mirror, teasing her long locks of curls, smoothing out her dress as she ran her hand over her breasts and down the length of her attire. "I cannot wait to see this gorgeous man, he might get lucky tonight," smiled in anticipation.

Meeting men had never been a problem for Chrisette. Allowing them to keep her was always a challenge. She enjoyed the freedom of doing what she wanted, whenever she wanted, and didn't see herself giving that up—at least not anytime soon. To her, fucking was just that, fucking.

She had spent her high school and college days being wanted by so many guys, she figured she'd use that to her advantage. Chrisette had particular types of men that she would bless with her paradise, mainly successful, clean cut, extremely attractive ones. All in all her thought process about getting hers was similar to how some men feel about 'running through' women.

She didn't get caught up in emotions and stayed far away from those who seemed to get too attached. If she wanted dick, she went and got it, no strings attached. The rush that came from fucking someone totally new thrilled her. Making them do what she wanted was even more pleasurable for her, it empowered her, and Robert was next on her list.

V

Arriving at Robert's address, Chrisette was beside herself at the exquisite homes lining the street. She had a four-bedroom, two-bath home, everything she desired and was very proud of that. What she saw before her eyes was unimaginable and made her wonder what Robert did for a living, and if he lived all by himself.

Chrisette road up the driveway and parked next to a Rolls Royce, outside of a four car garage. Looking at the house, she could see only one light on. It was on the first floor, and every other visible window was pitched black.

She pulled out her cellphone and called Robert; wanting to know that she'd arrived at the correct address. The phone rang and again went to voice mail. This time when she hung up the phone, she looked to the door of the house and saw Robert waving her to come in.

"Well, well, well. Look at you! You have no idea what you're getting yourself into," Chrisette said under her breath while walking to the door. "Good evening Robert, I was just calling you to see if I had the right place. You have a lovely home," she said, hugging him as they greeted each other.

"Thank you and I'm happy you could join me this evening. You didn't have any trouble finding me did you?"

"No, it was pretty easy. I've never been around here before. It's a really nice neighborhood."

"Please, have a seat," Robert offered as they entered the only room in the house that was lit.

"Would you like something to drink?" he asked.

"No, thank you. I'm fine."

Robert looked even better than she remembered. Their eyes met and it was almost as if they were speaking a language of their own.

"You look incredible Chrisette, but I don't have to tell you that. You look like you already know," Robert said, smiling.

"Thank you. So, what prompted you to invite me to your home? This is your home correct?"

"Yes it is. I thought it would be easier to offer you a chance to come see me than to impose and just invite myself to your home. I don't want you to think that everyone gets this chance. I like what I see and I know that you've had your eye on me the couple of times I was within your presence."

"You are right. I won't deny that I find you very attractive and wanted to see you again. You seem a little mysterious. Why is that?"

Chrisette asked, looking around this spacious room that was so quiet.

"Ask me what you want to know, I'm not too secretive."

"Well, I have to ask this first. What the hell do you do for a living that enables you to have a Rolls Royce in the drive way and this gigantic home? Do you have children, a wife? Do your parents live here with you? I can't imagine you living here all alone."

"Whoa, slow down. First, no I don't have children. I work for a government agency in D.C., but that's not what got me this. I made some really wise investments several years ago after getting an inheritance and this is the outcome. I'm thirty-six and I graduated from George Mason University. I have two sisters. I'm not married and no, my parents do not live with me. Anything else I can answer for you?"

"Investments huh…? I'm almost afraid to ask."

"You probably should be," Robert replied but with a slight smile to let her know that he was just kidding. "Tell me about you."

"I'm twenty nine, live alone, graduated from the University of Virginia, no kids, you already know where I work, and I love sex."

"Ha, ha, ha, is that right?" Robert laughed.

"Yes that is right. And I guess you should know, I'm pretty direct if you can't already tell."

"Yeah, I kind of picked up on that when you asked if I was going to chop you up. That's a good thing. I like that in a woman."

"So what will we be doing this evening, Robert?"

"The night is young. I'm spontaneous and don't plan too far ahead. We'll figure that out as time moves along. Is that cool with you?"

"See, that's what I mean about being secretive. I know you didn't invite me here without something in mind…A movie, something to eat. What is it?"

"Wow, I haven't had a night like that in about ten years. But if that's what you want we can do that."

"No, that's not what I'm just asking."

"Well actually, I've already prepared something for us to eat. As far as a movie, we can make one," Robert said.

"I'm not hungry, but I'm enjoying just listening to you talk Robert. Do you care to show me around your home, or is that a secret too?"

"Not at all, follow me."

It was a long walk through the hallway and up the first set of stairs as he showed her a game room, an office, a library, another room that looked as if it were just painted as a child's room. Or just someone who liked a lot of colors at based on the paint that was on the wall. Chrisette decided not to pry. Robert had already stated he didn't have children.

She thought that for a man to live in this huge, well-kept house with no relatives, somehow seemed very odd. It was hard enough to find men that had no children, weren't married, that were financially stable, and didn't have a whole bunch of drama. Here he was and so far, Chrisette could check all of those off.

They entered a room that was in the back of the house, it appeared to look like a master bedroom with an entire mirrored ceiling. It was decorated as if it were straight out of a catalog.

"So this is your bedroom, I assume?" she asked.

"You assumed right. Have a seat on the sofa over there if you wish. Would you like me to turn the television on or entertain you with more conversation?"

"It's a no on the T.V. and the conversation. But come sit with me."

Robert was leaning against the bed post. Instead of sitting on the sectional sofa that was in the corner of the large room, Chrisette climbed up on the high bed and invited Robert to accompany her.

"How do you know I want you on my bed?" he asked.

"Because you brought me to your bedroom to begin with, and we haven't seen the rest of the house, yet you want me to get comfortable in here."

"Good answer. What if I told you that I want you right now?"

"Tell me and see…"

Robert stood there in his Rocawear jeans, fresh pair of white Nike sneakers, and T-shirt, looking as smooth, relaxed, and confident as he could.

"I want you."

"Take me," she said, looking straight into his dark eyes.

Chrisette hungered for this man. A perfect stranger yet she felt that she belonged there with him and wanted to give him what ever he wanted. This was a total switch from the way she felt about getting hers. Robert somehow changed the game and Chrisette had the greatest rush that she'd ever felt.

Robert grabbed her hair, firmly but not roughly and pulled her close to him as he licked her lips and then kissed them.

"Take off your clothes," he told her and she complied.

She never took her eyes off him, loving how he looked at her like he was going to eat her alive. Once she was fully undressed, except for her heels, Robert turned her around. He kissed her neck and down her back. Chrisette began to breathe more rapidly, getting excited from the touch of his lips on her body. She quickly turned around, wanting to kiss him and pulled his shirt over his head, revealing a muscular physique and then unbuttoned his pants to find him in a pair of black boxer briefs with a dick that looked like it could bust through a wall.

She ran the tips of her nails up and down his dick while it was still inside his boxers. He had the sexiest body she had seen. The intensity of their kisses moved to tight grips on each others' bodies. Robert lifted her up, placed her on the bed, and rolled her over on her stomach. He bent down and kissed her leg to her ass and back, rubbing his hands on her body.

Chrisette again couldn't resist and had to turn around to look at him, she wanted to taste him, and nothing was going to stop her. She pulled down his boxer briefs and wrapped her hand around his big dick, knowing that she wouldn't fit it all in her mouth but she was damn sure going to try.

Robert reclined on the bed with Chrisette between his legs. She licked every inch of his dick then stroked it as she took his nuts into her mouth. He moaned, feeling her warm mouth attacking his package. She sucked his dick with the strongest suction he'd ever experienced, bobbing her head fast, as she hummed giving his dick an insane vibration. She did the same to his nuts, waiting for him to explode in her mouth. Robert palmed the back of Chrisette's head and just as he was about to cum pulled her head up.

"What are doing baby, why did you stop me?"

Robert didn't say a word but pulled her up further onto the bed, this time with her lying on her back. He put her long, shapely leg over his shoulder and kneeled in front of her on the bed. His fingers ran down her leg and meet her pussy lips.

"Open your legs," he ordered.

She spread them wider, feeling his fingers touching her clit and then going inside her.

"You are so fucking sexy, you know that?" Robert said, licking his lips and kissing her ankle resting on his shoulder.

"I can say the same about you. Why are you teasing me, give me what I want," Chrisette replied.

"What is it that you want?"

"Everything!" she answered, sure that she could withstand anything that Robert put on her.

"Remember you said that when we're through!" he said with a smirk.

Robert placed her leg that was on his shoulder, over to the side to fully spread her open wide as he lay down on top of her and kissed her intensely. He bit her neck, and sucked on her breasts like a beast, leaving passion marks all over her body. Chrisette welcomed every bit of it and could not wait to feel Robert put his dick inside of her. The head of his dick touched her pussy lips as they continued to kiss and she eased her hand down to guide it in.

"Not so fast…trust me, it's worth the wait," Robert said.

Chrisette was open in every sense of the word. At this point she wanted him to dominate and give her what she craved. No sooner than those thoughts ran across her mind, Robert made his way down to taste her pussy.

She could feel the heat from him breathing before his tongue forced its way in her pussy, and ran circles around her clit. Chrisette arched her back and turned her head to the side as she grabbed onto a pillow and held it tight. Robert had her legs in the air, refusing to let them down as she scooted in the opposite direction, unable to be still. His tongue moved at a speed unfamiliar to her. Chrisette was sure that nothing came close to how Robert made her feel. She could hear him enjoying himself while he moaned as if he got pleasure from her satisfaction.

Her pussy was dripping wet and Robert's mouth was catching every drop of it. Chrisette's body started to tremble before becoming completely filled with the sensational wave of excitement. His fingers were inside her massaging her g-spot while his tongue stayed on her clit and brought her to an incredible climax.

"Oooohh yeeesssss…! Lick my pussy, ooh-ooh, suck on my clit," she screamed.

His head was firmly planted between her legs and her mouth opened wide as she erupted. Never picking his head up, Robert lifted her up more and abruptly spread her ass cheeks apart to dive in with his tongue, sucking her ass. Chrisette was driven wild by the freak that she found in Robert.

"I don't ever want you to stop," she whispered hoarsely while pushing her body toward him. Within moments, she was on all fours and Robert was entering her pussy with full force.

"Agh, oh shit," Chrisette cried out in pain as he began pumping hard as soon as he got in.

Robert moved his hips roughly and held on to her hips, intermittently grabbing her ass. Her screams only made him smash her pussy harder.

"Can you handle this, huh? This what you wanted?"

"Ugh, ooh, yeah oh God, it feels so go-o-d! Fuck me, fuck me harder!" she responded, stuttering with her mouth wide open.

She lost all control as her pussy was now Robert's possession and he made it known. His ten and a half inch dick was too much for Chrisette. It stretched her pussy walls deeper. Her ass became red as he pounded her from the back with her back bent and head face down. She bit the sheets and could feel his nuts smacking her clit as he fucked her good. Robert couldn't hold back any longer from her pussy squeezing his dick with each stroke. He came inside her, and kept pumping, making sure she got hers over and over again. Slowing down, he started to caress her back.

"I didn't think you were going to make it," he laughed, referring to the punishment her pussy had just received.

"Hmm, hmm… I wasn't sure either baby. Now I just have to see if I can walk," she said, moving forward and expecting Robert to move from behind her when he grabbed her hips.

"Whoa, where you think you're going?" he said.

"Lets pick this up in about an hour, I must admit you put it down," Chrisette explained.

"An hour…? By then we'll be doing something else," he assured her.

Robert helped her up so that she still had her back against him but they were both kneeling. He reached around and grabbed her breast with both hands and asked, "Are you mine?"

Chrisette was caught up in rapture and without hesitation said, "Yes."

"That's what I want to hear," Robert replied, getting a tight grip on her hair and beginning to bite her neck and suddenly pushed her down on the bed. He slid his dick up and down the crack of her ass, seeing Chrisette push toward him, waiting for him to make his next move. And that he did. Robert grabbed both of her ass cheeks and spread them as he gently slid his dick inside the brown hole.

Chrisette wasn't fully prepared for it like she thought she might be and let out a loud scream, "Aah agh aaaahhhhh!"

She pulled the blankets off the bed. Robert started off with a nice slow pace as Chrisette got relaxed and then she started to play with her clit while he started to go faster and got a little rougher.

He showed her no mercy as he continued to pump and his body became stiff as he was about to cum in her asshole. He pulled his dick out, letting his cum run down her ass crack.

"Did you get what you came here for?" Robert asked a breathless Chrisette.

She rolled over onto her back, knees in the air and hands on her lower stomach.

"More than what I came for," she winked.

"Come on," he said grabbing her hand, holding it behind him as they walked into the master bathroom.

Robert turned on the hot water to the shower, letting the steam quickly fill up the room and then re-opening the glass door for them to both step in. In all of Chrisette's twenty nine years, through all of her encounters, she never took the time to really enjoy the level of intimacy that came after the sex and now Robert was unexpectedly giving that to her.

He began to wash her body, from head to toe as they shared a conversation of the eyes and she reciprocated the act. This was going to be a night that she would remember and desire again.

For the next few weeks, things were incredible for Chrisette. She'd seen Robert on several occasions and though she had a couple of nights with others, he was the one always on her mind. The mystery behind him still seemed to be there and that may be why Chrisette felt this strong attraction to him.

Tonight Chrisette was putting together her attire and jewelry for Alicia's wedding the next afternoon. This was something that Chrisette looked forward to for a long time, knowing how in love Alicia and Mark were.

Around 8:17 pm, Chrisette's doorbell rang. Who the hell could that be? She thought, running downstairs to get the door. Checking the camera, she saw a figure with his back turned and facing away from the door with a long black coat on. He quickly turned around, with his head down. All that Chrisette could now see was that he was wearing a suit.

"Who is it?" she called out through the intercom.

"Who do you want it to be?" he replied.

She opened the door immediately, it was Robert.

"What a pleasant surprise!" she said, giving him a tight hug.

"Why didn't you call and let me know you were coming over?"

"You said it yourself, I'm a pleasant surprise," Robert replied, taking his coat off and looking at Chrisette with bedroom eyes.

She stood there with a ponytail, in a red and white Adidas sweat suit, totally caught off guard by Robert dropping by. Chrisette was thinking to herself that she should go and change from the outfit she had on while running errands all day. Just then Robert said, "You look good in anything and nothing."

"You're sweet. So I take it you've missed me and that's why I get this unexpected visit?"

"Yeah, I guess you could say that but it's not just that I missed you. I needed something from you so I came to get it."

He got up from the arm of the sofa that he rested against and walked over to Chrisette who was sitting in a chair nearby.

"Needed? And what could that be, handsome?"

"You should know by now not to ask too many questions, just follow me."

Robert proceeded up the stairs, stopping about half way and turning around to kiss Chrisette. He backed her up against the railing, caressing her breasts and then moving his hand down between her legs. She moved to the steps, sitting down as Robert leaned against her body. Taking off each others clothes, Chrisette realized she was in for something good and was electrified just thinking about it.

Robert took his belt and wrapped it around Chrisette's neck, and started to kiss her again passionately.

"Let's go upstairs," Chrisette suggested and started to walk backwards so that they could continue to kiss each other on the way up.

Robert pressed her against the walls of the hallway, the whole way to her bedroom and upon entering, lifted her up onto her dresser. He took her breast into his mouth, sucking on it aggressively and biting her nipple.

"I want you so bad," Chrisette whispered into his ear.

"You're going to have to prove that," he responded, kissing her lips.

Holding the belt that he'd placed around her neck, he guided his dick inside her and long stroked her the way he knew she liked it.

"Is this my pussy?" he whispered to her as he tightened the belt around her neck and went deeper inside her.

"Ooh yes baby. Do what you want to it?" Chrisette said, opening up and pulling him deeper inside her.

She knew that she'd never been in love before and doubted that after only a few weeks this could be what she felt, but something had her addicted to this man. Her mind was blown and she didn't want it any other way. Although Chrisette was always confident about her sexual abilities, Robert took her to new heights. Something about the way he moved, the force he displayed, and the way he dominated her was making her obsessed. Anything that he desired she gave him, whether it was masturbating in front of him or allowing him to cum all over her body. It was a go. What started out as a rush now had her overpowered.

As the night went along, Robert took what was his until Chrisette couldn't handle anymore.

"I have an idea. How about you stay with me tonight?" Chrisette asked, knowing that it was going to be a chance that he'd stay.

They both knew how it went everytime and never stayed at each other's place.

"As tempted as I am, I have things to do very early. So I'll have to take a rain check. Believe me, next time I'm yours, beautiful."

Chrisette ran her hands across his chest and kissed it, "Okay, I'm going to hold you to that. I have quite a few things to do this weekend as well. I guess it would be wise to hold off on that for now."

Once Robert had left, Chrisette was ready to get some sleep

before Alicia's wedding the next day. It seemed like only a few minutes went by before the alarm went off.

"Damn…! I can't believe I have to get up now," she said, looking at the clock. But I'll do it for my girl. Then the slight smile appeared as she began thinking about how wonderful today was going to be. Her best friend was tying the knot.

She took a long, hot shower and made a few phone calls to see what time she needed to be at the hotel to meet Alicia, and help her get ready.

"Hey girl, it's your day. How is your morning going so far?" she asked as Alicia answered the phone.

"Good morning sweetie, I am soo nervous Chrisette! I can't believe today is the day. I can't wait to say those words to my soon-to-be-husband. I was thinking of him all night and wondering what he'll look like in his Tux."

"Everything is going to be perfect, Alicia. I should be there in about an hour. Is that going to be enough time?" Chrisette asked.

"Oh yeah, there's not much to do. I've gotten everything almost done, my mom is here and my two aunts, Tiffany stayed with me last night and so did Iesha. There are only a couple things that I need you to help out with. You've already done so much and thanks again for buying my dress. That was the best wedding gift ever!"

"I wouldn't have it any other way, I'll see you soon!"

10:37 a.m. and Chrisette was out the door. She wore a stunner gold Badgley Mischka dress that accented her skin tone and a platinum and diamond wrist bracelet with matching earrings. Chrisette would never intentionally outdo the bride but her gown was certainly a contender. She arrived at the hotel and gave her car keys to the valet as she went up to meet with Alicia. The hotel was actually where both the wedding and reception were going to take place. Chrisette saw many familiar faces, as many guests that were attending the wedding from out of town also stayed at the hotel.

Within a few minutes she was upstairs and entering Alicia's room, meeting with every one that was already there, including the new Maid of Honor, Tiffany.

"Hello Tiffany, how are you? It's been some time since I've seen you," Chrisette greeted, shaking hands.

"I'm doing okay, Chrisette. Alicia talks about you all the time and I was looking forward to seeing you again."

They made small talk and Tiffany seemed a little distant but Chrisette assumed it was probably due to her not feeling well as Alicia stated before.

"Well ladies, it's almost that time. I want to thank everyone for helping. This is such a special day for me, and I hope it is for all of you as well. As soon as my mom gets back and lets us know everything is set, we'll head downstairs and I'm getting married y'all!" Alicia screamed with excitement.

The male parties that were going to be in the wedding were on the floor just above Alicia's, and at the same time, getting ready to head down to get into their places. Twenty minutes later, Alicia's mother came into the room, and gave the signal to head downstairs. Alicia, dressed in a pearl white gown with a twelve foot train, the most beautiful bouquet, and most importantly, a man waiting at the end of the alter, began her walk down the isle. All of the bridesmaids and groomsmen had taken their places and the music of Keith Sweat began with the song, *I'll give all my love to you.*

Alicia visibly cried the entire way down the isle as her stepfather walked alongside her. There were two hundred and forty-seven guests, and they all had their eyes on her. During her walk down the isle, Chrisette had looked at all the people that filled the room and just before turning her eyes back to Alicia, she noticed a very familiar face. It was Robert. What is he doing here? She pondered, a little nervous and confused. I hope this isn't another surprise. I can't skip out on my girl's wedding for dick today.

The ceremony lasted nearly thirty-five minutes. Then they were officially husband and wife. Chrisette noticed that Robert had not looked her way the whole time which only made her wonder more why he was there. Soon everyone was exiting the room to go to the reception area.

Chrisette lost sight of Robert during that time as all of the people leaving made it difficult. She met up with Alicia at the reception and congratulated her as did the remaining wedding party. Tiffany stood nearby and made her way over. Chrisette released Alicia from their hug. She turned and saw Robert standing next to Tiffany.

"Congratulations Alicia!" Tiffany yelled and gave her a hug also. "Oh excuse my manners; this is my fiancé Robert Merris."

Chrisette's jaw dropped and it wasn't something that went

unnoticed.

"Wow, wow...soo you're engaged? Mr. Robert Merris?" She asked, not yet sure if she should bust Robert's ass or play it off like they were strangers for the time being.

"Yeah, we've been together for a little while now and we'll be getting married in a few months," Tiffany answered while Robert stood there with a red face, seemingly nervous and rubbing his head.

Chrisette was in total shock, feeling stupid for not even first finding out his last name during all those weeks she was with him. She needed to excuse herself but not before asking, "So Robert, are you any relation to Miranda Merris?" He didn't answer but again, Tiffany was quick to. "Yeah he is. That's his mother. I believe you work at her company from what Alicia's told me correct?"

Not wanting to mess up Alicia's day, Chrisette quickly answered, "Yes," and left the room but Alicia knew Chrisette too well and could see that something was clearly wrong.

Chrisette entered the ladies room and looked at herself in the mirror. Tears suddenly covered her beautiful face, and her heart felt crushed. There was no commitment between Robert and her, but somehow this revelation tore her apart.

He was honest about not being married, at least not yet. Now it all seemed like such a big lie. Not telling her that he was the son of her boss, there was so much that fell into place.

Alicia entered the ladies room shortly afterward.

"Hey girl, are you okay...? Talk to me and tell me what's going on!"

"Oh no, please go back to the wedding. I'm fine. We'll talk when you get back from your honeymoon. I'm so sorry you left to come be in here with me, but really I'm alright," Chrisette answered, trying to smile.

"Look at me, no you're not. And I'm going to stay here until you tell me what's wrong."

Chrisette looked down on the floor, wiped her eyes, and began to explain that she'd known Robert for a little while, and had been involved with him.

"So now you can understand why I left so suddenly. I just can't believe this happened, and that he's screwing both your friends."

Alicia stood in silence then fell to her knees.

"Alicia, what are you doing? Get up from there you're going to get your dress dirty. It's going to be okay. I'll get through this and don't worry. Robert and I are done!" She yelled, trying to get Alicia up off the floor. "Hey, what is it? Please say something," Chrisette pleaded.

Alicia shook her head and began to cry, holding her stomach and rocking back and forth in such a manner that Chrisette didn't know what to do.

"No, no, no, no! This isn't right. This is just not right," Alicia cried.

"What isn't right? Tell me, he has children doesn't he? Just another lie, I should have known."

At that moment Alicia looked up at Chrisette and said, "It's not that Chrisette. It's…its Tiffany. When I told you she wasn't well, I didn't mean she had a little cold or stomach ache. It's because she found out that she was positive. And you know what I'm talking about! She just told me last night that she got engaged and that she was moving in with him permanently. She promised we'd discuss it further after I got back from Italy. I know that she was dating for a while, but I had no clue it was that serious, and considering her situation, it would go in that direction. I don't even know if she's told him yet."

Tiffany, a former video vixen, well known for her body and some of the celebrities that she'd dated. She had also spent her early years at just about every college party up and down the east coast with numerous men. She had four children with three different fathers and not a clue as to who it was that changed her life this way. Having traveled the world, it would be hard to know something like that.

Though she learned from this devastation and vowed to never take anything for granted and abuse her body the way she did before. Because of her, other lives would be changed in the same manner. She made some of the same choices in life Chrisette did.

They were two strangers, living two different lives, and may now be connected in a way that neither of them would ever want to be. One thing that Chrisette would pray above all else was that she had the strength to be patient and take her time in life if only given another chance to do right, because it just isn't worth it to rush.

Biographies

Geneive Borne is the author of *Beautiful Bird* from *Lipstick Diaries* part 1. She has written part two for all readers who were intrigued and needed to know more about what happened to the main character, Dorel. *2 Beautiful Birds* is sure to answer any questions readers have about this chocolate smooth character as well as open their mind up to his new life. Genieve loves to write and is working on releasing her full length novel. Contact the author at www.streetlitreview.com

Arlene Brathwaite was raised in Albany, New York. A wife, mother and author, her debut novel, *Youngin'*, propelled her into the literary world. Her highly anticpated sophmore titled, *Ol'Timer*, followed shortly. Ms. Brathwaite owns and operates Brathwaite Publishing. *In The Cut* (Brathwaite Publishing, summer, 2009), and *Paper Trail, Youngin' Part III* (Brathwaite Publishing) along with *Cold Blood*, are upcoming titles written by the dynamic author/publisher. Ms. Brathwaite believes that an author should never be pigeon holed and is on a mission to prove this. Contact Arlene Braitwaite at www.brathwaitepublishing.com and www.streetlitreview.com

\Wahida Clark is at the top of the book game. She's the reigning the queen of Thug Love fiction. Ms. Clark is a national bestselling author whose works include national bestsellers: *Thugs and The Women Who Love Them, Every Thug Needs A Lady, Thug Matrimony, Payback is A Mutha, Payback With Ya Life, Sleeping With The Enemy* and *Thug Lovin.* Ms. Clark runs her publishing house W.Clark Publishing. She can be contacted at www.wclarkpublishing.com and www.streetlitreview.com

Sharron Doyle is a hardworking writer from New York. She wrote four titles while incarcerated. Her debut title, *If It Ain't One Thing It's Another,* has been met by outstanding, raving revues. Her highly anticipated, follow up novel, *When Love Turns To Hate*, will be released Spring '10. Ms. Doyle short story, was featured in *Lipstick Diaries*. Contact Sharron Doyle at www.streelitreview.com

Kiniesha Gayle was born in Kingston, Jamaica. She developed a passion for writing at nine years old. She earned a BA in Forensic Psychology at John Jay College of Criminal Justice. In 2002 she completed *King of Spades,* her first manuscript. The novel sold very well. After forming her own publishing company, KG Publishing, the busy Ms. Gayle released *Queen of Hearts* to great response. *Child Support,* her third novel will be released in 2010. Ms. Gayle was featured in *Lipstick Diaries.* Contact www.kgpublishing.com and www.streetlitreview.com

Brooke Green has been writing since the age of eight. Her hot, self published debut novel, *You Me and He,* was one of the hottest releases in 08. Ms. Green's follow up is *Candy* and will be released in Fall '09. A multi-talented Philadelphia native, Ms. Green is already making her presence felt in the field of literature. She owns and operates Full Circle Publishing, the company which has produced both her titles. Contact the author www.streetlitreview.com

Tracee A. Hanna is the author of, *A Little Bit of Sinning*, the novella, *Ultimate Freak-fest Fantasy*, and *The Masquerade Party*, featured in the New York Times Best Selling anthology, *Caramel Flava,* edited by Zane, and *Chocolate Cream,* included in Zane's anthology, *Honey Flava*. She wrote *Madame Travina's Diary* for the anthology *Ultimate Art of Erotica*. Tracee was born and raised in St. Louis, Missouri. She began writing erotica as an outlet for the secret desires of her overly inventive concupiscent imagination. Contact Tracee Hanna at www.MissTracee.com and www.streetlitreview.com

Katrina Jones grew up in a three bedroom apartment with her six other siblings and mother. Katrina Jones, a freelance poet and writer was born in Staten Island, New York and raised in the Bronx. Katrina got a feel for writing after reading a poem named Footprints in the Sand by Mary Stevenson. Poetry became her way out, reading also became her guide. Reading stories similar to her own life experiences and knowing of others, she was able to move from poetry to telling stories in words. Being able to relate to others, keeps her going. Wanting to inspire anyone who has a dream of becoming a writer, Katrina introduces herself to the world. Contact Katrina Jones at www.streetlitreview.com

Capri Love, a college student majoring in journalism, wrote her first poem at age seven. Her erotic poem *Storm of Bliss* was published in the October issue of Noire Magazine. Optimistic and talented, Capri resides in Atlanta, GA. with her son, Zaire. Capri Love is currently working on an anthology of short stories and a series of novels with plans of her stories crossing over to screen production. Contact Capri Love at www.streetlitreview.com

Caroline McGill is affectionatrely known as the Queen of Hip Hop Literature. Ms. Mcgill has written four top selling novels, *The Grudge, Dollar Outta Fifteen Cent, A Dollar Outta Fifteen Cent II: Money Talks, Bullsh*t Walks, A Dollar Outta Fifteen Cent III: Mo' Money...Mo' Problems.* She's currently finishing up *A Dollar Outta Fifteen Cent IV: Money Makes the World Go Round*. Caroline does it all for Synergy Publications. Her ascension began in Brooklyn, NY this means Queen Caroline is destined to rule. Contact the author www.synergypublications.com www.streetlitreview.com

Jada T. Roberts has been writing since the age of eight. Originally from Brooklyn, NY. Ms. Roberts fell in love with words from the time her mother introduced her to reading dictionaries word for word, periodicals, books particularly African-American literature. After sailing the seas in the US Navy, and reading several books in all genres, Jada decided to come to shore and write her own. Her first novel, *Junk Food*, will be published in late 2009. She resides in the DC area with her family. You may visit her website www.sheownspublishung.com and www.streelitreview.com

Aretha Temple has been writing since the 7th grade. She started writing poetry and soon discovered a passion for writing, expanding beyond just poetry. She began writing short and erotica. Her short story *Me, He, She* was featured in Noire Presents *From the Streets to the Sheets*. Aretha later had her own column Ree-Ree got the Scoop in Noiremagazine.com. Aretha's short story, *Honey Dip* is in the anthology *Flexin and Sexin.* Aretha Lives in Brooklyn, NY. She's finishing a novel, *Jane Doe*. Contact Aretha at www.streetlitreview.com and www.myspace/aretha

Zoe Woods is a multi-genre writer, who has collaborated with her husband in writing the urban fiction series, *Blood of My Brother.* A wife and mother, she is fairly new to the literary scene. Ms. Woods' ability to share her innovativeness has contributed greatly to her success. Presently, Ms. Woods resides on the east coast and is working on several publications and projects. She can be contactd at www.streetlitreview.com

The Augustus Manuscript Team
Tamiko Maldonado, Juliet White and Yolanda Palmer
Thanks to you all and the contributing authors for a job well done.
See you again in **LIPSTICK DIARIES 3**

GHETTO GIRLS IV

Young Luv

ESSENCE BESTSELLING AUTHO
ANTHONY WHYTE

Ghetto Girls IV Young Luv
$14.95 // 9780979281662

Ghetto Girls
$14.95 // 0975945319

Ghetto Girls Too
$14.95 // 0975945300

Ghetto Girls 3 Soo Hoo
$14.95 // 0975945351

THE BEST OF THE STREET CHRONICLES TODAY, THE **GHETTO GIRLS SERIES** IS A WONDERFULLY HYPNOTIC ADVENTURE THAT DELVES INTO THE CONVOLUTED MINDS OF CRIMINALS AND THE DARK WORLD OF POLICE CORRUPTION. YET, THERE IS SOMETHING THRILLING AND SURPRISINGLY TENDER ABOUT THIS ONGOING YOUNG-ADULT SAGA FILLED WITH MAD FLAVA.

Love and a Gangsta
author // **ERICK S GRAY**

This explosive sequel to **Crave All Lose All**. Soul and America were together ten years 'til Soul's incarceration for drugs. Faithfully, she waited four years for his return. Once home they find life ain't so easy anymore. America believes in holding her man down and expects Soul to be as committed. His lust for fast money rears its ugly head at the same time America's music career takes off. From shootouts, to hustling and thugging life, Soul and his man, Omega, have done it. Omega is on the come-up in the drug-game of South Jamaica, Queens. Using ties to a Mexican drug cartel, Omega has Queens in his grip. His older brother, Rahmel, was Soul's cellmate in an upstate prison. Rahmel, a man of God, tries to counsel Soul. Omega introduces New York to crystal meth. Misery loves company and on the road to the riches and spoils of the game, Omega wants the only man he can trust, Soul, with him. Love between Soul and America is tested by an unforgivable greed that leads quickly to deception and murder.

$14.95 // 9780979281648

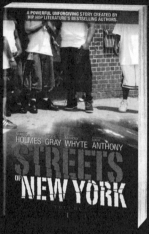 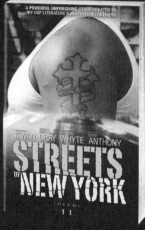 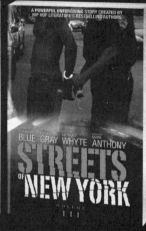